Spartacus

Spartacus

Talons of an Empire

R C Southworth

CLAYMORE
PRESS

First published in Great Britain in 2012 by
CLAYMORE PRESS
An imprint of
Pen & Sword Books Ltd
47 Church Street
Barnsley
South Yorkshire
S70 2AS

9781781590843

A CIP catalogue record for this book is
available from the British Library

Printed and bound in England
By CPI Group (UK) Ltd, Croydon, CRO 4YY

Pen & Sword Books Ltd incorporates the Imprints of Claymore Press, Pen
& Sword Aviation, Pen & Sword Family History, Pen & Sword Maritime,
Pen & Sword Military, Wharncliffe Local History, Pen & Sword Select,
Pen & Sword Military Classics, Leo Cooper, Remember When, Seaforth
Publishing and Frontline Publishing

For a complete list of Pen & Sword titles please contact
PEN & SWORD BOOKS LIMITED
47 Church Street, Barnsley, South Yorkshire, S70 2AS, England
E-mail: enquiries@pen-and-sword.co.uk
Website: www.pen-and-sword.co.uk

For my parents, no son could ask more of those that love him.

Prologue

The year was 73 BC and the Roman Empire was beginning to gather momentum. Its navy dominated the trading routes of the Mediterranean, while its legions began to look hungrily at neighbouring lands. The empire required land, wealth and slaves, commodities which they had in abundance but they still yearned for more. A third of the great city of Rome were enslaved but still they wanted more, the backs of slaves carried the aspirations of a great empire. Many of those slaves were sold into the ludus - gladiator schools. Here they would learn the art of warfare and become lethal killers. Many would die in the arena and all for the entertainment of the masses. Their masters became rich and cared nothing for the loss of blood, dignity and life. However, just 100 miles to the south of the great city stood Capua, a prosperous trading city eager to match the splendour of Rome. It was within this city the first blow would be struck for the slaves of the Roman Empire, a blow which would shake the very foundations of Rome.

Batiatus had been away, the slave markets had disappointed him again. He prayed that the Roman legions would soon go to war and bring new blood to the slave markets. He needed to stay ahead of his competitors. Luckily both Spartacus and Crixus were the envy of his peers. They filled his purse with coin but he knew sooner or later they would fall. If he just had a few more like them, his name would begin to be whispered in Rome itself. He entered his home and went straight to the balcony to observe the training area. It was dark and no gladiators would be there, but he liked to survey his own little empire. He spied a slave who had been castrated and hung on the wall to serve as a lesson to his comrades. Batiatus would not permit insolence and those who would try to escape would pay the ultimate price. He smiled as he looked at the corpse, bemused as to why the man should even try. Did he not look after them? They wanted for nothing and this was how they repaid a generous master. From the corner of his eye he saw an object, partly lit by the dim torches which circled the training ground. He tried to focus on it, trying hard to decipher its unusual form. As he did his hand moved on the rail, recoiling immediately from a sticky substance. The object's true form now announced itself to his mind, a body and then another and another. He raised his hand to his face and dark blood covered his pale skin. Panic gripped his insides, the urge to run matched only by his urge to find his family. He backed from the balcony into the safety of the main building.

Crixus slaughtered the children as though they were vermin. He held all Romans accountable for the death of his family and his enslavement, whether they were young or old. Spartacus turned away from the carnage in disgust, he wanted no part of these actions. He wanted to run, to protect his own wife and children but there was safety in numbers and he knew that staying with the gladiators afforded him the best chance of procuring passage to a distant land. He walked from the slaughter, bile rising in his throat. He needed to put as much distance between himself and the terror he had just witnessed. He reached an isolated room only for that isolation to be interrupted by a panic stricken Batiatus backing into it. Spartacus stopped still but it was too late, Batiatus turned and confronted him.

'What have you done to my family?' Batiatus part asked, part screamed.

'They are dead,' Spartacus replied. Though he did not wish their death, he had only hatred for this man and refused to feel pity.

'Bastards! I will have every one of you torn to pieces, starting with your family,' Batiatus ranted with insanity. The look of insanity changed to surprise as a gladius ripped through his torso, spilling his insides to the floor. Above him stood Spartacus, defiance radiating from every sinew

'You will not harm my family anymore,' he said, his blade sweeping down, puncturing the throat of his master.

The rebellion had begun, tens of men became thousands and then tens of thousands. Slaves throughout Roman lands rallied to the banner, eager to cast off the yoke of slavery. Rome was slow to react believing slaves incapable of forming a proper army, considering it at first just a local policing matter. However, a gladiator rose from the ranks to command. His skill in the arena would be matched by his skill to mobilise an entire army and Rome would pay the price for its slumber. Spartacus became the bringer of nightmares, Roman towns burned and Roman soldiers died in their hundreds. Rome had faced aggression before, mighty empires wishing to invade and take their precious lands but this was new, the enemy was from within and Rome stuttered in its response.

For two years the slave army made Roman lands bleed. For a while the plebs of Rome even believed the great city might fall. Finally the Roman senate were forced to act, legions were recalled to deal with the internal beast which had the citizens of Rome trembling in their beds. Two armies were dispatched to deal with the threat and these were not raw recruits but veterans made tough on the battlefields of the known world. From the south came Crassus, a political genius intent on winning military glory. From his campaign in Spain came Gnaeus Pompeius Magnus known as Pompey the Great, the best Rome had, a general used to victory. Each army raced to gain glory and the slave army was trapped. With no possibility of escape they turned to face the legions of Crassus in one last show of force against a cruel master. Spartacus had little choice but to fight but he could not battle both Roman armies at the same time. With so many of his warriors dead, including the mighty Crixus, Spartacus resigned himself to the fates. He gathered his army about him and as the legions approached the slave army roared its defiance. Vengeance and wrath clashed against perfect military precision.

Chapter 1

The orders were shouted and troops began to move and so the battle had commenced. On one side the experienced troops of the Roman legions moved in step. Ever onwards they closed the gap between themselves and the horde. The perfect rhythm of thousands of perfectly drilled professional soldiers moving in unison was a fearful sound, so much so it sapped the will of many opposing armies long before the violence erupted. The Roman legions were commanded by Crassus an extremely powerful figure within Roman politics but, as yet, untried as a military commander. He had chased this slave army around the countryside and they had evaded him at each step. However, with a further Roman Army approaching from the north under the control of Pompey, the slave army was now trapped and Crassus wanted victory before Pompey arrived to steal away his glory.

The members of the slave army watched the Roman legions steadily march on and knew that they must fight. Retreat was not an option and they could ill afford to be caught between two Roman armies. The more astute of the warriors, now faced by the true might of Rome, knew the end was near. For over two years they had roamed free in Roman lands, looting towns and growing in size. They had even defeated the Roman legions on a number of occasions but the armies they now faced were different. They were made up from veterans who were not easily forced to turn their back. A powerfully built gladiator, of which there were many within the slave army, glanced towards the sea hoping his family had reached the waiting vessel he had paid to carry them to safety far from the clutches of the Roman Empire. He glanced to his comrades, some were gladiators like him, others were impoverished Roman citizens who joined the slave army rather than sell themselves into servitude, but for the most part the army consisted of escaped slaves.

Rome relied heavily on the beaten backs of slaves and few

masters treated their slaves with anything but cruelty. It had only been a matter of time before a rebellion took place but the enormity of it had shocked even those who had warned against it. A revolt in a small ludus in Capua, where just a handful of gladiators had fought their way to freedom, had grown until the ranks of the rebellion swelled to as many in number as 70,000. The great empire began to shake and at one point it seemed that even Rome might fall to the rabble. However, the opportunity was lost and the gladiator, who had only ever wished to escape the lands of Rome, now knew he would die within them. The battle had begun and already the experienced legions were making progress despite the valiant efforts of his comrades. He stood with a number of other gladiators watching a detachment of Romans approach along the river's edge. If the advance was not halted then, with the enemy on the flank, the battle would be over quickly and the slave army cut to pieces in moments. He gathered some men around him and led the charge, releasing a deafening roar in defiance of those who would enslave him.

His eyes were heavy, like the chains which bound him, but he forced them open scanning the local area. Night was marching on, beginning to hide away the surrounding countryside. The chains were secured to a large tree stump which prevented too much movement, not that his weary body would permit much movement anyway. He managed to pick out a guard hunched over his spear sheltering as best he could against the cold breeze which whipped at his extremities. The guard faced away from him, secure in the knowledge the battle was won and the enemies of Rome lay dead or dying. The prisoner himself was bloodied and exhausted and awaited the death that would surely be delivered brutally and without mercy. His eyes searched out other members of his forlorn army. They had known going against the full might of Rome would eventually lead to one result, but still they had dared to believe, against all hope, this small band could escape the manacles the despotic empire had placed upon them. His mind began to wander to thoughts of his family, hoping they had made it to the ships on time and safe carriage to a far and distant place.

A large centurion approached the gladiator, grinning at the state of a vanquished enemy.

'Up on your feet scum, you have a visitor, though why such a man of importance would wish to have a meeting with the likes of you?' He spat out the words as if tasting rancid meat. The visitor approached. Two men walked at each side of him, although to call them men was such an understatement. These men were Goliaths, as dark as ebony with bodies which were made of granite stone. It seemed this was a man intent on showing his power.

'Well gladiator it seems you're having a bad day. The slave army is destroyed, as we speak the survivors are being taken to be crucified upon the Appian Way. Defeat was always going to be the only outcome. Now tell me, what should we do with you?' There was no malice in his voice more a mocking interest. The gladiator never spoke in reply he just stared unflinchingly at this man who held his very existence within his hands. A sharp burning pain smashed into the side of his face, the centurion had used his vine.

'Your Roman master asked you a question.'

'Kill me and be done with it!' The gladiator snarled back.

'It's clear to me that simply killing one of the men who challenged the might of Rome, no matter how foolhardy, is no reward for such courage. Your actions were misguided perhaps but nevertheless they were courageous. No, I think I have better services for your skills.'

'You think I would serve Rome? Then you had better kill me, for the release of the manacles only serves to free my hands to strangle Rome.' Again the vine struck bringing another welt upon the gladiator's features.

'Oh, I think I can restrain you much more adequately than with mere manacles, for instance let's see...' The visitor gave a wave of his hand and for the first time the gladiator's fight left him utterly and completely. Behind the centurion, figures were being dragged forward. To the gladiator's horror his family were brought nearer. 'You see gladiator it is my job to find weakness in both friend and foe and, if I do say so, I am rather good at it.'

'What is it you want from me?'

'What I want? I want you to do whatever I wish, when I wish it.'

'And my family?'

'They, or should I say all but one, will be released to a place where they can be watched. They will have comfortable carefree lives, unless of course you give reason for that to change.'

'All but one?' The fear was already in his voice as he asked the question.

'It is important you understand the lengths my masters are willing to go to, to ensure their plans are fulfilled.' With this the visitor nodded and, without a moment's hesitation, the centurion slit the nearest child's throat.

The gladiator roared, his powerful arms strained at his chains and just a flicker of anxiety crossed the visitor's face. For a moment he thought the chains would break.

'I am truly sorry to have to resort to such tactics, but do not think I will not act in that way again. Do I have your word or will we move to the next child?'

'You have it!' Cried the gladiator through the anger and tears.

'Very well. You will rest at a location I have chosen, you will regain your fitness and your family will be removed to a place of safety. I will arrange for them to visit you. Now have you anything else to say?'

'Grant me one request to cement our agreement,' the gladiator spoke through gritted teeth.

'You have a nerve. Very well if it's within my power,' the Roman replied.

'The centurion is a fine soldier at killing children and striking unarmed men, but let me show you what you get from me in this bargain.'

'Absolutely not, I need you alive for the time being. I will kill you when I require it.' The visitor was calm and clear in his response.

'If I can't kill one centurion then I am probably not the man for the job.'

The centurion butted in before the visitor could say anything in reply.

'Excuse me Sir I'd be delighted to show this gladiator what a Roman centurion of twelve years is capable of. Besides it's time a proper Roman soldier showed this scum how to fight, not the raw recruits this scum has bested.'

'Very well centurion. Gladiator you shall have your wish, but be warned should you lose your life, so too will your family.' The gladiator just nodded his agreement. 'Centurion make the arrangements, one hour I think.' The Roman aristocrat walked away without looking back.

The gladiator stared at his family. His beloved was beaten and bloodied but she stood proud, their dead son at her feet. Tears streamed from her eyes but she let out no cry. She cradled their young daughter close to her breast. Her eyes were lost in his, he felt her pain as deeply as any sword thrust. He noted the men around him, from the arrogant aristocrat to the centurion, down to the guards. Deep within him an oath was made, each and every one of the men who stood before him would die slow and hard. But only one today, the centurion.

More of the aristocrat's personal guard formed an unbreakable ring. Each carried a sword and shield but the gladiator didn't recognise the type or origin. Beyond them more guards held his family secure so, for now, he must behave as required. The centurion stretched his powerful limbs, limbering up for the fight ahead. Confidence oozed from him, for four years he had been legion champion. He had fought many battles and never received a scratch. He smiled, with a gladius within his hands he was invincible. He smiled at the gladiator.

'You have the honour of fighting Marcus Flavius. Your death at my hands will be an honour to your people. I have killed many with this weapon, Gauls, Greeks and many more have all fallen before it, which are you?'

'Thracian,' replied the gladiator. 'And it's a quality sword. I will look after it when you are rotting in the ground.' There was no malice in the way the gladiator spoke. Gone now was the anger, to be replaced as it always was, by a cold calculating killing animal. For the first time the centurion portrayed just a flicker of uncertainty. No-one else observed this except the gladiator who simply smiled.

'And your name Thracian, if the parents of scum like you deemed it necessary to name you?'

'You know not the man you challenge, I think you will know it by the end,' replied the gladiator.

'Plinius you worthless scab, give him a sword,' ordered the centurion. A young guard walked to the gladiator. He placed a blade in the gladiator's hand and whispered.

'By the gods, I hope you kill this bastard.'

The gladiator glanced at the young soldier, his face was battered and bruised but not from the recent battle. This boy had endured torment over a long period of time, it seemed the centurion didn't restrict violence to the enemy. He knew all about these types of men, they were a sore on life, whose only enjoyment came from the misery of others and the only cure was the same as a mad beast and that was death. Soon enough the centurion would be cured. The warriors began to circle. Flavius was powerfully built but the gladiator noticed how light he was on his feet. His uniform sparkled and was marked with hardly a speck of dust. This compared to the battle torn rags of the gladiator, gone was his armour but he was used to fighting without it. He had once fought naked to please the mistress of the gladiator school. The centurion went on the offensive raining blow after blow, all of which the gladiator parried. He stayed on the defensive just allowing the centurion to exert himself. The centurion began to blow his cheeks out hard. He had thrown his best moves against this man, but it had been like trying to hit mist. The gladiator smiled.

'You look tired centurion, maybe you should defend for a while.'

It was impossible, how could a slave move so fast? The centurion defended for all his worth but was giving ground constantly to the barrage of thrusts and slashes which came from the gladiator. Finally searing pain took him in the thigh, he hadn't even seen the stroke coming. It was not too deep, not troubling the arteries but enough to slow movement.

'Ok I need a rest, your turn,' said the gladiator, mocking him. Flavius screamed in anger. He launched himself at his foe, slicing wildly. He was rewarded with a cut across his forearm.

'Now, now. You know never to let anger beat you, you're fighting like raw recruit centurion.' The sarcastic emphasis on centurion, reverberated around the fighting ring.

It was funny to the gladiator, that here was the leader of many of these men, yet none of them showed anger at his downfall, in fact many seemed to show the faintest smile. Ten minutes later and six more cuts, Flavius was stumbling. None of the cuts had been disastrous but put them together and the loss of blood soon tells on a man, sapping his energy and speed. The gladiator was growing weary of this man. He raised the stakes, parry, parry, thrust and slash. Flavius' severed hand rose like a bird in flight and then crashed next to the feet of Plinius who calmly kicked it from the ring. The loss of blood was incredible. It was amazing how the man still stood, but he knew once he fell he would never stand again. He removed some of his armour to try and gain more speed but it just gave more opportunity for pain. The next slash opened a six inch gap in his stomach, his intestines poured from the wound like startled snakes. He attempted in vain to stem the flow with his bloodied stump, but the energy required was too much. He slumped to his knees and awaited death, his sword dropping from his hand. He looked at the victor.

'Who are you?'

The gladiator kicked the fallen man's sword a safe distance away and then bent and whispered to the centurion.

'I will say this, murderer of my son, so that you know before you die how you brought about your own downfall, for only a stupid man willingly challenges an unknown opponent.'

' Your name?' Spluttered the centurion.

'I am Spartacus,' the gladiator whispered. Comprehension spread over the face of the centurion, the next sweep of the sword brought Flavius to darkness forever...

Chapter 2

The centurion's end had taken place a week ago and still Spartacus had had no further contact with the aristocrat. Following the bout he had been taken a night's ride away to a country villa, where his wounds from the battle had been taken care of. Fresh tunics were made available and good food was bountiful. On the third day after arriving his wife and child were brought to the camp and six glorious hours followed. It was almost all they had both always dreamed of except, of course, for the watchers who were never too far away. There was no possibility of escape so, for now, Spartacus enjoyed the time they had together.

The time away from his family he spent regaining his fitness. The battle fought had taken its toll both physically and mentally. He was surprised at how seeing his men cut down had affected him. Being a gladiator he had become all too aware that friends were easily lost, and had also realised this prevented you from ever really forming true friendships. However, when he had reclaimed his freedom, fellow escapees became dependent on him and he also on them and, as time passed, real friendships grew and they were as brothers. They turned back into men rather than lethal weapons, they loved and laughed. The sadness at their loss tore at him as a fast running stream drags at the swimmer, trying to pull him to oblivion.

On the fifth day he was training with a wooden sword in the courtyard, when a familiar voice came from behind.

'I see a dangerous man is intent on staying that way.' The aristocrat eyed Spartacus impressed by the work ethic, many given this opportunity of good food and lodgings would have lazed in the sun but this man, this man was different. 'Walk with me gladiator.' Spartacus looked shocked this man wanted him to walk next to him with no guards. 'Oh I think I am safe enough, as I said before, the manacles which hold you cannot be placed on your wrists.' He said this with such unwavering confidence Spartacus was tempted to rip out his throat to test his theory but stayed his hands.

Spartacus lowered his training sword and rose to join the aristocrat. They ambled down a dirt track which led to a babbling brook which, only days before, was where he and his wife had enjoyed their time together.

'It's time for me to tell you what I know. Your name is Teres, named after a very successful ancient Thracian King, successful in Thracian terms that is. You were given the name 'Spartacus' by your Roman captors. You were of noble birth but your family lost their fortune due to the poor decisions of your father. Rather than starve, you joined the Roman Army. After twenty of your fellow Thracians were slaughtered due to an incapable centurion, you deserted after, of course, the centurion had been found butchered. It seems to be a recurring theme around you. After a year you were captured and sold into the gladiator ludus at Capua. Correct?'

'It seems you have me at a disadvantage,' replied Spartacus trying to disguise the wonder at what this man knew about him.

'That, you will find, is my business. Killing is your profession, information is mine and, like you, I am very good at it.'

'So what would you have me do?'

'All in good time. You may call me Cassian Antonius.'

'And judging by your wealth, a senator?' Spartacus suggested.

'No, I am what they call a facilitator. Rome is a cumbersome beast and politics often get in the way. Sometimes certain tasks need to be carried out quickly and without fuss, that is where I come in.'

'An assassin?'

'Oh that can happen, but my duties are far more extensive than that, to be honest killing is regrettable, but a necessity at certain times.'

'Like my son?'

'Spartacus, if I told you I regretted such action, you wouldn't believe me. That was an order from the people I work for and, although I understood their logic, I didn't agree with it. As I said, killing is regrettable. One day no doubt you will seek a reckoning; it's probably a race to see which one of us gets killed first.'

Spartacus wondered if this man had children of his own and would think it regrettable if one had been murdered.

'Down to business. In two days you will be joined by twelve men, their job is to follow your orders...um unless of course they contradict mine,' Cassian added.

'Who will they be?' Spartacus asked.

'Six will be men who I have used before in such tasks. They are good, very good, but they are followers not leaders. Another two will be the gentlemen you saw at my side when you so efficiently dispatched the centurion. The other four you will pick from a squad of soldiers which will use this villa in the next few days. A word of warning, choose well and best not use the name 'Spartacus' just yet. I am afraid you have rather upset a number of Romans in the past couple of years. I will return to give you your orders. Until then prepare well, you will need to.' Cassian put emphasis on the latter words. Spartacus watched the man go. So this man was a puppet to Rome like most others. Despite his self importance he took orders just like everyone else. What was required from him now was to do this man's bidding until he found the puppet master, which would be a day of true reckoning.

The next two days passed without incident, but on the morning of the eighth day a squad of legionaries filed into the courtyard led by a Goliath of an optio. He barked orders at his men and when the orders weren't acted on quickly enough he exacted a more physical approach. It seemed to Spartacus he enjoyed directing his fury towards a young guard who, after Spartacus had moved in closer, he recognised as Plinius, the guard who had handed him a sword to kill the centurion with. Spartacus was about to intervene when Lucius the villa charge hand began to speak.

'Soldiers of Rome, my master apologises for not being here to welcome you, however that is not important. What is important is you listen clearly to my instructions. This man,' he gestured towards Spartacus, 'has been selected for special duties for Rome. Four of you will be selected to join this man and will be rewarded justly; the others will assist him in any way necessary to help prepare for his mission. Whilst under this roof this man will be treated as your commanding officer. Are there any questions?'

18

Lucius ended his announcement abruptly and briefly waited for questions. As none arrived he quickly turned and left to go about his business.

Roman soldiers had learnt through experience they did not question orders, however that did not mean they had to like them. The optio spat on the ground. It was clear this was one Roman who disliked obeying non-Romans. Spartacus ambled across to the men. He walked up and down the line, an occasional tut issuing from his lips. His secondary vision kept the optio in view, and he noticed the man was getting more and more angry.

'Strip to tunics only,' Spartacus blasted out quite suddenly and a number of the men flinched. 'Soldier your name please?' He gestured to Plinius. The young soldier stood proud and screamed out his name. 'Good man, be so kind as to fetch me, let's say, four of the training swords.' He said it in a matter of fact way, but the boy still scurried off, clearly eager to impress. Spartacus wasn't sure if the young soldier had recognised him, but he would no doubt soon find out. The boy returned in double quick time with the blades.

'Right, three best swordsmen to the front,' he barked. The optio immediately stepped forward, this Spartacus had expected. Then a tall, deep olive skinned man, thin and wiry stepped forward. He had the longest arms Spartacus had ever seen. He made a mental note to beware of the reach and then, to his surprise, a short man who, apart from his head, was covered in thick black hair stepped out of line. Spartacus noted he didn't rush out, he sauntered but, as unimpressive as his movement seemed, Spartacus noticed his eyes were everywhere, completely alive, noticing everything. He observed Spartacus the same way as he was being observed.

'OK gentleman you've retired, Rome has conquered the world. You're sitting on your perfect chair in your perfect settlement, the farm is making money and you are at peace with the world. Then along comes this bloody foreigner who fucks your best bull and shits on your favourite pair of boots. What are you going to do?' Sniggering broke out in the ranks. The optio silenced them.

'Ah optio, just the man, what are you going to do?'

'With respect sir, I'd cut his balls off.' He stared at Spartacus, sending out the message that's just what he'd like to do to him.

'And you other two?' He gestured to the others. The tall guy simply ran a thumb across his neck. 'And you?'

'Never seen a man shag a bull, I'd ask was he on top or the bull?' Spartacus smiled.

'Good answer, what's your name?'

'My mother called me Drakis, sir.'

'And what do the men call you?' Spartacus asked, wanting to know the man.

'They call me Bull, sir.' A huge smile spreading on his face.

Spartacus erupted with laughter and struggled to stop smiling for some time. He told the men, apart from the three who had stepped forward to whom he gave blades, to get comfortable. The men were still smiling and chattering when Spartacus gave his next order.

'Right gentlemen, kill me.' Spartacus spoke in a calm, secure manner but his words still had weight. The remaining crowd of men stopped, they couldn't believe it, one man against three. This man was either like a God with a sword or just plain stupid. They edged towards stupid.

Immediately the optio and the tall man crouched, ready to attack. Bull on the other hand held back simply observing. The tall soldier again and again used his impressive reach trying to throw Spartacus off balance, but it was clear he relied too heavily on the same moves too many times. The optio lunged, but Spartacus simply moved to the side, tripping him up on his way by. As he did so he crouched low and wasn't surprised, the tall man had used the same move and his blade whistled over his head. Spartacus simply punched the man, knocking him out cold. Still Bull stood watching. Returning to his feet the optio attacked from behind but he was too slow and too loud. Spartacus again side stepped his advance, this time bringing the flat of the sword slapping into his face. His nose splattered, throwing blood and mucus at least two feet into the air and he collapsed to the floor unable to see his opponent let alone fight him.

'You're good, a real professional,' said Bull.

'Oh just lucky I guess. You like to observe an opponent don't

20

you,' replied Spartacus.

'It's always a benefit to know an opponent's strengths and weaknesses.'

'Not too many weaknesses I hope.'

'A few,' Bull said confidently.

They circled one another, a few testing moves to see how each other moved, then both rained in full bloodied attacks. Neither was able to break the defence of the other and, after what seemed a lifetime, they broke away from one another, each breathing heavily.

'Well Bull have you learnt enough from me yet?' Said Spartacus, breathing heavily.

'I think I have the measure of you,' replied an equally tired Bull.

'Good, then I can switch to using my proper sword arm.' Spartacus' face portrayed just a slight smile, whereas for the first time Bull's face displayed a look of complete and utter disbelief. From that point on the dual was totally one sided. Spartacus' cuts and thrusts were delivered with more speed, accuracy and power and it wasn't long before Bull was felled. But there was no vicious hit or taunting, Bull had fought well and deserved respect. Spartacus offered his hand which Bull accepted and used it to heave himself to his feet.

'Right, all of you the weapons you brought with you are to be checked in with Lucius. It is time to be washed and ready for a feast which our generous host has provided for us. Bull and Plinius you will come and see me when I have finished speaking. The rest of you eat and sleep well, for tomorrow we will be busy.' Spartacus thought to himself how easy it was to command men, no matter the origins. These soldiers did his bidding as easily as the slaves who rallied to his cause to fight against Rome, but he didn't simply want them to obey him. For what he had in mind he needed them to love him, love him so much they would betray their own people. 'But that's for another day,' he spoke quietly to himself and moved to talk to Bull and Plinius.

He grasped a pitcher of wine and poured them all a drink. 'Tough day,' he mentioned in a throw away fashion. 'How long have you been with the legion?' He enquired, although he was eager for them not to feel he was interrogating them in any way.

'Three years for myself, the boy joined us about six months ago.' Bull said. Spartacus noticed that Plinius bit his lip as the word 'boy' was used.

'Clearly this Plinius wants to prove himself. Well he may just get his chance if he lives long enough, if any of us live long enough,' he corrected himself. 'What made you join?' He knew this was a tricky moment. Much of the legion was made up from the scrags of mankind. They were running or hiding usually, or had reached the bottom of society and it was either jump in the Tiber or join the legions, both usually ended in death, it was just the Tiber was a little quicker. Surprisingly Bull was quite open.

'My mother was Greek and my father a Roman centurion and, like most centurions, was a bastard. So when I had the chance I skipped, joined the triremes first with the navy but transferred over to the legion as I must be the only Greek who can't stand the movement of a ship. My father pulled strings and here I am, about the only thing he ever did for me that didn't involve that bloody cane, bastard.' Bull spat as he finished.

'Plinius, what about you?' Spartacus smiled. Nervously the young man re-counted how he and his brother Aelius, had joined when his family couldn't pay the landlord; it was either that or starve. 'Where's your brother now?' Spartacus asked, but could tell that maybe he shouldn't have asked because Plinius turned away. Bull interrupted.

'The boy and his brother joined together. At first they were doing well, showing a lot of promise. Back then our centurion, Flavius, was a sword sparring freak. At first I thought he just loved it as an art form but what he actually liked was the opportunity to bully. One morning he was undertaking his usual torment on a new recruit, young Plinius here. He took it too far and broke Plinius' arm. I remember because Flavius never stopped laughing, right up to the point when Aelius knocked him cold. Everyone except Aelius was sent back to barracks. We were quite a distance away but we could all hear the screams. When Flavius came round he and our dear optio kicked Aelius to death, and for what? Aren't we supposed to stand up for one another, a bloody crying shame that was.' Spartacus stared at Plinius still with his back to the two men and then at Bull.

'Both of you go and get some food I'll see you in the morning.' Spartacus watched them go, thoughts turning over in his mind.

The next morning Cassian joined the camp. From the moment Spartacus saw him he could tell there was something wrong. He was talking to messengers constantly, sending them hurtling on their way. His composure seemed less than normal, which had to that point been the very essence of calm, complete control. The morning passed and it was well into the afternoon when Cassian finally came to speak with Spartacus. He seemed agitated and really didn't say much, generally just passed the time of day and retired early. Spartacus knew the look that had portrayed itself upon Cassian's face; it was of a man whose plans had taken an unexpected turn. This was something Spartacus had learned to live with while he had commanded his slave army.

Spartacus put Cassian from his mind and went and trained. He spent time with Plinius teaching him technique and while he was not showing the boy the art with the sword he had instructed Bull to do so. Spartacus was aware of the optio continually throwing insults Plinius' way, but the boy seemed oblivious, he was so focussed on learning the sword. It was clear he had a plan and Spartacus guessed it involved the optio and revenge for his brother Aelius. Finally at the end of the day Bull asked.

'So Teres, what is this mission?'

Spartacus glanced in the direction of Cassian's quarters.

'To be honest Bull, I haven't any idea, but tomorrow I think, will bring news, but I will say this, I will require yourself and Plinius and would be honoured if you were to join me.'

'Yes sir,' both soldiers snapped to attention.

'No men, I believe this will be dangerous beyond usual soldiering. I ask you not as soldiers but as men, I ask you not to follow me into the depths of hell, but to stand at my side as we cross the threshold, together.'

As he said these words he held out his hand. Plinius shook the hand of Spartacus, as Spartacus knew he would. Bull stood and grasped Spartacus by the shoulder and said,

'To hell then.'

Chapter 3

The training continued over the next few days and it was hard, pushing each man to his very limits. Spartacus was surprised to see how quickly the men were improving. He had thought they would stick to the tried and tested methods of the Roman legions, one which flourished and relied upon endless drill and fighting in formation, but they had grasped that whatever mission they were to embark upon, it would require different skills. This type of warfare required a much greater personal skill, it was a raw, beastlike way of fighting, and where those that had learned best would remain standing, with the foe bloodied and dying in the dirt. Although he had been impressed by the men wanting to learn, he recalled the savagery of the arena in which he had learnt his own trade and he feared few of these men would have lasted long fighting under the sun in the arena at Capua.

He smiled thinking he was lucky to survive that place and reminded himself it was impossible to second guess who would walk from the arena alive, for a man's desire to survive often outweighed his skills with a weapon. Deep within all men there is a beast which needs only to be set free, and even the most unlikely candidate could become a God amongst the blood and the sand. When victorious he would experience the crowd cheering which enthused the warrior to a point where he almost thought of himself as a God, that is until the next time he stood at the gates waiting for his next bout to begin and the fear began once more to rise within him.

The days were long and hard and suddenly Spartacus was tired. All his life he had been wielding one weapon or another, fighting enemy after enemy, whether it had been as just a boy when he quarrelled with his father, whose savage tongue was his weapon of choice, or later fighting for Rome against its barbarian enemies, or in the arena against others forced to fight against their will. He didn't join the men that night for feasting and a goblet of wine, and for this he reproached himself, for he needed to know them better, but the spectres of his past were playing heavy upon his heart and mind and all he craved was solitude and sleep.

Spartacus spent a troubled night, images of those he had lost swimming in and out of his mind's eye, the worst of which his son. The glint of a dagger, the splash of red and gone was that wonderful child who he had loved so deeply and who he had allowed harm to be befall. The shame and grief awoke him, tears rolling from his eyes, mixing with the sweat so common to a disturbed rest. His eyes fixed upon a shadow in the doorway.

'I'm sorry did I wake you?' The figure spoke and Spartacus realised it was Cassian. He didn't bother to answer the Roman but instead swung his legs from his bed.

'I have brought something for you Spartacus. I hope you will accept it in the manner it is offered.' There was no confidence in the man's voice, merely a meagre hoping. Spartacus growled.

'What is it?' The anger of his dreams still haunting him.

'You will need to come with me,' Cassian said. He didn't wait for a reply, but turned his back and walked from the room.

Spartacus heaved himself from the bed and slipped on a tunic. Following Cassian from the main buildings he headed towards the babbling brook. He crossed a small wooden bridge and climbed a small hillock which overlooked the brook and surrounding valley. Spartacus spied a small grave which had been installed, marked with a small lantern and which had been topped with a marble stone.

'I brought your son's body back here, and seeing your family enjoyed this area so much I thought, I thought well …it's done.' Cassian stumbled over his words.

'And this makes your murder of him wash away does it?' Spartacus tried his best to be angry but, to be honest, he struggled, for his real anger was at himself, for all fathers are duty bound to protect and, no matter how impossible the odds, a failure is still a failure and a source of everlasting shame. Spartacus crossed to the small grave and read the inscription; tears came freely as he begged for forgiveness from his son.

'You know, when Batiatus allowed the champions of Capua to

have a single woman to be their mate and no other would be permitted to touch them, I thought it a kind of freedom. Then less than a year later my son Thrax was born. He had the strength of a lion from the first time he grabbed my finger, and for a while we were happy. At night they left the ludus and I stayed, confined to my room. As time went on I spoke to Batiatus about why he had allowed such a freedom to gladiators. He just laughed and said, 'What freedom? I have chained you and your family to this place forever.' I looked at my son, then five summers old, and decided he would never live as an ox to serve man. Within the year I was gutting that fat slob Batiatus like a fish.' Spartacus finished talking and just stared at the grave. Cassian made to move away.

'Wait!' Said Spartacus. Cassian turned and, for the first time, Spartacus looked straight at him. 'You have my thanks for this thing you have done.'

'Debts often come in different guises Spartacus,' and with that Cassian nodded and walked into what remained of the night.

Spartacus watched him walk away, a mixture of loathing and gratitude gnawed at his insides; this was an uncommon man who left Spartacus feeling bewildered at best.

Spartacus never returned to his bed that night but instead tended the grave until the call to breakfast. He sauntered down to the kitchens, the previous night's happenings turning over and over in his mind and he didn't regain himself until he met up with the other men. The men had grown accustomed to each other by now and idle chat sparked into life easily. All but the optio joined in, he seemed to resent the comfortable, happy aura that seemed to have developed between his men, but he held back from chastising them too obviously because Spartacus was never far away. It was clear that hatred existed between the two.

The morning marched on with the men being put through their training. They began with weapon training, not only with swords but with javelins and slings. Spartacus believed it important that the men he would eventually choose should be able to rise and meet any challenge. As the afternoon approached Spartacus ordered the optio to take the men on a run around the villa's grounds, as he did so Cassian hailed him.

Cassian was seated at a large wooden desk, papers covered the entire surface and, at first, the man looked transfixed by the number of documents. Eventually he looked up, smiled and motioned to Spartacus to take a seat.

'Your training goes well I hear. Have you selected your men yet?'

'Two are with me, I am still reviewing the qualities of the other men,' Spartacus replied. In truth he had seen little in the other men to fill him with confidence, many were just professional soldiers. They could obey orders all day but ask them to think for themselves and it got tricky. Cassian poured wine for them both and stared, as if in deep contemplation, for a few moments at Spartacus before speaking.

'Tell me Spartacus, what do you know of Rome, not the city but the people of Rome?'

'I only know of the people who have taken my liberty and order the world to conduct themselves as the Romans do, or meet with the sword and death.'

'That assessment is partly correct, I wish I could sit here and declare some higher purpose, but I cannot. Let me tell you of the real Rome. Some time ago a great general named Sulla ruled Rome with an iron fist. The senators feared him, the plebs only saw a man who gave them great victories. Once Sulla defeated his great rival Marius nobody could stand against his will and Rome was truly a dangerous place to live. Then Sulla died and many thought Rome would cease to be such a sinister place. This, however, was not the case. Since the death of Sulla there has been a power struggle within Rome between those who would gain power, and that battle rages as we speak. Those who don't seek absolute power throw their allegiance behind someone who does, for if you don't have a powerful ally in Rome then you will soon be feeding the carrion.'

'This is all very interesting but what has it to do with me?' Spartacus interceded.

'To succeed in this mission you will need to understand the type of men you serve and those who will want to stop you at any cost,' Cassian replied. 'There are three types capable of gaining power within Rome; firstly those from the position of family and tradition.

Few of the Roman hierarchy can claim true Roman status stretching back more than a hundred years. The fact those families have done so shows a quality of survival few can match and, as such, others are keen to join their cause. Second comes military, a successful general will have support of his legions which strikes fear in the heart of most of the nobles and also gains supports from the plebs, who feast on great victories. Thirdly comes wealth, and I mean true wealth. A man who is capable of buying senators will always have power and person to do his bidding. Anyone who fits into these categories has potential to rise to the top and anyone who fits into more than one is almost guaranteed to attempt it.'

'And where do you fit into these categories?'

Cassian smiled. 'My grandfather was a Greek merchant. I have never served in the military and I have wealth, but not to the levels required so, like you Spartacus, I do others bidding and, like you, I do so to survive.' He placed emphasis on the 'survive' part of the statement.

Spartacus never replied but inside he almost laughed. Like me he thought, you are nothing like me.

'Which brings us to the task ahead. One such man who wishes to be the ultimate power in Rome is Marcus Lucinius Crassus, a man who not just fits into the category of those with wealth he practically is the category. Without doubt he is the richest man in Rome and, quite possibly, the world, but as for his military qualities, he has lacked the victories of his rivals. Despite putting your little rebellion down Spartacus, I am sure you will agree his tactics were hardly startling. So the natural thing for his rivals to do is to concentrate on weakening his wealth, for once that has gone his potential to rule has gone.'

'How could this little band do such a thing to such a wealthy man?' Spartacus queried.

'By removing, step by step, the areas and people who make him wealthy, which is why shortly we will be travelling to Utica, once a great city of the Carthaginian Empire, because at Utica there is a man known as Dido. He is our mission.'

'What we just walk in and cut his throat?'

Cassian smiled. 'It would seem an easy solution but one which wouldn't suffice in this instance. Dido is a powerful man in his own right, with not only friends in Carthage but Rome also. You see, Dido controls most of the pirates which operate in Roman waters and therefore, to a certain extent, he controls trade.'

'So why not send in the troops?'

'For two reasons, Dido would know of any impending attack long before the troops would be knocking at his door, and secondly of his friends in Rome they block any call for action. To be fair most of the senate hold coin in their purse from either Crassus or Dido, so that option would never be viable. The only way to prevent Dido from supporting Crassus is to take away Dido's wealth to the point he becomes worthless to Crassus.'

'But how? If you can't kill him or send in the troops?'

'Like I told you before Spartacus, I find the weakness in people, those flaws which expose their own downfall.' Cassian had a glint in his eyes as he spoke now.

'And this Dido has a weakness?'

'My dear Spartacus, this man has two. He has tried hard to make them work in his favour but weaknesses they remain.'

'Women?'

'Oh no. To be honest I don't think Dido's cloth is cut that way. No, his first flaw is he's a gambler, and when I say gambler, this is gambling on the very edge. The higher the risk, the less he can resist. The second is the arena. He has organised for the last three years a tournament called 'The Blood of Baal', where the entrants must pay a king's ransom and have a team of six gladiators just to enter. Each team of six fights each other until the final round when whatever is left of the team will fight Dido's three champions. The winnings are enormous. Dido will always bet huge sums however, because his champions have never been beaten, he has never had to pay up. It is our mission to change that.'

'Our mission?'

'Yes Spartacus, I will travel with you. I have given orders that your family be taken to my home and they will be treated with dignity. They will not be slaves. I have afforded to them the most secure place that I can - with my family. So you see Spartacus, failure is not an option. It will not be long before Crassus knows of what we intend to do and failure will leave us open to his wrath. However, success does not assure our safety but it does keep the support of those I serve.'

Spartacus thought of the perils ahead and yearned for the days of the arena where there were no politics just blood. You either won or lost. Rome was like a city of mist, the clarity of the road ahead was always unclear, ghostly figures moved in the mist but were they friend or foe? Was it a hand of friendship they held out, or a dagger to cut a throat?

'Crassus will know we are intending to travel soon though, I hope, will not be aware of the destination. He will know I have gathered a great wealth and wagons to load it into and I have gathered some men about me. When we leave Spartacus the route will be as dangerous as the destination and we must be prepared.'

Chapter 4

A few weeks passed without interruption. Cassian remained in the villa with Spartacus and the men. He discussed constantly with Spartacus the qualities of each of the men.

'We will need more than the four I asked you to choose.'

'Where are the six men you said were coming to join us?' Spartacus enquired, he had wondered about this for a number of days but had waited for the right opportunity to raise the subject with Cassian.

'A couple of my farm hands found them yesterday. They were hanging from a large tree which signifies the end of my land. A clear message has been sent, I believe, that Crassus knows we are up to something.' As he spoke, Spartacus noticed the sure signs of grief creeping into the face of Cassian. He had seen this look many times, a proud man expected to take such things in his stride, never letting such matters bring him down to the level of mere mortals, but the signs were there. The slight quiver of voice and lip, the refusal to look anyone in the eye. This man had suffered a loss.

'You knew them well?' Spartacus probed, although he did not know why. What did he care for this man's grief? Cassian merely shrugged, a clear attempt at hiding his true feelings.

'Five had worked for me for some time - good men, loyal men.'

'And the other?'

Cassian raised his head and, for the first time, looked Spartacus squarely in the eyes and Spartacus knew this man was in pain.

'My brother! Crassus has killed my brother.' It was not screamed or said through sobbing, it was said quietly as if an important duty was being added to a list and in many ways Spartacus believed that is what it was. Cassian, in that moment, had added Crassus to a list. He continued 'I believe I under estimated the reaction of our foes in this matter, we will need to take as many men as we can muster for the journey to the coast.'

'As for the men, most are adequate with sword and all have the ability to follow orders,' Spartacus replied. 'I am sorry for your loss,' Spartacus added quietly and then moved to join the rest of the men. He was angry at himself for caring enough to say it, why should he care? Hadn't this man ordered the death of his son. Well, if he believed Cassian then that order was not his but from a higher office. So did he believe this Roman, when all Romans he had met thus far had proven to be deceitful? Yet since that very first day Cassian had shown himself to be a man of honour. Spartacus thought the world had gone mad - Romans you could trust, never!

It was decided over the next couple of days all the legionaries would travel if they so wished. It would be a mission only a volunteer would be expected to embark upon. Each man would receive a small fortune on completion of the mission and given the option to leave the ranks and join normal society. The offer was completely mind blowing to the common soldier, who ordinarily had to serve for many, many years, and the chances of reaching the end of that service without death or serious injury were very slight. Cassian had chosen only men with no families, so to collect the reward you had to survive. If you survived then the mission would have to succeed, for failure meant only the carrion would know your graves.

All readily signed up. They were all provided with new clothing and equipment. The Roman legionary regalia was washed away, leaving the citizen beneath. From now on there would be no commanders other than Cassian and Spartacus. They would obey orders the moment they were asked to do so, and failure to do so would mean death with no appeal. This was a fact the ordinary soldiers within the legions were used to, unless you were lucky enough to serve in a legion which was commanded by one of the few officers who knew how to treat men. If you were not so lucky then cruelty and untimely death were commonplace. They were used to risking their lives for someone else's whim. This, at least, offered them the chance to make it worth the gamble. Even the optio seemed at ease at giving up his rank, the chance of real wealth overcoming even his oversized ego.

The next morning was greeted with great activity. An hour before Cassian had released his decoy. Two wagons, and around twenty slaves had been dressed up to look like an armed guard. However, it was made clear to them if they were to meet with trouble then they were to flee, and not try and rescue the wagons. If captured they knew nothing of importance which could harm the real convoy. A short time later the real convoy set off, after Cassian's spies had observed riders dressed all in black leave and start shadowing the initial convoy.

'It will give us a few hours - half a day at best before they realise what's happened, and with the trail I have picked maybe a good deal longer,' remarked Cassian.

'Unless they have more lookouts posted along the way,' replied Spartacus, unsure of the plan.

'Oh they did have, but they only look to the skies now,' Cassian replied with a grim determination. Spartacus had noticed the difference in the man since the news of his brother. The loss seemed to motivate this man to succeed even more. Such a loss had broken many men but Spartacus was relieved Cassian's judgement had stayed true, and logic was winning where emotions could have triumphed. How, or if, that would change if Cassian were to meet Crassus he did not know, but that was for another time, and for now, as the mission finally lurched into progress, it was clear much blood would be spilled before it reached its end.

As it was, little happened on that first day. Cassian had decided upon three wagons pulled by huge oxen, with spare oxen trailing behind each wagon. One wagon carried the gold and some supplies, in the second was armour, swords, helmets and all the required items to keep a gladiatorial team at its best through a tournament. The third carried more supplies such as animal feed, which these beasts seemed to consume in massive quantities.

The night wore on and the convoy rested for the night. Guards were posted and Cassian decided that fires must be lit. To reach the tournament when the men had not had proper nourishment or warmth would see the attempt at winning quickly falter. Cassian gathered the men around after all had eaten their fill.

'It is time for honesty gentlemen. You have sworn to fight on this mission. It is possible some will never return home, so I believe you should know certain facts – the first is that we fight to prevent a man taking control in Rome who would surely bring it to its knees. As such, we have in our midst a man who stood for that very ideal. This man sought the end of Rome and, if truth be known, Rome created the man who would cause them so much trouble. However, this man is to be trusted and obeyed, for the success of this mission will rely upon him.' Cassian gestured to Spartacus to come close. 'This man, who you know as Teres, is none other than Spartacus, leader of the slave revolt. I will know whether anyone here has any problems?' Not a hand was raised or a voice heard, except a little chortle from Bull.

'I knew I recognised your fighting style. I saw you at Capua when you defeated Petrocles, the champion from Pompeii. What a fight, he pushed you that day.' Spartacus smiled.

'He had seen better days. I was not likely to humiliate him for the baying crowd. At his best though I think the match may have had a different result.'

'I don't think so, he may have been quick and strong but he lacked the moves to unlock your defences.'

'I am grateful for your kind words,' Spartacus replied.

Cassian then told the men of what lay ahead, describing the mission in some detail and emphasizing the difficulties which faced each of them. Spartacus was surprised, knowing that if one of these men was a spy for Crassus then they now had the full picture to report on. Cassian seemed to understand what Spartacus was thinking from the look upon his face.

'It is also clear that one or more of you may well be a spy placed within our ranks. Let me make things quite clear, the names of every man on this mission have been placed on a list. That list has been given to the man I serve. That individual has undertaken that if any one man returns from the mission when it has failed then they will suffer death, and I doubt it will be a quick and easy fate. Moreover, if the man runs he will have one of the most powerful men in Rome, with unlimited resources, dedicated to tracking him down. There will be no place in which you could hide. I hope that is clear, the mission is to succeed or die. Glory or death.'

Despite the magnitude of the mission ahead, the men settled for the night well. A small amount of wine was permitted and tales were told beside the fire. Men shared their past, including Cassian who told of his family's rise to wealth and of his family; a wife and two boys. Aegis, one of Cassian's bodyguards, sang an ancient song which had a haunting melody which lulled the men into tiredness.

'That song, from where does it come?' Spartacus enquired.

'My homeland is far to the east. It is the song my people sang the night before a battle. It is not a celebration of war but tells of the sadness of losing comrades in a battle that must be fought.'

As Aegis spoke he seemed to drift to a far off place, a feeling Spartacus knew well. He too often thought back to happier times, where he played as a young boy with his brothers pretending to be great warriors.

Spartacus thought to himself that if young males only knew what being a warrior entailed they would happily live out their days as farmers, never wishing to pick up a sword. Spartacus was aware that even as a victor in battle you were still the loser. Each defeated foe's face that Spartacus had slain still haunted him. Each terrible final scream that had issued from a dying opponent rang in his ears, a night's sleep was often disturbed by the ghosts of the past coming to visit him. Their unrelenting unhappiness, not at losing their life but at the chance to find a lasting, peaceful happiness which all warriors yearn for. The chance to return to a simpler existence had been taken from them. He doubted whether many warriors ever truly found peace for, even if they survived, the chains of those they had killed still weighed heavily about their necks, securing them to a life of blood and tears, which they only wished against all hope to forget.

'Do you hope to return to your home once the mission is over?' Enquired Spartacus.

'My home is no more, torn apart by wars that left only destruction. Gone are the chiefs, the soothsayers, the people. Only dust remains and when I die my body will turn to such dust and the winds will blow me to rest with my kin.' As Aegis spoke the words it was with such gentility, the fight was gone from him. A giant of a man, skilled in war and savagery, but Spartacus knew he had accepted whichever fate the Gods had decided for him and, for now, his soul was at peace. Spartacus envied the man, for he was a mix of hatred for the sins which had been done to him and self loathing for the acts for which he was responsible. Many times he questioned whether he was any better than those who had done him so much harm. He had, for a long time, excused his actions as a result of being enslaved and mistreated by his Roman captors. However, that did not hide the thrill he had experienced within the arena, or the satisfaction at cutting Roman throats when he later met them in battle. Aegis observed him.

'I see the mighty Spartacus has many questions within his soul.' It was not phrased as a question, but as a statement of truth. Spartacus didn't reply but merely gazed fixedly into Aegis' eyes and acknowledged his statement with a nod.

'It is not always possible to answer the past, merely to learn from it and hope the gods steer us on a better course in the future. It does not help to dwell too long in the past for the future is just a heartbeat away, blink and it has gone.' He spoke in such a calming way Spartacus felt at ease and able to offer a smile.

'I see that killing is not all you are good at Aegis. Let's make a new future at least between us, let us be friends upon this quest.' Spartacus spoke heartily.

'I considered us comrades the moment the task began. It would not do to die amongst strangers. At least a little sadness is required whenever a soul passes into the next world,' replied Aegis.

Spartacus and Aegis talked into the early hours, discussing the mission and the men, but mostly discussing Cassian and his character and how, even to Aegis, the man was something of an oddity. Aegis had been carrying out duties for Cassian for quite some time and, at first, the young aristocrat had seemed like all Romans - arrogant and dismissive of any other race. But, with time, Aegis had noticed Cassian often went out of his way to better the lives of those who served him, and indeed treated those same people with dignity, at least with as much dignity as there could be between master and slave. However, the questions about Cassian being so different to other Roman nobility were questions to which Aegis had no answers. Spartacus was indeed becoming intrigued by Cassian.

The following morning dawned like the first, with no sign of an enemy ready to strike. However, as the morning was giving way to the heat of the afternoon, the scouts pointed out a dust trail rising about half a day's march from them. Cassian quickly doubled the amount of scouts, trying to ensure the enemy would not be able to steal past the convoy and lay a trap further up the track. Constant reports came back to Cassian. It seemed the pursuers were approximately twenty in total, not enough for an all out attack. However, about half of their number seemed to be carrying bows which could make things extremely tricky. It was hard to defend against an enemy far beyond reach. As it was, the riders gradually drew closer but made no real effort to come in really close.

Aegis returned from a patrol with details of what seemed to be the reasons for them holding back. It looked as though the riders had pushed their mounts to breaking point over the past day, trying to find the convoy. It was clear from the condition of the horses that these beasts would be in no condition to fight a skirmish. It would make sense for them to rest now as they now knew exactly where the convoy was located. It would seem the next day would be the last for some of the men on both sides.

The convoy continued making its slow progress, picking its way slowly through the countryside until the time came to rest both man and beast. The enemy were closely watched and, in turn, they carefully observed the convoy. Spartacus took his turn to view the enemy, eager to see the type of men they faced. He moved in close enough to be able to see the dark riders were in high spirits, supremely confident in their own abilities and it seemed they sensed they would soon be enjoying the wealth of the convoy. There would definitely be no attack that night and why would there be? The wagons slowed progress to a steady crawl and the riders knew their intended prey could not race away from them. They were in no rush, they had the luxury of being able to plan when and where to deliver an attack and the men of the convoy could do nothing about it.

Spartacus returned to camp, his place watching the riders taken by Bull. Cassian had set his guards well, the camp would be informed well in advance if the riders did decide to attack in the night. The camp personnel were in a relaxed mood knowing their sleep would be guarded and so they dined and told stories just as they had the previous night. There were just a few tell tale signs of nerves as there were occasional glances towards the darkness and the enemy that lay within the creeping shadows.

Chapter 5

The morning started calmly enough with Cassian's scouts keeping track with the riders. He had also selected six men to head up the track early. Spartacus asked Cassian why he had sent men away as he thought they would need all the men they could muster to guard the wagons.

'Half a day's ride from here is a bridge and, it has to be said, the quality of the bridge is a little questionable. If the convoy can reach it then it may be possible to bring it down before the riders can cross. If that is possible we will guarantee ourselves at least two days respite from our pursuers.'

'And if we don't reach the bridge?' Spartacus replied.

'Then trade along this route will have been disrupted for no good reason, but being dead I feel we will have strayed beyond the anger and retribution of the authorities.' Cassian smiled and continued, 'come Spartacus, with these wagons we have no hope of outpacing these black riders, we need to slow them down using all of our trickery and I have a few tricks left yet. We have at our command, counting every soul on this convoy, combatant and slave, thirty-three men. Last reports put their number at twenty five. They cannot come straight at us but with those bows they will attempt to thin us out first. We need to prevent them from doing that. I fear that on this day they will have the advantage but, if we survive, this day that advantage may switch.'

'Very well, I think the plan is as good as it's going to get. May I suggest that we protect the oxen as much as possible and, if I were you, I would forget about riding on horseback, the target would be difficult to resist. And maybe you should dress in clothes which don't shout out that you are the leader of the convoy.'

'Is that concern Spartacus?' Cassian asked, through a cheeky smile.

'It's concern for my family. If you die, they die so, against my better judgement, I will just have to keep you alive.'

'Then for your families' sake and mine, I hope the reports of your skill have not been exaggerated.' Cassian slapped Spartacus on the back and continued, 'come Spartacus, you will have plenty of time to kill me but that's for another day. For now let's concentrate on those who need to enter the afterlife sooner.' Spartacus nodded and followed Cassian to the head of the column.

Cassian gave orders, including the oxen being fitted with what looked like huge overcoats and he noticed Spartacus observing.

'My own design - heavy hide. It may slow the beasts down but it may also deflect any stray arrows coming their way, though I doubt a direct shot will be put off.'

The convoy rumbled down the track and, despite the earliness of the hour, the heat was oppressive. Water was poured onto the beasts to prevent them overheating. The men however cared little for the heat, their eyes glancing around the surrounding countryside trying to catch sight of the mysterious black riders who offered to bring all of them doom. The convoy's scouts had announced the riders had spread out on both sides of the convoy and melted into the bushes, with only occasional sightings being made from that point. Cassian had brought his scouts closer in, they dismounted and took up larger shields for protection.

Talos, the youngest of the convoy's men brought water to Cassian and Spartacus. He was a bright boy, eager to learn and he had spent much of his free time watching Spartacus train. They drank with enthusiasm and haste. Spartacus bent to place the water ladle back into the bucket but, as he did so, it slipped from his grasp. He made to retrieve it and heard the familiar thwack of an arrow finding its mark. He raised himself, poised, ready to leap into action when required. There in front of him the world stood still. The young man had not screamed when the arrow had hit. The arrow's shaft protruded from what was left of his eye socket. The front of the shaft was nearly a foot in length from the back of his skull. Brain and blood decorated it now. Strangely, it seemed to Spartacus it was the only colour in this scene for the boy was pale ghostly white and already dead.

Only the Gods knew what force kept the boy on his feet but then, without a whimper, the body slipped to the ground. Yet still

40

the world had not started again, not until a scream shattered the stillness. One of the scout's horses called out its agony, thrashing wildly trying to remove the shaft buried in its flank, its flailing limbs catching a man squarely in the chest, launching him from the track.

Spartacus observed the mayhem that threatened to overwhelm the convoy. The mission was in danger of ending before it began.

'Get these wagons moving and somebody kill that bastard of a horse! Keep your shields up and stay close to one another and shout out if you see any of the bastards.'

Spartacus moved from man to man giving clear instructions. More men fell, but the convoy moved ever onwards. Those that were wounded were thrown, without ceremony, onto a wagon. The dead and those who were dying lay where they fell, the carrion would eat well tonight. He called for Aegis to join him. He noticed, as Aegis moved to him, that for a large man he moved like a predatory cat, ready to strike at any moment and the arrows of the enemy seemed always to hit where he had just been or was going to be. Spartacus couldn't decide whether it was a good idea to keep this man close or as far away as possible.

'Hot work my friend,' Aegis boomed.

'It will get hotter if we don't give those bastards something to think about,' Spartacus replied, ducking as a shaft hurtled above his head.

'What is it you have in mind?' He quizzed.

'Well I am afraid you and three others will have to be amongst the dead today.' Spartacus held up a hand when Aegis went to speak.

'Purely for the onlookers in the trees, you are to wait until the wagons and its enthusiastic followers have passed from vision, then I want you to come up on them from behind.'

Aegis smiled. 'I understand.'

'They seem to be working in groups of three or four. May I suggest that the first two groups you kill quietly but the third you make scream and put the fear of the Gods into the rest.'

'Why not kill them all?'

'Because by the time you have worked from group to group this convoy will be fit for nothing. Those riders won't be so trusting of the ground in front of them if they have heard their comrades fall and half their number are dead.' Spartacus said with a grim determination, knowing that it was a dangerous mission. However, he also knew he was needed here and Aegis seemed the best equipped to get the job done. Aegis nodded in agreement.

'Consider it done,' and, without another word, he had gone.

Aegis, Muto, Thulius and Gnaeus had succeeded in appearing dead, as the black riders passed by, though in truth the opportunity for a close inspection was not possible. The riders stayed in the trees and wanted to keep the pressure on the convoy. So the dead lay undisturbed, until four ghostly figures rose voluntarily and quickly melted into trees, unobserved by the riders who were too concerned with an enemy to its front. Aegis picked his way through the undergrowth. He had taken the lead, signalling to his men when to hide and when to advance. They moved without sound, the black riders who were once the hunters had, unbeknown to them, become the hunted.

The trees thinned slightly and less than twenty paces ahead a group of three black riders appeared in front of Aegis. He surveyed the area and became aware of a further rider, ten paces in front of the initial three. The riders were cautious, allowing only one man to move forward whilst the rest looked for men charging from the convoy or helped to pin point targets. The furthest rider loosed his arrow. It arched into the air and then gradually began its downward journey. It embedded, with a thud, into a wagon. The shooter cursed his luck, for the huge warrior who had been giving orders to the rest of the men scurrying around the wagon had only just moved from the spot the arrow now occupied. He turned, expecting ridicule from his comrades only to be shocked by the fact that they were nowhere to be seen. The curse which he had begun to utter was never heard, for a huge black hand clamped around his mouth. His brain had little time to register the panic, before a blade smashed through his back tearing all before it.

The second group of riders fared no better, all succumbing to the stealth as lethal warriors arrived without warning. Aegis moved onto the third group. There was no time to dawdle for his

42

comrades on the convoy were dying and it was not long before his skill at tracking found the next small group of riders. Because of the position of the riders the chance of getting close without being spotted was unlikely and so the timid approach was abandoned. Aegis and his men charged, sounding their battle cry as they went. Three of the riders fell easily, the shock of the enemy emerging from the trees causing them to hesitate, a hesitation which would see them slain. Gnaeus however had stumbled on a tree root and his enemy had fired an already notched arrow. It took Gnaeus in the right shoulder and, before he could react, his enemy had drawn his sword and slashed at him. The blow hit Gnaeus and his throat erupted, turning the world around him into shade of scarlet. The rider though had little time to celebrate his victory for Aegis wrenched him bodily from his horse, the warrior landing a huge fist into the riders face. The dazed rider looked up from the ground to see three enemy standing over him, swords drawn. He smiled weakly trying to ingratiate himself with them.

'Seems your day is not going to improve,' Aegis threw down his sword as he spoke and pulled a razor sharp dagger from his belt, the rider's eyes widened in terror.

The deadly shafts continued to rain in. Burying into any exposed flesh, be it man, horse or oxen although the oxen seemed to have been largely left alone. On the whole Spartacus could only guess these men in the woods wanted to take anything of value and to do so they would need the wagons. Spartacus had worked out the riders were working in six groups, two from behind and two on each flank. However, the arrows coming from the rear had gradually slowed and now they seemed to have stopped altogether. He wondered if that was the work of Aegis and his men, or simply whether the riders were re-positioning so they could cause more carnage. All he could do is hope, for up to now six men had been killed with a further nine injured and two of those would not see another sunset.

Suddenly a terrible scream filled the air. It came from the flank of the convoy, and it was swiftly followed by many more. Clearly the riders had heard the same screams, for the arrows at first slowed and then came to a total halt and it was clear that they were investigating the sounds. Spartacus smiled, he hated missile warfare. If you fought you should fight looking your opponent in the eye and not cowardly hiding behind a bush. He just hoped that Aegis and his men made it back to the convoy safely, for it was in need of good men.

Sometime later Aegis and his men came into the camp calling out first to ensure they were not mistaken for the enemy. He approached Spartacus and Cassian, a broad smile on his face. Blood covered his torso and limbs.

'You are injured?' Cassian inquired.

'No my lord the blood is that of our enemies and unfortunately that of Gnaeus our man who has not returned with us,' Aegis replied, his smile faltering as he spoke of a fallen comrade. 'The riders have gathered further back to lick their wounds, but fourteen of them shall never again raise arms against us.'

'You have done well,' Spartacus said, 'but I fear it will not be long before they return to torment us with more of those damned arrows.'

'The men we took down had only limited amounts of missiles. Soon they will need to meet us face to face.'

'You see Spartacus, as I said the advantage begins to change.' Cassian spoke without arrogance, it was merely a statement of fact.

'I pray you are correct but for now they still get to choose when and where to fight, that is advantage enough. I suggest we send out scouts and pinpoint where they are exactly, for we need to reach the bridge soon, so both man and beast can rest.'

The scouts were sent and it was not long before they returned with news. The riders had moved up ahead of the column, tracking its movement from a safe distance, obviously unsure of their next move. Every once in a while a rider would come within bow range and lose a couple of arrows towards the convoy, but the woods had thinned now and the riders could be seen as they drew closer. Men had time to take cover and before long no arrows came. It was clear the enemy would need to be closer from now on. They clearly had no intention of charging in and, as the day marched on, they moved further away from the convoy, even slipping behind it to a point where the scouts had to move further away from the convoy and

44

the rest of the men could relax.

The convoy ambled on up the dusty track until, just as the sun was beginning to dip in the sky, the small bridge came into view. The men who had been sent ahead had already made camp on the far side. The smell of roast rabbit wafted across the water and Spartacus could almost taste it. He glanced behind to ensure no last gesture was being made by the black riders and was happy to see the track clear.

The heavy carts rumbled across the bridge, it creaked like a ninety year old man rising from a favourite chair. Eventually, a safe distance from the bridge was attained and then the fires were lit. It took a while for the heavy embers to take light but eventually the bridge erupted into flames, lighting up the night sky. It lit up the opposing bank where what was left of the enemy rested. They arrogantly made camp and even acknowledged Spartacus' men with a casual wave. The sentries were set but it was clear to all that enough men had died this day and it was time to rest.

The rabbit was good, succulent from first to last bite and the wine quenched the dry, bitter thirst that all had endured that day. Surprisingly the men were in high spirits, they had survived, and although they mourned those lost, soldiers could not afford to dwell too long on the fallen for it would numb the senses to the dangers which still lay ahead. The ghosts of the past would have to wait until simpler and safer times gave the respite from immediate dangers. Cassian sent a messenger on his way with a dispatch which he later explained was addressed to a local land owner with whom Cassian had dealt with many times. The man owed Cassian certain debts which should guarantee the man's services and obedience, despite the gentleman in question being positively the most vulgar individual Cassian had ever had the misfortune to meet.

Later, Cassian, Spartacus and Aegis sat huddled by the fire and discussed the losses of the day. Twelve men had died in all and two of the wounded would soon join them. Another two would take no further part in the mission, although Spartacus was pleased to see that Cassian had assured them that the wealth promised to them would be theirs when the mission was completed. So the band had lost nearly half its number. Seventeen men remained to see out the rest of the mission. Spartacus was starting to dislike the odds. Sensing this Cassian moved to reassure him.

'That will be the worst of the land journey, the rest of the tracks run close or through friendly owned land. Those riders will need to travel two days to cross that river and they will find little help along the way. The majority of Crassus' agents have been, shall we say, convinced to be quiet.'

'I pray you are right, at this rate we will be pulling the carts ourselves,' Spartacus replied.

'I do hope not, this is a new tunic.' Cassian joked.

The three men burst out laughing because, the usually immaculate Cassian, literally looked like he had been dragged around the Colosseum. His entire figure was a mix of blood, dirt and dust. Spartacus remarked.

'Finally Cassian you know what it is to be a soldier.'

Chapter 6

The night passed without incident. The enemy riders still lazed the morning away when Spartacus and Cassian strolled through the camp. All of the survivors had remained within the camp meaning the previous day's exploits had not stirred the thought of flight within them. The two mortally wounded had not lasted the night and they were buried quickly without too much fuss. Cassian seemed not to want to upset the upbeat feeling within the camp. Fires were stoked and the morning meal was taken. A drop of wine went a long way to cheer the men even more. Shortly after the last of the plates had been hungrily cleared of food, news came from the scouts that riders were approaching the camp. However, they were not approaching from the river side, instead they approached from the track which the convoy was to follow. Nine riders were dressed in all the finery you would expect from a wealthy Roman landowner, the tenth was the messenger Cassian had dispatched the previous night. He still looked filthy and had obviously not been treated as an honoured guest by one of the nine others who Spartacus could only guess was the man Cassian had spoken of previously. They reigned in alongside Cassian. A few of the men had to scamper quickly to the side to avoid being trampled under hoof.

'Cassian, by the Gods look at the state of you man!' The words were spoken by a toad like man, who it seemed to Spartacus did not really suit his clothes. Here, he thought, was a man who dressed in the finest clothes the world could offer and yet still looked like a giant horse turd.

'Crannicus,' Cassian replied, 'your journey went well I hope?'

'Better than yours I dare say,' he replied and continued, 'you there,' gesturing towards Spartacus, 'help me down.' It was not a request, but an order, an order from a man who was used to giving them.

Spartacus didn't speak but simply helped the overweight lump

47

of a man from his horse, no easy mission in itself as, despite the power and strength possessed by Spartacus, both nearly went sprawling to the dirt. As Spartacus straightened, the man let out a loud belch which was only matched in volume by the terrible odour it produced. Spartacus almost gagged and thought of the Roman ballistae. Breathing their balls of fire was preferable to being within range of this man's bodily functions. He glanced to Cassian, who seemed to be secretly trying to give his apologies without alerting Crannicus. He then addressed Crannicus himself.

'You received my list of the items I require?'

'I did, all are ready at my villa at no small cost to myself may I add,' Crannicus said sternly.

'You will be well rewarded for any materials we need.'

'That's all very well and,' Crannicus paused to again let lose a titanic belch, which seemed to scare the birds from the trees, 'good but I had plans for those wagons,' he had continued without missing a beat.

Cassian, on the other hand, was constantly trying to stay up wind of the man and, as such, his conversation was becoming stunted.

'Like I said, you will be very well paid and I need not remind you of certain other matters.'

'You need not, I am well aware of those matters. The items are ready and may I suggest while you are at my villa you and your men take a bath, for you are quite disgusting.' His last words were spoken as he casually scratched at his genitals.

'Errrmmm, yes that would be most kind of you,' Cassian stumbled by way of reply.

With that Crannicus returned to his horse and was helped aboard by the ever eager Plinius, who was rewarded by Crannicus breaking wind, the noise of which resembled a thunder clap which hit poor Plinius directly in the face. The group rode away, with Crannicus simply nodding to Cassian as he left.

Spartacus approached Plinius and slapped the boy on the shoulder.

'Did I not tell you this mission would deliver to us untold dangers?'

'Give me the black riders any day. I once cleared the dead from a battlefield, it took us two days but I have never smelt anything as bad as what comes from that man's arse,' Plinius replied.

Bull who was standing to the side erupted into side splitting laughter and, struggling to speak, managed.

'Your eyes are watering.'

Even Cassian was struggling to contain his amusement.

'Maybe I should raise the payment for this mission, for even I did not realise its true dangers.'

The convoy moved away shortly afterwards. The mood was light but all the men took a nervous glance back towards the black riders on the opposite shore. Still they slumbered. Cassian noted this to Spartacus, surprised at the lack of movement from the enemy.

'They will not follow our path.'

'How can you be so sure?'

'For dead men follow a different track.' Spartacus said it with such finality that Cassian knew it to be true.

'But how?'

'I have always been a fine swimmer, my mother taught me as a boy. The guards were looking towards the bridge and I simply worked my way around and took each one in turn. I think they had allowed too much drink to be consumed for they never stirred from their dreams.'

'Then why not tell the men?' Cassian asked, whilst trying to hide his amazement at the actions of the man before him.

'Because these men have to be on the edge, it will keep them alive. If they believe danger is lurking at every corner they will be on their guard. If not, they will die and I will do my damnedest to make sure that does not happen.' As Spartacus spoke he moved away, wishing to be alone. For all his bravado about protecting the men, he knew it was a forlorn hope on this mission and, as battle hardened as he was, he could never truly reconcile himself to killing sleeping men. Sometimes he thought the simplicity of the arena was easier to deal with.

With the wagons moving at their usual slow pace and a wagon smashing a wheel, it was nearly nightfall before the convoy pulled into the courtyard of Crannicus' villa. The man may have been fit only to sleep with swine but, by the Gods, he knew how to show off. The villa was a picture of opulence. Fantastic mosaics adorned the walls. Marble statuettes, mainly of beautiful women, gave the gardens that other world feeling where nymphs were common place. The gardens themselves were amazing, so vibrant with all the colours imaginable, making it a spectacle to behold. Even in the poor light Spartacus doubted he would ever see a place more beautiful. It confused him how a man who clearly took so little time over his own presentation could create such a place. Cassian seemed to read Spartacus' mind and attempted to bring clarity.

'You wonder about the compatibility of the home and the man?' It was said as a question, but delivered more as a statement.

'It had crossed my mind.'

'You see Crannicus has two major gifts as a man. The first is he loves big business, the thrill of the success, and the second is the woman he chose to be his wife.'

'She is responsible for this?'

'Oh yes. She is named after the Roman goddess Flora who, if you were not aware, was the goddess of flowering plants and spring. It seems her parents could not have chosen a better name for her and, as her plants, she seems to lighten the heart of whoever looks upon her.' Cassian seemed to be lost in thought as he spoke.

'So beautiful?' Spartacus smiled at Cassian. He almost felt the urge to tease him, for he obviously had feelings for the woman.

'You misunderstand me, she is attractive in a simple way. It is more the vigour for life she brings to a room when she enters, you will see for yourself,' Cassian answered, a slight red flush upon his face.

Spartacus could not help but be intrigued. Any woman that could disarm a man such as Cassian merely by entering the room would indeed be worth meeting because, so far, there had been little to distract the man.

The hall was full of splendour as was the rest of the villa, to the point that Spartacus felt a little self conscious. He had seen lavishness before when back at the ludos. Batiacus had thrown lavish parties to win favour with important guests and at such parties the best of the gladiators were often put on show, like prize beasts. However, even Batiacus would have stumbled over his usually silken tongue at such beauty. Crannicus rose and hailed his guests, saying that his home was theirs and quickly called for more wine for his honoured guests. As he did so a female entered the hall waited on by two maidens. Crannicus turned to acknowledge her.

'Ah Flora, my dutiful wife. Please come meet our guests, I believe you know my friend Cassian.'

'Of course! Cassian, my dear friend, it has been too long since we last talked of politics,' she replied. There was no usual proper nod and acknowledgement, and instead Flora launched herself and hugged Cassian as a long lost friend would do. Crannicus seemed annoyed at this show of emotion.

'As you see Cassian, my wife still struggles to adhere to the proper protocol on such occasions.'

'Why Crannicus, I feel if everyone greeted each other in such a way there would be little war in the world,' Cassian replied.

'Well said my dear Cassian! Now tell me, how are the boys and my dear sister Epionne?'

'She and the boys are well thank you, but my dear wife becomes ever more annoyed that she cannot compete with your wonderful gardens,' Cassian winked as he replied.

'Now she should leave an older sister something to cling to, after all my younger sister got the beauty, at least let an old maid keep her garden. Besides I have told you that villa of yours is built on dust, fit for nothing.' She teased Cassian.

'As for looks both sisters were blessed and as for my villa, well on that score you may well be right. Maybe next year you can help me find a new place to build.' Flora erupted into exited giggling, clapping her hands together.

'Oooo, yes, yes!'

Spartacus knew what Cassian meant now. Each action, each word that Flora performed kept every man, woman and child completely transfixed. She was like a ball of energy, each person watched her hoping to catch hold of a single burst of energy and ride it.

Eventually all were seated and much food and drink was

51

consumed except, Spartacus noticed, Cassian who seemed to drink slower and slower, but seemed to become more and more slurred in his speech, a fact that was lost on the rapidly becoming intoxicated host. As the night wore on the ladies, slaves and men left them. Those remaining were few and even those who seemed to hold high office with Crannicus slipped away. Seated now at the table were Crannicus, to his right sat Cassian so, if need be, both could whisper comment without fear of being overheard, Crannicus' eldest son from a previous marriage Tictus, and what Spartacus supposed was advisor to Crannicus, a slim, wily looking gentlemen by the name of Veotus. All were listening closely to Crannicus.

'You come to my home, make demands of me, the cargo you brought with you can only be guarded by your own men and you will not even tell me what you're up to. Seems a pretty poor state of affairs Cassian.' Crannicus sneered as he spoke and his words were met with nods of approval from both Tictus and Veotus.

'The reason for my men guarding the cargo is because they have fought and some have died to get it thus far. It would seem disrespectful to simply hand it over to someone else's care when they have no understanding of your worth Crannicus.'

'What! Men do as they are told or they face the whip, you're too soft Cassian.'

'And the reason I do not enlighten you further is because I will not place your home at risk.'

'Risk. No fool would dare raise a hand to,' Crannicus began but was interrupted by Cassian,

'You know the type of men I deal with Crannicus, they could snuff out your lives and business as quickly as extinguishing a candle flame. I have no wish to tell my wife of her sister's death.' At Cassian's words Crannicus just grumbled his discontent but no more was said on the matter.

The night wore on, and with consternation, Spartacus noticed Cassian was letting slip certain details of the mission ahead. Damn fool he thought, if you cannot hold your tongue when you drink you should not hold a goblet. It was not long before the party disbanded completely with the mask of over friendliness

52

descending again. Crannicus was hugging and slapping his fellow party goers upon the back with gestures of never ending loyalty. In a short while Spartacus found that he and Cassian were walking in the cool night breeze totally alone, the villa slipping into slumber.

'Well that went well,' Cassian stated, still slurring his words.

'You think so, you bloody idiot,' Spartacus struggled to keep his anger in check. 'Why did you go blurting all that stuff out, you may well have killed us all.'

Cassian stood straight as if to argue, then a broad smile stretched across his face.

'Yes I was convincing.'

Spartacus checked himself. Gone was the slurring and the silly manner in which Cassian had held himself, now stood in front of him the calm, calculating Cassian of old.

'For some time Spartacus I have known that within this household there is a traitor. I believe it to be one of the three men we have just spent time with. I decided to use that. What happens next will determine which of the men is our enemy.'

'What do you mean?'

'Simple, if it's Crannicus it is unlikely we shall leave this place tonight, he has many men and will most likely kill us all in a few hours. If it's the son Tictus he too will use men, although I doubt he will have more than twenty he can call on who would not go running to the boy's father and he would need to take what we have away from the villa. Then finally there is Veotus. He would be the information gatherer, those snippets of information would not have passed him by. He will most likely excuse himself within an hour of us leaving tomorrow and then give that information to our enemies.'

'Or it could be two of them, or all three.'

'Possibly. There is no way of knowing, but I do know this; if it is the information they wanted they now believe we are heading for the wrong port, to board the wrong ship, to an incorrect location.'

'So now what do we do?' Spartacus enquired, marvelling at the man's forethought.

'Why my dear man, now we go to sleep. I have been holding my breath most of the night rather than take in the foul wind that

Crannicus emits, it's left me rather tired.' With that he gave Spartacus a gentle slap upon the shoulder wished him good night and retired. Spartacus thought: sleep you have just told us we may well be murdered in our beds. At what point would that enable any man to sleep?

Chapter 7

The night passed without incident which still did not prevent Spartacus awaiting one. He slept very little, constantly aware of every sound that could be the tell tale sign of impending attack. The night though eventually turned to sunrise, and the beautiful gardens turned wondrous as they were bathed in the golden red of the early sun. He paced the preparations which were already in full swing for the convoy to make its next journey. Fresh oxen and wagons would help prevent delays. Cassian joined him half way round, they discussed the new wagons and the supplies that would be needed. Flora and Tictus entered the courtyard.

'You will have to forgive my father for not being here to say farewell, unfortunately too much wine has had its effect,' Tictus said without too much conviction. Flora launched herself at Cassian and embraced him deeply, her mouth close to his ear she whispered.

'Be careful dear friend, the path ahead may be dangerous and not all in this house may wish you to succeed as much as Crannicus and myself.' Cassian spoke quietly and without really thinking.

'Crannicus?' He said questioningly. She guided Cassian away from the others and chastised him as a mother would a small child.

'You never understood did you? Crannicus only wants to make me happy and if helping you makes me happy he will do whatever it takes.'

'Forgive me, my words were unkind. May I kiss my favourite sister goodbye?'

'I would consider it a great insult if you did not.' They kissed and once again she hugged him tightly. 'Please be careful.'

The convoy trundled on, the already warm sun soaking the men's bodies, making them feel at peace with the world. Both Spartacus and Cassian barked out orders, both knew they could ill afford the men to slip into melancholy.

Cassian had private words with Plinius and once the convoy

was clear from view of the villa the boy mounted a horse and sped away from the convoy. Cassian noticed Spartacus watching.

'He goes to see who leaves the villa.'

'You chose the boy?' Spartacus asked, as if questioning the choice.

'He is a fine rider and I have given him instruction only to watch and bring back news of potential threats, that is all. Besides, we cannot carry passengers, all must do their bit.'

Spartacus made to answer back but realised Cassian was right, the boy needed to earn the respect of the men but, more than that, the boy needed to prove to himself that he belonged within the group.

Plinius noted the two men leaving the villa, they were heading towards him. He dismounted and hid in the shadows, there was plenty of cover and the men seemed locked in conversation and as they drew closer he recognised the men as Tictus and Veotus.

'You should go back my young master, I feel these lands are a dangerous place while that convoy travels through it.'

'I do not fear my own lands Veotus,' Tictus replied. 'What I fear is the reason you leave so early and to what end?'

'I simply have a personal matter to deal with and wished to complete it before my duties at the villa begin.' Veotus spoke calmly but Plinius could tell he was uneasy.

'I saw you last night speaking with that man from the convoy, what was your business with him?' Tictus pressed.

'Business? No business merely conversing with the man.'

'If you go against my father's wishes you will be made to pay Veotus, my father...' The words were cut short. Tictus never saw the blade concealed in Veotus' sleeve, it ripped into his side, tearing muscle and sinew.

Tictus managed to push himself away from his attacker, falling from his horse and landing heavily upon the ground. Veotus laughed and dismounted.

'You think I fear your father, the bloated puss filled leech? The man I work for could buy your father twenty times over! I am sick of listening to your family, so full of self importance, you're just scum.' With that he pulled back the head of the young Tictus. 'Now

56

the only question is, do I kill you quick or slow?'

He never saw the heavy branch being swung but he did indeed feel it land. It knocked Veotus sideways, making him sprawl across the dusty track, landing heavily in a clump.

'You're one of Cassian's men,' Tictus spoke though gasping for breath.

'Yes! My lord we must get you back to the villa,' Plinius replied.

'No! Cassian, he must know of the treachery of Veotus and one of his own men – is Veotus dead?'

'No I am not. It seems I will kill two boys today.' Veotus spoke the words as he climbed to his feet and, as he did so, the familiar scraping of a sword from scabbard accompanied it.

Plinius rose, he too drawing his sword. He thought of what Spartacus had told him; observe your opponent, use his failings against him, whilst maximising your own strengths. He looked at Veotus, he seemed bigger somehow. This, he thought to himself, is probably going to hurt.

'Well boy! It seems you have joined a man's game, what a pity to die so young.'

'I don't like being called boy and before this day is out you will give me the name of the traitor,' Plinius spat the words back at Veotus.

Veotus attacked, his superior strength forcing Plinius to keep parrying and retreating, time and time again the boy was forced to yield ground.

'Throw down your sword boy, I was slitting throats before you were born, do it and I shall kill you quick.' Veotus continued, 'what could you do to this traitor anyway, you will never leave this place?'

'Then tell me his name,' Plinius replied, narrowly avoiding a slash directed towards his throat, 'or do you have so little confidence in your own ability?'

'Why surely you already know, who is the man who helped kick your brother to death? Oh I know everything about you boy, your optio spills information as a cow spills milk. For a little money he tells a wondrous story.'

'The optio?' As the words issued from his own mouth, Plinius realised he had always known.

'Too bad that information will have to keep you company in the afterlife,' Veotus sneered. Plinius smiled.

'I think not.'

Veotus could not believe it, the boy was moving so quickly and gone were the defensive moves, this was a full blown attack. Veotus screamed his anger and tried to cleave the boy in two with one blow. He missed by a hair but the swing unbalanced him, sending him sprawling to the dust. As he rose he felt burning agony as steel ripped through his ankle bone. He turned and fell flat onto his back, screaming his woe as he tried in vain to reattach the severed foot, and looked in fear at the approaching boy. Plinius kicked Veotus' sword away and plucked the dagger from within Veotus' sleeve, bringing an elbow crashing against the nose of his opponent as he did so.

'Well old man it seems this is a game I play well and, do you know, I like it.'

Aegis spotted the approaching horseman and informed Cassian of their arrival. He moved to the back of the convoy trying to work out the figures. One was sitting upright, one was slumped in his saddle and the third seemed to be tied to the horse. He wondered what on earth was going on. As they drew nearer he recognised Plinius. Spartacus joined him, an equally confused look on his face, Plinius called for help as well as wondering why they all stood there, with their mouths gaping.

'Plinius! What in the name of Gods has happened?' Cassian demanded.

'Do not blame Plinius, he did well today.' The gasping voice came from Tictus as he half climbed, half fell from his horse. Cassian rushed to his aid.

'Tictus, what happened?' He questioned, as he saw the blood drenched tunic.

'I accompanied Veotus from the villa as I was suspicious to the reasons he left so early. A short time later I pressed him for answers but was too slow to see the danger. If it had not been for Plinius here, I would be dead.' As Tictus spoke Aegis worked on his wound, using unknown herbs from the satchel which never left his side.

'I am sorry my lord, I went against your wishes but, upon hearing the conversation, I thought it best to intercede.' Plinius spoke not knowing if Cassian would be angry or not. He knew that Tictus was family but he also knew there was no love lost between the two.

'Your actions were that of a true warrior Plinius, you saved a man and killed his attacker,' Cassian replied.

'Oh he's not dead, he passed out from loss of blood but I tied the wound. I thought you would have need to speak to him and the man from whom he gained information.' Plinius gazed around as he spoke but could not see the optio.

'Your optio has proven to be less than reliable Cassian. Veotus gave him up as he thought he had Plinius, over confidence seemed to be his downfall.' Tictus spoke casting a loathing eye towards the figure now starting a low moan.

Cassian gave orders that Veotus should be taken down and restrained and Aegis should go and fetch the optio who would be blissfully unaware of the proceedings as he was scouting to the front of the convoy.

'Bull if you would be so kind, I believe you will probably find certain monies within the belongings of the optio, paid to him by this scum to deliver all of us to the afterlife.' Cassian gave the order as calmly as ever, but it was clear there was a rage growing within him. Then he sent a messenger to Crannicus to inform him of what had happened.

The optio was in a chirpy mood. He tied his horse against a tree and strolled to the small stream. As he bent and drank some of the clear fresh water he thought of the stupidity of Cassian. Why the hell should he risk his life on a suicide mission? He would wait until they reached the port, slip away unnoticed when it was convenient and catch some small boat to some god forsaken place. With the money he had procured from Veotus it would be the easy life from now on, and he might even slit that little bastard Plinius' throat before he went. He noticed the shadow looming over him and looked up to find the foreboding figure of Aegis.

'You silly big bastard you scared me half to death what do

you...' The phrase was never finished, the large powerful fist connected with his jaw and darkness overtook him. The next time he opened his eyes it took a while to shake the dizziness from his head. He tried to focus, his eyes slow to adjust. When they were finally clear they were met only with horror. He was staring directly at the beaten and bloodied face of Veotus. He tried to turn away but had been tied so that he could not move. His entire field of vision was that of the crumpled corpse, fear began to rise within him.

'Ah good, our guest of honour is awake. I was worried you would sleep all day and miss the proceedings – it seems Veotus chose eternal sleep.' The voice was Cassian's and it was clear to the optio that his fate was sealed.

'I am a soldier of Rome, there are rules,' the optio argued, but even to himself he knew it was a forlorn hope.

'Indeed you are and, believe me, I am all for Roman military tradition. Let me see, what is tradition within the military for a man who places his comrades at risk, who would rather see their deaths than do his duty?'

The fear spread clearly across the optio's face for he knew of a punishment, a punishment which brought pain like no other. He had seen it a few times within the service, he could remember smirking at a prisoner as he had soiled himself in preparation for what was to happen.

'Ah I see the practice of bastinado is not lost upon you, that is good.' With that Cassian leaned in closer so only the optio could hear him. 'You would see your comrades die, you would risk my family for a few coin, think on that with every bone that breaks, you treacherous bastard.'

The optio was pulled to his feet and led to an alley, but the alley was not lined with buildings instead it was lined with men, each armed with a large cudgel. The optio stared around. He saw Cassian join Crannicus, Spartacus and Flora who had gathered to see his punishment. He heard Cassian tell Flora she should not watch but she refused his advice, stating that she would happily watch any man die who would place her family's lives in danger.

Aegis prevented the optio from moving backwards with a blade held up against his back. He watched for the signal and it was not long before it came. The optio was pushed into the alley. He raised his arms to cover his head and felt some relief as he realised the first blow had missed, but then there was agony as timber met bone. His forearm was smashed and, as he stumbled, another blow took three ribs. He moved ever on, blow after blow landing. He could no longer protect his head and it too was opened to the onslaught. Finally he fell but still the blows rained in until, at the end, just one shadow appeared over him. The shadow was just a blur and the optio could not recognise who stood above him but he did know the voice.

'It was only a matter of time, you killed my brother for fun you bastard. I hope you never find rest.' Plinius swung the final blow, smashing the optio's skull to pulp. He then simply walked away into the woods nearby. Aegis went to call him back but Spartacus stopped him.

'No, let him go. He needs time to think - the thought of revenge has burned so hot inside him for so long he requires time to work out what to replace it with.'

Plinius moved to the shadows of a large tree. He knelt, unseen by the rest of the camp and his last action as boy would be to break down and cry for the loss of his brother, for the actions he had taken to avenge that loss but mostly from this point he was no longer a boy. Plinius stayed in the small clump of trees all that night, luckily with all that had happened the convoy never moved from the location he had left it in. Occasionally Spartacus or Aegis would secretly steal into the trees from a distance, just to check on the young man. At one point they came upon each other, both making lame excuses as to why they were in the trees, followed by an awkward silence then both slouched back to camp in a way that resembled a child who had been caught stealing. The two came close to Flora.

'How is he?' She asked.

'I was looking for rabbits,' Aegis blurted out.

'I was ..." Spartacus stumbled at the same time as Aegis. Flora threw her head back in dismay.

'Men. Bloody useless!'

Chapter 8

The morning came and activity was at a maximum. Crannicus and Flora prepared Tictus for his journey back to the villa. Flora mothered Tictus and, for once, Tictus seemed glad to receive the attention from his stepmother, with all previous disputes left firmly in the past. Crannicus approached Cassian.

'Before, I did your bidding because I had to, from this point my brother I do it because I should and because I want to.' Cassian held out a hand but Crannicus took him in a full body hug. 'Be careful, I have nearly lost a son, thank the Gods he will survive. I have no wish to lose a brother.'

Flora burst into tears.

'You men, why does it take such events for you to behave as you should?' She gently punched her husband's chest.

'Crannicus, I am honoured to be called your brother,' replied Cassian who was clearly taken by surprise at Crannicus' actions.

'One more thing, when Plinius returns tell him that he will have a home here and I shall call him son and Tictus will call him brother.'

'I will, I think the young man has done us all a great deed,' Cassian added.

The convoy moved away, heading towards a port which would speed them across the sea. Plinius returned as it was leaving, Aegis and Spartacus both observed the young man as he joined in step with his comrades.

'He seems taller,' Aegis remarked.

'Indeed he does,' Spartacus replied.

The small convoy, well equipped and refreshed, made good progress despite the slowness of the oxen. Spartacus had wondered whether the slaying of the optio in such a manner would prove detrimental to the men's morale, however it seemed to generate a more solid bond between each of the men. He had wondered himself whether it would not have been simpler to just slit the optio's throat, but Cassian had insisted that the manner in which he died must be at the hands of the other men, for it was those same men who he had put in mortal danger. Spartacus had to admit, not only to Cassian but to himself, that it was the right thing to do no matter how barbaric and distasteful to watch. Important lessons had been learnt, firstly, that although Cassian was not of a military background he still possessed the spine to carry out discipline no matter how extreme, and secondly that Cassian would not permit disloyalty, those who were disloyal must be prepared to answer for their actions.

The day passed without incident. Bull and Plinius managed to catch some rabbits so fresh meat was on the menu. Unusually, Spartacus and Cassian decided to eat away from the men, giving them the chance to discuss the next steps of the mission.

'Tomorrow we will reach a small port little known to the authorities. It belongs to my father who purchased the land at the height of his trading days. It will help us catch the boat I have arranged and it will also throw off any would be eavesdroppers as I am sure Crassus' agents will be expecting us to enter one of the larger ports,' Cassian informed Spartacus.

'Then do we sail straight for Utica?' Spartacus enquired, for he knew that although Cassian gave him parts of the plan he rarely revealed the complete truth.

'No. From there we travel to Caralis. It will give us a base to do further training and, once away from the port there, I have friends who will keep us from prying eyes,' Cassian seemed less than sure of this part of the plan.

'You seem somewhat disturbed by this part of the plan,' Spartacus remarked. Cassian smiled.

'There are no certainties in this game we are playing – Caralis is about as lawless as a Roman province gets. The port itself is a hive of cut throats but we dare not arrive at Utica early, the hour of our arrival is key to the success.'

'What do you mean, I thought this Dido fellow was only interested in the money?'

'Oh he is, but if we were to arrive early he would have no alternative to report our presence. If we arrive as the registration for the games begins he will be too busy. Not only that but we will be very public in our intentions and we will make it so public he will not wish, or dare, to lose face.' Cassian seemed to come alive as he went through the plan.

'This Dido, what more do you know of him?' Spartacus wanted to know this man, he liked to know all his opponents.

'His name should give you a clue. He named himself after a Carthaginian Queen who supposedly founded the great city of Carthage and sacrificed herself rather than become the wife of a tyrant.'

'But surely he would take the name of male warrior, by the Gods Carthage produced enough of them?'

'That's the point, this man thinks beyond the normal, being different to the point of insanity. When he first called himself Dido it is believed five men laughed at him and, to this day, they say five sets of genitalia hang above his so called throne.'

'Do you believe the rumours?' Spartacus asked. Cassian laughed.

'No not at all. Dido, shall we say, was his stage name. Dido was an arse whore servicing the rich and powerful who had certain vices. He made his name through blackmail and intelligence. Before long he was more powerful than many of his previous clients.'

'So what stops this man simply killing us the moment we reach the games?'

'He will want to no doubt, but he will have his name to save. The games have become known as a haven from all authorities, his supporters know nothing of his links with Crassus. He will honour the bet we make with him, especially if we make it so loud and so enormous all will stop and observe.'

'It seems to be a gamble,' Spartacus pointed out.

'A gamble! It's a bloody ridiculous plan but it's all we have. Suicide it may be, but if it works then it will rumble like an earthquake in the pockets of the powers that be in Rome.'

Spartacus did not know why, but he became angry.

'You forget Cassian, my family's lives are forfeit if I fail this mission. I would like to think they have a fighting chance.'

'Then let us make a deal Spartacus. Will you honour your

word?' Cassian's eyes burned into Spartacus.

'I always have,' replied Spartacus, still fuming at Cassian's jest. His anger matched the intensity of Cassian stare.

'Then swear to me you will fight with me on this mission and not attempt to escape.' Cassian looked Spartacus squarely in the eyes.

'And my family?' Spartacus replied, unsure to where this conversation was going.

'Remove family from your thoughts – will you fight with me and the men?' Cassian had become intense.

'You have my word,' Spartacus agreed although by the Gods he did not know why, after all what choice did he have.

'Then observe,' Cassian thrust towards Spartacus a parchment, 'your family were freed the very night we left my villa. They stay with my family as guests, free to come and go as they please with, may I say, a handsome allowance.'

"But...but why?' Spartacus was almost dizzy with the magnitude of the situation.

'I trespassed against you Spartacus, my actions were forced but no less grave. I have learned of the type of man you are and pray to the Gods that one day you may forgive me, for I certainly will not.' Cassian spoke with tears within his eyes. 'Man should not make war on children or use them as bargaining chips.' Spartacus looked at the man and realised he was as much a slave as himself and, although he found it difficult, his words were gentle.

'Cassian, I can never forget that day but it is clear to me you were not responsible for that act against my son. I will fight by your side and die by your side if necessary. What you have done for my living family has eradicated any actions against it in the past and I will honour my word to you, but under one further condition.'

'And that is?' Cassian asked still feeling his shame.

'When we complete this mission and I see you safely back to your family and I grasp mine safely in my arms, you will give me the name of the man who gave the order to kill my son.'

'You will have it, though I doubt that day will ever come, after all it is an insane plan.'

Both men laughed long and hard, the tension in the air broken.

They both knew a friendship had been forged, and in a world of deceit and betrayal each had a friend they could trust.

They reached the small port owned by Cassian's father the following day just before dusk. The boat was already waiting for them, its sleek silhouette cut an impressive figure. The captain made for the group as they moved into the small square between a handful of buildings. He too cut an impressive figure, although sleek it was not. Spartacus had never met a pirate but, if he had, he would expect him to look like the captain. His skin was burnished to a golden bronze from many days out at sea. There was no uniform, but from how his men reacted to him it was clear there was only one captain aboard his boat. Cassian introduced him to Spartacus.

'This rather energetic gentleman, Spartacus, is Lathryus, the finest seaman this part of the world has seen in many a year.'

'Ah too kind Cassian,' the fellow boomed, slapping Cassian on the back nearly hurtling him down a nearby well. Cassian steadied himself and took a huge breath of air to replace that which had just been removed from his lungs.

'This is Spartacus, he has a number of talents,' Cassian winked at the gladiator.

'A true pleasure and any friend of Cassian's usually ends up dead but until then let us be comrades in wine.' Lathryus erupted into laughter at his own jest. 'Do not fear for your cargo, my boys will look after it or the swine will answer to me. Let's get drunk and talk about my exploits.' He laughed again. 'Tell me Cassian, did I ever tell you of my exploits fighting the dragons of the nether world?'

'I believe my knowledge of that wondrous tale is somewhat lacking,' Cassian smirked.

'Really! That's probably because I haven't made it up yet. Never mind, bring the wine and I will indulge you of my magnificence, and stories of me besting such creatures that would make a normal man's cock curl,' again he roared.

Lathyrus wandered off to chastise one of his men, while he did Spartacus took the opportunity.

'Is he for real?' He asked Cassian.

'His tales are piss in the wind but do not be misled to consider the same of the man. His sailing exploits are legendary and the man is the finest bare knuckle fighter I have ever witnessed, maybe even a match for you without weapons,' Cassian replied.

'Then it seems tonight we drink,' smiled Spartacus.

'Oh and do not try to out drink the man, by the Gods his stomach has no end.' Cassian spoke in awe.

The night with Lathryus seemed to last an age and Spartacus did not know which would falter first; his legs from the drink or his jaw from the laughter. By the Gods the man knew how to enjoy himself and although he barked at and scolded his men often, they seemed to adore their captain. Cassian explained that each of the men had grown rich on the booty he had won for them. Indeed many could have left the sea forever and lived a life of relative luxury but many stayed, for the money yes but also for the life serving such a man. One by one the drink took the men, falling to happy slumber on wine and roasted boar. Spartacus praised the man who had made it possible, for the future was unclear and all men should sample such a night before tackling the unknown.

The morning light streamed into the small hovel, the light trying to force open the eyes. Spartacus resisted, but the light searched for weakness and eventually burst through like a torrent through a weakened dam. He tried to stand, but a mixture of throbbing head and numb body forced him to sit again. The door burst open and, for a moment, Spartacus thought an attack was imminent, but standing at the door was Lathryus and his booming voice rang out again.

'Come on you lazy bastards. The tide waits only for the Gods, which you pair are not! The way you two drink is girl-like not God like.' With that he was gone hurling abuse at some other poor soul. Cassian stirred.

'I can't feel my legs. Do me a favour go kill that big bastard.'

After a while Cassian and Spartacus finally managed to emerge from the hovel, to be greeted by a wondrous sight. The boat was fully loaded, the men already boarded and all the two of them had to do was try and look dignified as they made their way to the boat.

'Nice of you to join us ladies, please do step aboard,' the captain boomed.

The sailors laughed, obviously used to such nights. Cassian's men made a feeble attempt to laugh but most just went back to looking green and sullen. It was not long before the boat began to move. Spartacus stared out, wondering what the Gods would throw at this rag tag group of men next. His thoughts though were interrupted by the swaying of the boat and its effect upon his rather delicate stomach. He gulped down air to try and prevent the feeling of nausea, but the salty sea air only made matters worse. He could not resist any longer and rushed to the rail and vomited which made the rancid taste of the previous days wine haunt his mouth. His action triggered a chain reaction and many of his men joined him, even Cassian was compelled to empty his stomach contents. Lathyrus boomed his laughter.

'Let this be a lesson to you lads,' he spoke to his own men, 'these land lovers drink like little girls at night and complain like old men in the morning.'

His men cheered his words. Spartacus felt the urge to throw the oversized blaggard into the sea but another urge overwhelmed him and again he rushed to throw his head over the rail, accompanied by whoops of joy from the sailors.

As time slipped by the nausea lessened and Spartacus gradually gained his sea legs though when meal time came he refused the remnants of the previous day's roasted boar. Many of his men took the same course of action, only testing their delicate stomachs with dry bread. The sailors and Lathyrus however ate heartily and with substantial quantities of wine, the night's revelry obviously having no ill effects upon them. Cassian, walking very uneasily, joined Spartacus and they observed Lathyrus in awe.

'The man is not of this world,' Cassian remarked. Just watching the man even made bile rise to his throat.

'The big bastard must already be dead for that lot not to affect him,' replied Spartacus, shaking his head in disbelief. Both slumped down, resting their weary bodies against the rail, the weariness taking them as though both had fought in battle and both were truly amazed as Lathyrus called for more wine.

Chapter 9

The call went up that land was sighted. Many of Cassian's men rushed to see if it was true, few had enjoyed the sea voyage and prayed to be back on a firmer footing soon. The harbour was a hive of activity with boats of all sizes, cargo passing from port to boat and vice versa. But for a Roman province there was little to suggest Roman law was in force. Lathryus boomed.

'Ok men, you will be making landfall very soon. A word to the wise, keep your purse and your cocks close. The thieves will take your money and cause a whole lot of misery, whereas the whores will give you a whole lot more.' The men laughed, but the point was taken. Caralis was a place to be on your guard against a whole range of misfortunes, some more tempting than others but every much as dangerous.

The unloading was completed in double quick time. A perimeter was set up as the unloading took place to prevent prying eyes and wandering fingers. The trouble was in protecting what they had a clear signal was being sent there was something worth stealing and it was clear the message was getting around.

'I do not like it Cassian, the scum round here will gut you like a fish for a handful of coin let alone the cargo you carry,' Lathyrus said, concern clearly etched upon his face.

'We have little choice. It is the closest landing area to our training camp and we dared not risk landing in Utica any earlier,' Cassian replied but his concern also showed.

'You could have stayed on the boat, cramped yes but free from harm.'

'Your concern honours me dear friend but the men must train. The task ahead is a deadly one and I would have them at their best. Though to be honest the offer was tempting.'

'Ah you always were a stubborn bastard Cassian, let's hope this time it doesn't get you killed.' Lathyrus spoke shaking his head as he did so. Cassian thought the same but he could not see a better way and hoped his stubbornness did not prevent him seeing any better alternatives.

When the convoy was ready to move Cassian gave the order. They would first travel to a warehouse on the outskirts of the port. It was owned by Cassian's father who had such buildings dotted around most of the known world. The problem was it had been out of use for some time, Caralis had become a too unstable port for guaranteed movement of goods. The men were on edge, they could see as well as Cassian that danger was near. Every step they made, every word they spoke was eagerly observed and listened to. This place was lawless and the men who inhabited it were the lowest scum in the empire to whom a man's life was worth the contents of his purse or indeed the load on his wagon.

The wagons had completed half of their journey when a hooded figure stopped to speak to one of the front guards. The guard nodded and approached Cassian.

'My lord, the man says he knows you and wishes to give you a message.' The hood prevented a clear view of the stranger but from his movements it was clear that he too was nervous.

'Check him for weapons and bring him forward,' Cassian said cautiously and was relieved to see Spartacus draw his weapon and move in close at his side. The check was completed and the figure brought close. Cassian recognised the walk but just could not put a name to it. The figure was obviously concerned about being seen in the convoy's presence, but having a conversation whilst marching through hostile ground was not going to be easy. The figure stopped and began to speak in a hushed voice.

'Forgive the secrecy young Cassian, I would liked to have spoken more freely but it seems you are already drawing unwanted attention.' Beneath the hood a faint smile appeared. Recognition finally dawned showing itself on Cassian's face,

'Old friend it has been too long, what news have you?'

'You visit Caralis in troubled times my friend. Crime is at every corner, the old merchants have all but left with a new order controlling all.'

'This I can see for myself. Is my warehouse still standing?' Cassian quizzed.

70

'Standing it is, but a most unwanted set of lodgers are currently residing there and have been for some time.'

'Then they owe a good deal of back rent. I shall endeavour to collect and promptly evict them.' Cassian eyed the stranger with determination.

'I see the boy I once knew has become a brave man, but has he grown intelligent as well as brave?'

'Only time will show that. Tell me do I have your support?' Cassian asked, fearing the answer to be no.

'Your father once saved my life. I promised myself that one day I would repay that debt. Besides, I grow weary of the scum that now make a mockery of this once fine port.' The stranger spoke with clear venom, and reached up and removed his hood.

'Trabus, my old dear friend it has been far too long.' Cassian's face broke into a broad smile, momentarily forgetting the danger of the moment.

'Cassian, my dear man. Your family, are they well and why on earth would you risk that happiness to venture to this piss hole?' The sadness of what Caralis had become shown too clearly upon his face.

'Needs must. I will tell you all the finer detail later but, for now, we must reach the warehouse and tomorrow on to the villa of Albus. Tell me friend, would you join us?' Trabus smiled.

'It seems I have shown my enemies where my allegiance belongs. They will not forgive it and I do not ask their forgiveness. They deserve neither respect or loyalty. I guessed where you would be headed, my men are waiting there now ready for orders.'

'How many do you command?' Cassian spoke hopefully, hoping that Trabus would have a small army at his command.

'I have only fourteen men. The numbers have dwindled over the years, better wages and loose women soon pull men to other quarters, but these men are loyal and are good to have near when the blades are in use.'

The convoy trundled on, each of the men watchful for any disturbance. Cassian was amazed at the change which had taken place in Caralis. The last time he had visited it was a bustling, wealthy port dealing with merchandise from all over the known world. Now signs of squalor and degradation were everywhere. Filth ran in the streets, flies buzzed overhead feeding on the filth. The people too had changed, gone were the eager buyers and sellers to be replaced by drunks and whores. The empire had failed here, law and order needed to be restored, not that squalor did not have its place in a properly run Roman province. Indeed poverty was around every corner even in Rome itself, but here it was the overriding normality. These people had lost their self respect and it showed on their faces. They attempted to wash it away with the sour wine they consumed, but the shame was etched on each of them which could not be washed away with all the wine in the world.

Every other building seemed to be a whore shop, women blatantly flaunting themselves and showing their wares to any passer-by whether interested or not. Cassian heard Spartacus chastise Plinius to 'Keep his fucking eyes on the street.' Cassian smiled for it must be difficult for a young man not to be distracted by such thoughts, but in times like this distraction could lead to death.

Spartacus did not like the cramped streets, it made for poor movement when fighting and he wouldn't be surprised if a fight was looming. The air was filled with tension. A number of times he had noticed someone in the crowd rush off, as if reporting upon the convoy's every movement. He wondered if this new member of the convoy could be trusted because if he couldn't, then this small band to which he was a member was in real trouble. In the time he had spent at the head of his army he had grown accustomed to being well informed but now he lived off scraps Cassian threw his way and he did not like it. If danger was going to strike he would like to at least be able to make an educated guess as to when and how, but that was a luxury which was gone and, like the men, he hoped that Cassian knew what he was doing. Spartacus moved in close to Plinius again.

'Listen Plinius, those whores bring only misery, besides we have more pressing matters than what's between your legs.' This time Spartacus spoke gently as he regretted the harsh words to Plinius earlier and he succeeded in making the young man blush with embarrassment.

'Sorry sir, it's just I have never...' Plinius again blushed crimson, eyes fixed firmly down at the road.

'I know, but it will happen soon enough and hopefully with a girl with more to give in the heart department and less in the disease department. Besides, probably best to stay alive and to do what we need to stay alert.' Spartacus spoke the words but as he did he realised just how young Plinius was and wished he could transport the boy to safety, where he could grow to an old age preferably shagging some local girl to his heart's content. But he could not so he decided to keep the boy alive, so that one day maybe he could enjoy such a life. He patted Plinius on the shoulder and the young man brightened, a new determination came across his face to do his duty. His back straightened and his eyes once again scanned the crowd not dawdling on the whores but searched for intended mischief of another kind.

Spartacus moved back into position only to see a drunk sidle towards him. Spartacus eyed the drunk and observed that, despite his ungainly walk and nonsense talking, the man's eyes were alive and observing all. He saw the man was also holding his right arm close to his waist as if concealing something.

The drunk moved closer to the convoy, moving towards the second wagon, Spartacus prevented Plinius going to meet the drunk with an arm across the boy's chest.

'Back in line Plinius, I will deal with this.' Spartacus spoke not with gentility but with the authoritative voice that leaves its recipient under no illusions that the order must be obeyed. Spartacus moved to the drunk and arranged a smile upon his face.

'Right dear friend, what is it I can do for you?' All the time his eyes watched for movement from that right arm and the possibility of danger.

The drunk had done this many times. His master on a number of occasions had asked him to judge the metal of the men who he would liberate of certain possessions. The ruse had worked so often the drunk had lost count. He would amble up to the intended victim and, at a certain point, would crouch low, pretending to be suffering from cramps. The victim would offer help and the drunk would slit his throat and disappear into the crowd. Pursuit was not possible, for the rest of the men would need to tend to the victim and guard the convoy. It was all too easy. The act would spread fear amongst the rest of the guards and, before long, his master would have more treasures to add to his wealth and the fear of his name would be elevated even more. Ah thought the drunk, the big bastard had stopped the boy, very well your throat will cut as easily as the boy's and hopefully there will be a bigger reward for doing it.

Spartacus saw the man crouch and heard the man squeal his discomfort. He leaned forward and asked if he could be of assistance. Quick as a flash of lightening the drunk drew his dagger, it glinted in the sunshine. He swept the blade upwards, a smile upon his face, expecting soon to feel the familiarity of flesh being torn by his dagger's edge. The drunk's eyes widened in disbelief, his arm was being held firm by the powerfully built man, whose eyes mocked the pitiful attempt. He felt himself lifted by the throat a clear foot from the floor.

'I take it you want to send a message to your master – well by all means let this be the message, and it's one that we should not be prevented from carrying out our business.' Spartacus spoke aloud, all around eyes were glued to such a show of strength. The drunk was carried to a nearby door. He let out a terrible scream as he saw his own dagger move quickly and powerfully towards him, a scream which was cut short as the dagger pinned him through the mouth to the heavy wooden door. Spartacus walked away, the twitching body of the drunk left suspended on the door. Cassian approached Spartacus again his face filled with awe.

'We could have questioned him you know.'

'I am sick of all this deceit, the next fucker who gets in my way I'm going to gut.' Spartacus marched away.

Cassian was joined by Trabus who was equally amazed by the show of pure aggression and skill shown by Spartacus, and felt the urge to ensure understanding.

'Ermmm, by the Gods I hope that man is on our side?'

'He is,' Cassian replied.

'His loyalty, is that beyond question?' Trabus posed.

74

'He is the man I trust above all others – but I am afraid that is as far as this discussion goes.' Cassian answered curtly and Trabus knew the conversation was over.

A number of thieves and cutthroats were observing the convoy when Spartacus had performed his act of Herculean strength and aggression. The plans they had been making within their minds had evaporated, along with the courage in their hearts. As negative as the effect upon those wishing harm to the convoy, the exact opposite was the case for the men of the convoy who marched at Spartacus' side, heads held high.

All had come to admire and respect the skills the man had with the weapons he used, but it was more than that, for Spartacus had shown himself as a leader who thought of more than his personal glory and wealth. He was a man who considered the lives of his men. It was something rare in a leader which too few had observed back in the ranks of the legions. They glanced around not only at the crowd checking for danger, but also at the men who marched alongside them, a sense of purpose and solidarity echoed in step. Only Cassian stood apart, he still felt like an outsider and he believed he still had some way to go before these men trusted him. He tried to cast off the feeling, trying to tell himself that was the way of things, but deep down he vowed to change their attitudes.

Chapter 10

The convoy stopped short of the warehouse. The crowds had thinned this far from the centre of the port. Trabus made a signal and his fourteen men emerged from secluded spots to join the main band of men. They briefed Trabus and Cassian on what was happening within the warehouse. So far it seemed that the men inside were unaware of what was approaching. Apparently the men inside belonged to the house of Apelios, a powerful local trader come bandit who tended to take rather than barter for items, and could gather a good deal of men should it be required.

'Well Trabus, what is this man Apelios like?' Cassian asked.

'He gives Greeks a bad name. He is vicious, not the sort of man you want as an enemy Cassian. The trouble is he's not the sort of man you can make a bargain with unless you have a huge advantage.' As Trabus spoke he shook his head in dismay at the task facing them. Cassian glanced at Spartacus.

'What do you think?'

Spartacus was still annoyed at how the day had proceeded.

'How many man do you think this Greek can muster not counting those inside the warehouse?' He asked of Trabus.

'I would say at least fifty, that's nearly double our force. Not to mention the timing of the attack would be in their favour,' he replied bleakly.

'Then that settles it. We cannot bargain with the man, he will not burn the place down because he will want whatever is in our wagons, so I suggest we just kill the bastard. The time has come to put niceties to one side.' Cassian just shrugged.

'Seems like a plan to me.'

Trabus grimaced to himself knowing that there really was only one course of action. Apelios must be stopped and the only way to do that was to stand against him, but Trabus and his family had lived in this port for a long time and any unsuccessful action against Apelios would certainly see that come to an end. He looked at Cassian and wondered if the boy he once knew had it in him to challenge an old war horse like Apelios. He remembered the time he had spent with the boy's father and wished his old friend was here now. He would have known what to do with the likes of Apelios. He looked to the skies and gave a short prayer to the Gods, let out a lengthy sigh and joined Cassian and Spartacus in the planning of the next move.

Spartacus and Cassian entered the warehouse, behind them filed ten men. It was important they showed strength, the rest were left to guard the wagons. They walked as calmly as possible into the dark dusty environment, as casually as their nerves would allow. A group of three men were seated drinking wine and laughing, these were men secure in the fact that nobody dared challenge their authority. Standing to the group's right were another two men who had stopped what they were doing to observe Spartacus and his men. A quick glance up into the second tier and there were another two, and coming from behind some large wooden crates to the rear of the warehouse came another two.

'Remind me to congratulate Trabus on his men's observation qualities,' Spartacus smirked as he spoke.

'Hmm, a little work needed, six have quickly become nine,' Cassian remarked. 'Make that ten.' He nodded towards what seemed to be the feet of a tenth member asleep.

A man, who was in the centre of the three seated, stood and took a long look at the new arrivals. He produced a black toothed smile.

'Yes gentlemen, what can I do for you? I am afraid if you seek business this is merely a holding area and if it's trade you require you will need to go and see Apelios.' Emphasis was placed on the name as if to shoot a warning to those who wished to cause trouble.

'My name is Cassian and I believe, and I am sure it is a harmless mistake, your master seems to have taken over my warehouse. Now I am not one to be unreasonable but if you gentlemen would like to vacate my warehouse I am quite willing to forget any owed rent.' Cassian smiled serenely and spoke as if passing the time of day with an old friend. The man was thrown for a moment but quickly regained his composure.

"You're kidding right! Maybe you are new here because Apelios does not make mistakes.'

'Oh, in that case if you and your men would run along and ask him for the monies which are owed I would be most grateful,' Cassian said, again keeping calm and eloquent in his approach. The man clearly showed his annoyance at being dismissed as a young child would be.

'I tell you what, how about you and your men here walk away now and maybe I will let you keep your balls? Although when Apelios hears of your attempt to take this warehouse he will probably feed them to you.'

'Oh what a shame, it seems we are at an impasse. I suppose we shall just have to kill you then.' Cassian smiled his sickly sweet smile and, as he uttered the words, Spartacus and the men drew their weapons.

'Oh really, well let's see what you make of Androcles first shall we.' The man laughed as he spoke.

Spartacus had observed the men in the room but had momentarily forgotten about the feet. He quickly glanced to the area where they had been but now the area was empty. Suddenly a huge figure erupted from behind some crates, brushing them aside and two swipes later, from what looked like a blacksmiths hammer, two men were down. The blows had taken the first on the skull and shattered it on impact. The second had taken the hit in the chest, he lay on the floor blood pouring from his mouth, he would never rise again. Spartacus was amazed to see the rest of the enemies had not bothered to fight. They were happy to see this monstrous human being do his work, work he seemed to be very accomplished in. Another one of Cassian's men fell beneath the hammer and then one of Trabus'. Spartacus yelled for them to stay back and he moved into position to take the man down. The trouble was the man did not obey the simple rules of combat, he just charged, his great power meaning any opponent felt compelled to retreat. He towered above Spartacus and seemed almost as wide as he was tall. The sheer power of the man knocked Spartacus off balanced and it was all he could do to avoid a huge smash with the hammer before he had time to recover. The giant of a man caught him with a kick that sent him sprawling. It felt as though a team of oxen had ploughed into him. Androcles roared in triumph and the rest of his men cheered with him but this, in turn, gave Spartacus the chance to recover. He glanced at Cassian and winked, Cassian though could only stare back with anxiety.

Spartacus stood in front of Androcles and looked as a small child in comparison to the huge mountain of a man who faced him. He smirked and said.

'My, my, now you're a big bastard. All those muscles, are we compensating for something not so big?'

Androcles roared his annoyance and again lunged at Spartacus who had succeeded in exactly what he had intended. The lunge was ill thought out and over reached itself. Spartacus merely took a step backwards and flicked his blade upwards, taking three fingers from the colossal hand. His opponent screamed in agony and charged in blind fury. Spartacus knew it was coming and half ducking, half rolling to the side, with a deft slash he took the giant behind the knee. His opponent crumpled and, before the man could recover, Spartacus was upon him removing his head with one blow. As he did his other hand went to his belt and pulled a dagger, and a moment later it embedded into the chest of the enemy's spokesman. Shock and disbelief etched on his face as he slipped to the floor, blood already bubbling from the corner of his mouth.

Four more of the enemy fell beneath the swords of Cassian's men though, in truth, the determination for a fight had left them as soon as Androcles had fallen. The rest scrabbled fleeing from the building. The skirmish was already over but they would not be pursued for Cassian would not lose men down the foreign streets of Caralis where the enemy had the advantage. Trabus entered the building.

'By the Gods Cassian you have stirred up a hornet's nest now. Apelios will want your balls,' he said, shaking his head in disbelief. Cassian turned towards Spartacus.

'You know, since I have met you people seem awfully keen on removing parts of my anatomy.' He smiled as he spoke.

'Trust me it is something you grow accustomed to,' Spartacus replied. Cassian turned back to Trabus.

'How long do we have?'

'Apelios will need to gather men and he is not the sort to charge in here. He will want to know what he faces first. Vicious and deceitful the man is, but he's no fool.'

'Then we have some time to prepare,' Spartacus interrupted, 'we best make use of it.'

The wagons were brought in and orders given. Men scampered this way and that while Cassian, Spartacus, Trabus and Aegis made plans. Every now and then one of them would rise and walk around the preparations that had been made, order alterations if any were needed or instruct on new plans. Trabus gave the group all the information he could on Apelios, discussing at length the man's strengths and weaknesses, and information on his headquarters and the type of men he commanded. Aegis and Spartacus gave most instruction on what needed to be done for the defence of the warehouse, while Cassian told the group where they needed to be to keep to his plan for the mission to succeed. The problem was that defending the warehouse, although keeping the wagons and hopefully the men safe, left little room for them to continue their journey to the villa of Albus and the opportunity to train for their mission. In the end they called a halt to the meeting. They needed to spend time with the men, for they knew this would be one of the most dangerous stages of the mission. They were in a foreign place where they had little room for manoeuvre, where they faced a local enemy used to this type of fighting and was doing so in his own territory. It made for a bleak outlook.

Plinius had settled himself on some old crates away from the rest of the men and seemed in deep thought. Even Bull had tried to cheer him without success. Spartacus had observed this and wondered what disturbed the young man. He knew it could not be the upcoming fight, for Plinius had faced all the mission had thrown at him without so much as a flinch. No, this was something more. Spartacus acquired two goblets of wine and joined Plinius. At first nothing was said, both drank from their goblets and an unusual calm settled between the two of them. Spartacus knew that Plinius wanted to say something but an invisible force seemed to hold the boy's tongue still. It would need a statement of trust to come from Spartacus to loosen the boy's will to remain quiet. He would need to know he could trust Spartacus and so Spartacus must share a part of his soul if he was to try and soothe that of Plinius. Then hopefully the boy would be able to concentrate on the present dangers.

'What do you know of me Plinius?' Spartacus asked.

'What do you mean?' The boy answered, a confused look upon his face.

'I mean, what have you heard and what do you make of the things I have done since you have known me?'

'When I joined the legion I heard stories of how the beast from Thracia broke from his chains in Capua, slaughtered the good honourable Batiatus and raised an army which put thousands of Roman citizens to death.' Plinius blushed as Spartacus eyed him. 'And then you killed the centurion, a man I loathed. You trained me so that I might stay alive, and you seem to have forgiven Cassian for an act which I never could.' As Plinius made the last statement he could not look at Spartacus but fixed his gaze firmly to the ground.

'Now let me tell you the truth as I see it. Capua erupted in violence, I did not start the rebellion as many seem to believe. I did not even lead any of the men, the trouble is, under Roman law, if one slave rebels then all the slaves under that household are put to death.' He paused for a second, wanting to get each word correct in his mind. 'So rebel I did and, I admit, it was my sword which took the life of Batiatus. I sort of grew into one of the leaders because of my military background. Roman towns were attacked and terrible things happened. It was survival and we did what we needed to, and then it ended in blood and defeat.'

Spartacus gulped back the grief which suddenly overwhelmed him. 'Then as you know my son was murdered and, as hard as it is to look at Cassian sometimes and to deal with the burning hatred that sometimes ignites within me, I have to remember that although he gave the order it was not his will to kill my son. Revenge is a luxury that men of our standing can ill afford to carry around like a banner. We need to fold it away and place it in a safe place where we can use it when required.' He paused for a moment letting his

81

words register with Plinius. 'What I am saying is although it is not easy, the death of our loved ones cannot be the reason to throw away our own lives for who will remember them? When the chance for revenge comes take it, if you must, but do not expect it to take away the pain.'

'I killed the optio, I thought …' Plinius' words trailed away.

'You thought it would lessen the weight you felt inside. The weight of loss cannot be removed by revenge. For a while the anger we build up seeking revenge lessens the feeling of loss and so we cling to it, stoke its fires and feed it, but in the end it is the loss we must deal with.' Spartacus felt his own pain churning his insides.

'Have you dealt with the loss of your son and do you not seek revenge?' Plinius' eyes now sought a kind of answer to it all from Spartacus.

'No not yet, my son's loss still weighs me down, and as for revenge – I will have a reckoning with the man who made the order but I will not let the yearning for such a meeting rule both my head and my heart. You are a good soldier Plinius and a fine man. Look to the future not the past, your brother protected you and lost his life doing so, do not allow that sacrifice to be in vain. He would have wanted you to live and not be forever veiled in a blanket of grief.'

Tears were in the boy's eyes now and he turned away not wanting to be seen. Spartacus knew the conversation was at an end and he walked away holding back his own grief with every step. Spartacus thought of the conversation he had just endured with Plinius, the content of his words nearly provoking laughter. For it was revenge that acted as food for his own spirit, the hatred cradled deep inside. He had known little but anger for what seemed a lifetime, long before his child was murdered before him, but he hoped to make clear to Plinius that to live with the hatred burning like the fires of Mount Vesuvius was only possible if you learned to harness them, for to let them burn freely would consume and destroy.

Chapter 11

Time passed and Spartacus wondered if there would ever be an attack. He was glad to see Plinius had snapped out of his melancholy and was taking an active part in the defensive work. He glanced at Trabus who was showing signs of anxiety, time and time again checking the same part of the defences.

'What's up old man? We are not done for yet.' He tried to be enthusiastic.

'Less of the old, there's plenty of life left in me yet. I worry more for my household rather than myself,' he replied, the concern still on his face. The words he uttered though seemed to spark the beginnings of an idea deep within the thoughts of Spartacus' mind. He called for Cassian and with Trabus they huddled in a corner.

'What do you think?' Spartacus quizzed the two.

'It's madness,' said Trabus, 'but I do not see what other choice we have.'

'How many men will you need Trabus to complete both tasks?' Cassian asked.

'Six should be enough, two to go to my home and the others to make the surprise for Apelios,' he replied.

'So now it is more about timing. It's probably best if you and the men were to sneak out now in case we get surrounded, besides the sooner your household are removed the safer it will be for them,' Spartacus informed.

For the first time Trabus looked at Spartacus without suspicion in his eyes. No words were spoken but, from that moment, all mistrust was gone from him. If he would put the household of a stranger above his own safety, which keeping as many men close as possible would do, then Trabus would consider him a friend. Cassian spoke.

'The second phase should take place just before the sun rises. It's important that it been seen.'

'Oh, it will be,' Trabus replied, and for the first time the look of confidence was evident upon his face. The men were chosen and the six of them and Trabus, hooded cloaks in place, slipped from the warehouse and the hopes of all the men rested squarely with them. Watching them go gave Spartacus mixed emotions. He knew they had to go for the good of all, but they would have no way of knowing what degree of success they had achieved until the morning, and by then it may be too late.

It was not long before the lookout called out. The main road approaching the warehouse was teaming with men, armed with an assortment of odd weapons none of which filled the heart with joy. Cassian and Spartacus watched the procession, Spartacus cursing.

'Bloody Trabus! Can the man not count? There must be at least seventy of the bastards.' He shook his head.

'It matters not Spartacus, we are trained men they are just men with weapons.' Cassian tried to sound upbeat.

'You say this to me, may I remind you of a slave army who bested a number of your Roman legions.'

'You forget one thing my friend,' Cassian smiled, 'this time you're on our side.'

Spartacus simply blew out his cheeks.

'You know the most annoying thing in the world Cassian?'

'What's that my friend?' Said Cassian, still smiling broadly.

'Bloody endless optimism, it drives normal men to despair.'

'Very well then Spartacus I will refrain from happiness while we go speak to this bastard. Oh, by the way, if you get the chance gut the pig.' Cassian winked as he walked to the door.

Spartacus joined Cassian at the door. A figure had moved away from the main crowd and approached within a spears throw and casually leant against a post.

'Cocky bastard isn't he?' Spartacus observed.

'Ah, he feels on firm footing. His prey is cornered, he has numerical and time advantage, he believes he is in complete control of the situation,' Cassian suggested.

'Well he bloody well is!'

'It would be proper if we just gave him a little to think about.' As he spoke Cassian sauntered out to speak to Apelios. If he had nerves they did not show and Spartacus had to admit this was one rich Roman with balls.

Apelios observed the young, arrogant Roman emerge from the warehouse. He had, of course, heard of Cassian and the special duties he carried out for the rich and powerful back in Rome. This though was Caralis and here there was only one law, and that law was written by Apelios and no jumped up fuck from Rome would change that. If he let the insult of Cassian taking back his warehouse and killing his men go, then his power would slip and Apelios was no fool. He knew once it started to slip then momentum would gather and soon another would stand in his place. This Roman must be firmly put in his place. He looked past the Roman to the heavy doorway. Standing in full view was a man whose body looked as if carved from rock, an involuntary shiver ran down his back for the man was looking straight at him, and the eyes of the man seemed to speak and they spoke of death. He quickly dragged himself from that moment, it did not do to dwell on such matters. He decided he would deal with this Roman quickly, lay down the law and the snivelling little shit would run back to Rome with his tail firmly between his legs like the arrogant young pup he was.

'You have travelled far young Cassian,' Apelios spoke quietly but there was no mistaking the malice he issued.

'Yes, and I would travel further if you would be so kind as to remove yourself from my property, then my men could rest properly before we continue that journey.' Cassian's words stung Apelios. He was tempted to order the attack at once, but bit back his anger at being dismissed in such a way.

"Very well. Plain speaking it is. You will leave this place I have need of that warehouse for the use of my men. You will forfeit your wagons, their cargo and, of course, your weapons.' Apelios gave Cassian his most intimidating stare as he spoke, but Cassian brushed it away like swatting a fly.

'Apelios, you seem to be under the illusion that I give a fuck what you want. If you come into that warehouse your men will die. You will lose the hold you have on this port and, if you attempt to delay me further, you will lose your life.' Cassian now returned the stare and it was ice cold. The sudden change from firm but pleasant manner to downright aggressive had thrown Apelios, this is not the way it was suppose to happen.

'You... you... cannot win!' He blurted out the words, gone was the cool, calculating animal many in the port knew.

'I already have. These are just formalities.' Cassian turned and walked away as he spoke, leaving Apelios hanging there, completely aghast at what had just happened. It took a few moments to regain his composure, then he turned and stormed back to his men.

Cassian returned to the warehouse where he and Spartacus observed Apelios screaming and shouting at his men. It was obvious Cassian had succeeded in making Apelios extremely angry and both knew angry men made poor decisions. They both waited and hoped for him to make the mistakes. It was not long before it came. Apelios was so eager to smash away the defences and chase out the arrogant Cassian he ordered around fifty men to make a direct assault against the main entrance. It was a blundering attempt, the fifty charged towards the door and all seemed to believe they would simply be able to roll over those guarding it. Suddenly missiles from the second floor started to land within the ranks. Men fell, when the slingshot and javelin rained in, they in turn brought down others who could not avoid them.

When they reached the main entrance it was blocked by a heavy upturned cart and they would have to clamber over it. They faced a major problem; the defenders were there in force and they were not wearing the light tunics of the attackers. The defenders had adorned their full gladiatorial armour. This had two effects, firstly it gave the defenders confidence - protected against many of the blows which came their way, and then it sapped the confidence of the enemy because they suddenly realised they were not fighting the usual street scum that they were used to.

Apelios pulled his men back to safety. Eleven dead men and two so badly injured they would take no further part in the day's activities made him check his anger. He realised he would need more than just brute force to win this day. Spartacus' men had done well, they breathed heavily as the enemy retreated. They had lost just one man, although all who had fought at the entrance were covered in cuts and scrapes.

Trabus and his men picked their way through the dark and grimy streets, sticking to the backstreets where possible. The inhabitants seemed to possess a sixth sense where trouble was concerned. Trabus thought they were like the animals that sense a dark cloud and scamper for cover long before the storm hits. Few of the locals could be observed on the streets and he thought it best to split the men to avoid unwanted attention. He pulled his men in close. He gave instruction to four of the men, who huddled in close for his words.

'Right you know what to do, do not fail for you know what Apelios will do if we do not succeed.' The men didn't reply but merely nodded in agreement and slipped away melting into the darkness.

Trabus and the other two men carried on to his household. As silently as he could, he gathered the entire household trying, where possible, to calm the panic which was so close to erupting. He snapped out orders, making them concentrate on the task in hand, rather than the possibilities that could lay ahead. As they moved away to complete those tasks, Trabus and his wife were left alone in the hall to his villa. He looked into his wife's eyes.

'Forgive me my love, I fear I have placed you in great danger.'

'What has happened my love?'

Trabus told her of all that had happened and again asked for her forgiveness. She held his hand tightly and moved closer to him.

'My love, I was just a girl when we decided to make our lives together. I have, in that time, been blessed with a husband who has provided for his family but also tried to always be an honourable man in all his dealings.

'But...' She held a hand to his lips, preventing his words.

'I have seen what Caralis has become and how that has affected the man that I love. I know you would have moved long ago to prevent Apelios if it was not for your love for your family. We will face what the Gods bestow upon us.' She ended by holding the man the years had not diminished in her eyes. He held her too, and gently kissed her cheek fearing that this would be the last time he would do so.

The wagon was stacked with all Trabus could load into it, and it pulled away as quietly as it could. It carried all he held dear. He looked upon the face of his wife and could not stop himself being amazed that so many years had never diminished her beauty and, for a moment, he was lost in her eyes. The wagon passed from view, and the last of his men were sent to guard its way. He returned to his home and sifted through a few documents, ensuring nothing of importance had been left behind. There was a small, almost undetectable sound which came from behind him. He smiled the smile of resignation.

The men inside the warehouse watched as Apelios gave his orders. Men separated from the main group and disappeared from view. Within a short time they returned carrying ladders.

'This man learns quickly,' Spartacus said, with a rueful look as he dressed a small cut on his forearm.

'Yes...pity that, and I would prefer it if you did not throw yourself into every fight.' Cassian replied, but even as he said it he knew it a forlorn hope, Spartacus was not the type of man to stay in the background as others died.

The enemy started to fan out, circling the building looking for an easy way in. With the numbers within the building so low it would be difficult to defend everywhere at once. Once again the charge order went up and the enemy swarmed towards the building. This time the missiles had less effect, with the volleys not being concentrated in one area but scattered trying to defend the building on all sides. The enemy pressed and the defenders threw them back as best they could.

At one stage the enemy gained ground on the upper tier but Aegis and a small group who had been held in reserve valiantly charged. Aegis roared like a demon and hurled himself at his foe. All the enemy fell, smashed like kindling by a mighty axe, but men were dying on both sides and Spartacus knew they could not last if things remained the same. That attack failed and the next and the two following that, but the defenders were being worn down. It was relief when they heard Apelios pull his men back on the final attack, and it seemed, for the time being, the fighting was over for the enemy began to make camp. Food and wine were brought from one of Apelios' many households, the enemy revelling in the fact that the defenders were so low in number, for when the sun rose it was evident the warehouse would fall.

'Why do they stop attacking?' Cassian asked Spartacus, but it was Aegis who answered.

'The leader knew his men were close to breaking, too many comrades had fallen. He will fill their bellies with food and good wine, then their heads with tales of a vast fortune and then, come the morning, they will charge like devils once again.' As he spoke Aegis looked around at the dead and dying, few had come through the ordeal without damage, even Cassian nursed a badly swollen lip. Spartacus had joked he must have tripped over his tunic but he took it in good spirits.

'Then when the morning comes, let us hope...' Cassian never finished the sentence as a shout came from outside. It was Apelios, with a figure at his feet. It was difficult to see who, as darkness had swept down and only torches lit the place in which the sprawled figure lay.

'I have a gift for you Cassian, something for you and your men to think on – until the sun rises that is.' He turned and walked away. However, two of his men lifted the figure and brought it closer to the warehouse, before nervously skitting away to join their leader. Before Cassian could stop him, Spartacus leapt over the barricade and hefted the figure to his shoulder and returned to the relative safety of the warehouse.

It took some time to recognise the figure, so beaten were his features, but to everyone's amazement it spoke.

'A glass of wine would go down well.' The words only just audible.

'Trabus,' Cassian cried, 'What...?' he began, but a bloodied hand rose to stem his questions.

'Cassian, let me speak for I fear I do not have long. The plan is still in place, I was taken after I got my family out.' Trabus struggled to catch his breath.

'Do not worry about that, you need rest my friend.' Cassian held the head of his battered friend, as he gazed down at him he knew it would not be long. Apelios' men had done their work well, Trabus' body had been broken and shattered, the only miracle was that he still lived.

'My family have been sent to Albus, please...' Trabus struggled. Cassian interceded.

'They will want for nothing my friend, they will be as my own family.'

A pained smile crossed the distorted face of Trabus.

'Thank you my boy.' Trabus seemed to drift but continued to speak. 'Did I ever tell you about me and your father...?' Trabus spoke more.

'Trabus...Trabus, old friend.'

Spartacus closed the old man's eyes and looked around. So many dead and yet this loss seemed the hardest to take. He could feel the sadness descend upon the men and knew that the fight was lost. The next time the enemy came they would rip this place apart and all here would die. Trabus would have company on his final voyage.

Chapter 12

Spartacus and Cassian jerked upright. They had somehow managed a couple of hours sleep but now were aware of shouts coming from the enemy's camp. They rushed towards the main door. Lots of movement from outside made Spartacus shout to his men, trying to put some spark back into their weary bodies. He glanced over to Cassian who was straining to see what was happening.

'Well it won't be long now. Let's see how many of them we can take with us,' Spartacus growled.

'Look,' Cassian replied, pointing towards the east, 'and there,' pointing over Spartacus' shoulder.

'By all the Gods, Cassian they did it. Trabus' men, they did it!' He cast his eyes down at old Trabus and felt the old man did not deserve to be laid to rest in an old dusty warehouse. Cassian, reading his thoughts, said.

'We will take him with us, his family can pay their respects at Albus' villa.'

'I think first we need to get out of here. We best make ready.' Spartacus strode off to make the arrangements.

Cassian stood watching his enemy, their blind panic evident. He smiled to himself. Apelios was bound to be distraught. If he stayed then he risked losing everything. Cassian could see the now four fires raging in the port, all of which he would guarantee were the property of Apelios including his very own headquarters. If Apelios left to deal with the fires then he lost out on the chance to claim the wagons and whatever prize they hid. He guessed he was going to be an extremely angry man indeed.

Apelios could not believe it, he watched the flames destroying what he had spent so long building up. He glanced back at the warehouse and asked himself what wealth did it conceal? He did not think for too long, he had to protect what he had. The arrogant Roman could wait, but he vowed to himself, if it killed him, he would have a reckoning with that bastard.

He dispatched men to the various fires but told four men to stay behind and watch the warehouse while he himself took the largest group and headed off to his headquarters. With each step his resolve strengthened to take revenge upon Cassian. He did not know how he had managed to get by his scouts and put a torch to his property. He then thought of the old man, Trabus, who he had not bothered to question. He had thought the old man to be just looking out for himself and trying to escape the troubles. He swore and cursed his own stupidity and picked up the pace, for now his concerns were more pressing. A part of him, the cautious part which lay buried mostly dormant in the past few years, warned him of re-igniting the feud with Cassian and the tall stranger he had observed at the door, for the thought of the man made him uneasy. He had no wish to meet the man's gaze again.

The four guards settled down, happy at the ease of their task. They did not even bother to watch all the sides of the warehouse, surely the men inside were so battle scarred they offered no threat? Three of them curled up around the dying embers of the makeshift fire, whilst the fourth sat slumped, his back against a fence, his eyes observing the main entrance to the warehouse. For a short time his good intentions held him to his job, ensuring nobody left the warehouse but, as the exertions of the previous night's battle wore down his resistance, he too slipped into slumber, blissfully unaware of the danger he faced.

The figure had taken his time working his way around from the back of the warehouse just to be sure no trap had been set. He moved quickly to the first guard already lost in a world of his own. He hardly stirred before he died, and had no opportunity to warn his comrades. The figure moved quickly and efficiently to the next man, all the time checking the surrounding area for concealed enemy. There were none and he continued his work.

Spartacus held his victim and drew the knife quietly across the man's throat. He was the last of the four, but that did not mean Apelios didn't have friends close by, so he killed quickly and efficiently. It was important that no lookouts got away. The wagons needed to move as quickly as possible and, hopefully, they would be long gone before those that mattered became aware of it.

The wagons were loaded inside the warehouse, every attempt being made to conceal their intentions to leave. The men covered the heavy wheels with animal skins to soften the noise they made and they removed their armour. With the dead and badly wounded taken out of the equation it meant just eight fit men to drive the three wagons and indeed to defend against attack. The lack of numbers was an issue, they needed six good men for the upcoming tournament. At this rate they would not be able to fill the quota. Of those that were able to fight all needed serious rest, many sported minor injuries which, if left untreated, could become far worse. Spartacus had seen many a good man felled by what seemed, at first, a trivial injury. He glanced over at Plinius. The boy had fought well and had even stopped Aegis from being gutted up on the second tier. Any problems the boy suffered in times of peace seemed to dispel when the battle horn sounded. He smiled, he had heard himself described the same way.

The wagons moved away. The men, still weary from the previous night's exertions, tried their best to be alert to attack, but all knew that if one came the chances of survival were little. Aegis stayed behind. He was to set the warehouse alight when the wagons had moved away a safe distance. Cassian was determined that Apelios be left nothing for his troubles, and all believed that the fallen friends within the warehouse deserved a decent funeral pyre and did not want the enemy to disrespect the bodies in any way.

Cassian climbed aboard the wagon next to Spartacus and for a while both sat in silence, each only raising their heads at the occasional noises which disturbed the silence. A startled rabbit broke cover and skitted around looking for a safe place to hide.

'The men fought well,' Cassian said tiredly.

'Never seen Romans fight so well as a team and as individuals, as they did last night,' Spartacus replied.

'We lost some good men; Trabus, Marius, Matro, all good men …' Cassian's voice trailed away as he listed the names.

'Battle cares not of the quality of a man – it takes as it sees fit.' Spartacus knew Cassian had seen his first real battle the night before, and he also knew what the man was feeling was guilt. The guilt of all leaders who had lost men in their command.

'When dealing with my peers in Rome many of them yearned for battle, eager for the glory of the thing.' Cassian shook his head as he spoke the words, 'if only I could tell them the true nature of the beast.'

'Even then they would still wish for it, for until you experience such an ordeal the mystique and glory dims any argument put forward. Cassian, do not reproach yourself for those who have been lost. Honour them yes, but do not let them weigh heavily upon your heart. For to do so will prevent you making the necessary decisions in the future which need to be made. Besides, though it pains me to say it, we need you.'

'Spartacus, I fear you begin to read my spirit like parchment. Can I hide nothing from you?' Cassian attempted a small smile.

'In part. I have grown to know you Cassian but I know how you feel because it is what all sane men feel when the battle is over and the mind reflects on such horrors. I was still a boy when I killed my first enemy, and not much older when I lost the first man under my command. To this day I see their faces when I close my eyes, eventually they begin to pale as terrors and you must treat them as old friends who accompany you along the long road.' Spartacus spoke with such solemnity it shocked Cassian. The silence descended upon the two once more, each lost within the thoughts of their own minds.

The time and the convoy moved ever on. There were nervous glances, endless looking back towards Caralis in fear of an enemy desiring retribution and swift destruction, but none came. Then an extra glow could be seen in the port. Obviously Aegis had done his work well. If Apelios became aware of the fire he would know his prey had slipped the trap, but Cassian knew sufficient time had passed and they would reach the relative safety of Albus' villa.

Cassian said a private, short prayer to the Gods for a friend lost and for those valiant men who had served him so well. He hoped the choices he made were the correct ones, but decided there and then to banish regrets and would no longer look along the path they had taken, but only that which they must still journey upon.

He spurred the wagons to move faster. He was keen to reach the villa. More plans must be made and there was still much to do. It was with a joyous heart when, finally, the villa came into view. Aegis joined the wagons shortly before they entered the villa. He gave reports that no more of Apelios' men had ventured towards the warehouse. All were too busy with the fires that had been lit, and no enemy had followed him or the wagons from the port. He did bring news that two of the buildings razed by Trabus had been totally destroyed, but, as far as he could tell, the rest including the headquarters had been saved. Therefore Apelios would still have power to yield within Caralis and still posed a serious threat to the mission.

Cassian grimaced at the thought of Apelios, still capable of causing them harm. After all they would still have to make the return journey once the men were rested and trained to take part in the most vital stage of the mission. Aegis also brought with him two men who helped Trabus in burning Apelios' property. It was perhaps a mark of their respect for their previous master, the clear sadness they showed upon hearing of his death. Cassian offered them the choice of joining the convoy and serving with the rest of the men or serving the family of Trabus. He would not accept an answer immediately for it was not the time for hasty decisions.

The wagons rolled through the large wooden gates of the villa and it was immediately obvious why Albus had no problem with men such as Apelios. The walled villa was guarded with a high proportion of men, all of which looked capable of doing an extremely professional job. The inside of the villa courtyard was functional, not at all like the fine villa of Crannicus, although to be fair few came up to that standard. Inside a sinewy, tall figure held up his arm in acknowledgement of Cassian's arrival. The man had a gaze that could freeze a stallion in mid gallop. His shoulders were strong and straight, with his chest pushed out. It was clear this was a man of military background and the guards on the walls seemed to echo the man's character, for they moved quickly and efficiently in any task asked of them.

'I did not know whether you would make it through Cassian. Larger groups than yours have fallen to those within the port.' He spoke with a knowing, confident voice.

'Many of us didn't make it,' Cassian replied, gesturing to the wrapped body in one of the wagons.

'Who?' Said Albus.

'I am sorry Albus, it's Trabus. I did not want to leave his body behind and I will need to speak to his family.' Cassian was sorry for he knew Trabus and Albus had dealings with one another over many years. There was a slight flicker in the eyes of Albus as he observed his friend's body, but the military training kicked in almost immediately.

'Of course. They dine down by the orchard, I will send for them immediately.' Albus made to call a guard but was stopped by Cassian.

'If you would allow, I will go and break the news. Better they hear before they see the body and, if you would be so kind, Albus my men have endured much I would be grateful if their needs be fulfilled.'

'Of course Cassian, forgive me I will see to it immediately.'

Albus, despite being a man of military background, showed a great deal of respect and consideration to the men of Cassian, even helping a couple of the injured from a wagon. Cassian strode away from the wagons and out of sight. Spartacus did not envy the young Roman this task and believed it easier to take life than to inform the loved ones of one that has been lost. He had only had the dreadful task once and the terrible, hollow scream of grief had haunted him for many weeks after the deed. The thought of it even now made his insides churn. He climbed down from the wagon himself, his muscles crying out their tiredness. He wished for nothing more than to bathe and sleep. As he looked at his men, their bodies covered in blood from the battle and the dirt from the road, it was almost impossible   to tell which was which. They stared blankly and hardly moved, resembling the statues within the gardens at Crannicus' villa. He would need all his skill to reinvigorate these men for the remainder of this mission, they seemed as shadows lost in thoughts of the past.

What was left of Trabus' household were dining down by the stream. For a moment fear tugged at Cassian, for he had been a young boy the last time he had seen Trabus' wife Celese. Although the memory of how kind she was stayed with him, her face had vanished completely from his mind. It would be unforgiveable to have to ask which person she was. As the fear raced through him he heard a gentle voice, a voice which conjured up memories from the past. He remembered falling as a little boy and a sweet voice soothing his pain, then a warm hug and kisses, the memory of which still filled him with warmth. He turned to the voice which reminded him of those pleasant times and he knew the woman. As he approached her she turned to meet his gaze.

'Ah I know that little boy, it has been too long young Cassian.'

'Much too long Celese, I wish...' His words failed him, how could he deliver such news to such a gentle spirit.

'Now I will not have to dry your tears again Cassian. Let my heart cry enough for both of us and you have no need to utter the words, for my heart told me of my loss. I knew that my husband may not return but I feel honoured that I had him in my life for so long.' As she spoke she placed a gentle hand against Cassian's cheek, genuine concern for the boy she had not seen in many years. Cassian, for his part, was truly astonished that at a time like this Celese still cared for others.

'He was a good man.' The words seemed too small for what Cassian wanted to say, for a man so normally gifted and eloquent in his speech.

'He was.' That was all she replied, for her it was the complete story and nobody could sum up her Trabus any better.

They conversed for some time, not on the sadness of Trabus' passing but on the household of Trabus and, within a short time, Cassian was aware the household was in good hands. The house of Trabus would not falter and slip away with the passing of the man, she would not allow it. Celese would honour the man by ensuring all was well with his household and securing its future.

Chapter 13

The pyre was built high and Trabus' wrapped body placed gently on top. His family wept for their loss, and the men who owed so much to the man, stoically held their tears inside, for it would not do to shed them before the women, but still the tears flowed within. The pyre burned brightly and although the scented spices attempted to hide the smell of the burning flesh they never really concealed it. It clogged the nostrils and tasted on the tongue, only those so deep in grief were not aware, the loss of the man consumed all.

Cassian had been unusually quiet after performing the task of informing the family of the demise of Trabus. He was trying to converse with Albus and ensure the men were comfortable but Spartacus was aware that even the usual high spirits of the young Roman were at a low ebb. The ceremony, though right and proper, was unlikely to soothe the mood within the man and the rest of the camp. Spartacus spent his time, though really only wanting to sleep, talking to each man in turn, judging each of them, sharing a joke or two if possible. Only Bull stirred from his slumbering spirit, and it seemed to Spartacus that a man such as Bull was worth ten other warriors, for he invigorated others whenever he could. He remembered that Bull's father was a centurion and decided Bull must have inherited the qualities from his father. To keep men going when, often, they would prefer to give up. It was a fine quality and a dangerous one, which set him apart from the normal soldier.

The night moved on, with the ceremony past the crying died away and men, who on the previous night faced death, began to relax. Food was consumed and wine taken in huge quantities. It was not long before laughter broke out from all quarters. Men, rather than looking back in horror, spoke of each other's bravery and the daring deeds they had achieved. All saluted the brave Trabus and other comrades who had fallen but it was different from earlier. That night men celebrated the fact they were alive. Spartacus saw the change in the men, saw how quickly they had stepped away from the abyss of despair and marvelled at the speed in which they recovered. He smiled for the mission was still on.

The following day was used as a rest day, although the men were not allowed to laze about drinking wine - not that many could bear to smell the stuff after the previous night. Each man was taken to the baths and, after being cleaned thoroughly, they were massaged, the tiredness being driven from each muscle. All cuts were treated by Aegis and his mysterious herbs, much to the dismay of the resident healer. The men chose Aegis not only because of the respect they felt for him, but the men were of a military background and they believed most Roman healers to be butchers, whose only answer was to cut and saw. Everything they did was as a group. They ate together, a huge pig was roasted on a spit down by the orchard and was hungrily devoured by the men. Cassian and Spartacus both joined in, for they too needed the feeling of solidarity just as much as the men.

Plinius had taken to talking to a young slave girl and the men teased him about it although, Spartacus noticed, never teasing him when the girl was near. They boasted of his skills to her, it seemed they too wanted the girl to see Plinius in a good light. Whenever she was near, the young man blushed and he initially stammered quite badly when he attempted conversation with her, but eventually his confidence grew and he spent more and more time with her. The first day ended and the men looked more and more like their old selves. All were excused guard duty, Albus' men performed all of those, so when sleep time came it was complete and without fear of attack, a luxury the men had not enjoyed for some time.

The next day the men were put through the basics of arena fighting by Spartacus. Each man chose a sword and shield which was unusual within the arena. It was too late to train them in the use of other weapons and, besides, in such a deadly tournament a man should use what he is most comfortable with. The arena offered different challenges to normal Roman soldiery. The enemy rarely came just from the front, the battle raged all around. Many a good gladiator had been speared from behind whilst concentrating on foe to the front.

The men they would fight trained endlessly night and day to perfect their art but they trained as individuals, seeking glory for themselves. The one advantage Spartacus' men had was that they were used to working as a unit. He knew this was their best chance for both victory and survival. They worked in the morning using the heavy wooden swords which would strengthen the arm. As the training weapon was heavier than a real sword, when the battle came, a proper sword would feel light in the hand. They sparred with Spartacus as an opponent. He used the sword firstly and then moved onto the fuscina, a vicious looking trident which was used in conjunction with an inretire, a net designed to tangle the opponent and leave him to the mercy of the fuscina.

There were other weapons but merely variations on the two main types and it was these main weapons Spartacus concentrated upon. Time and time again the men were felled by him but they rose immediately, eager to learn all he could teach them. He taught them tricks of the trade to throw an opponent off guard and told them to kill immediately they had the chance.

'No quarter will be shown in this tournament and so we will not give any and, besides, a wounded man can sink a dagger into flesh just as well as an uninjured one,' he explained.

Only Plinius managed to knock a sword from Spartacus' hand. Unfortunately for him it was when he was fighting with two swords and no shield and it was not long before the still held weapon was lying at his throat, but all the men cheered the efforts of Plinius, who puffed out his chest in recognition of it.

The slave girl watched Plinius and she applauded the young man. Seeing this Plinius again blushed a rich scarlet but inside his heart skipped a beat. Cassian too had noticed this and when the men disbanded he called Spartacus to him.

'Spartacus I believe the young man has designs on that pretty slave,' Cassian smiled as he spoke.

'Certainly, but he needs to keep his mind on what he is doing, not on what's between her legs,' Spartacus replied earnestly.

'Then I suggest we hurry things along. The boy needs to let off steam I believe, and quickly for otherwise he might burst.' Cassian turned to the girl as he spoke and gestured she should come near. The men moved from the square to bathe and it was an ideal time for a chat with the girl, out of sight of Plinius.

'What do you have in mind?' Spartacus asked.

'I am a deal maker Spartacus. I am sure I could offer the girl a deal which would tempt her to open her legs for our young Plinius.' He winked as the girl drew near.

'My lord,' the girl said, bowing her head slightly.

'Ah my good girl, no need for all that. May I ask, what is your name?' Spartacus noticed that Cassian again used his sickly sweet tone as he always seemed to do, when he was making a deal.

'Chia, my lord.' The respectful tone was hard to drop. The years of service had taught the girl well but Spartacus noticed a flame in her eyes, this girl was no docile servant.

'May we speak candidly my dear? Plinius, one of my men, has taken a shine to you and I fear his mind is elsewhere when he does his duties. Due to his age I feel that he is slow in his advances towards you. I wondered if it would be possible for you to speed things along? Obviously I mean no offence,' as he continued in this tone, he placed a number of coin on the wall next to the girl.

'My lord, may I too speak candidly?' Chia was cool and calm, not at all awed by the position of the man she now faced.

'Why of course dear girl,' Cassian replied.

'My lord, if I am to be paid to have sex, my talents far exceed the coin you have placed in front of me. But you ask me will I fuck Plinius? Yes I will, and a better man he will be for it. Now I have duties, may I return to them?'

'Errr, well yes of course,' Cassian stammered his reply as the girl turned and walked away from them, leaving the coin where it lay. Cassian stared blankly after the girl, until his wits returned.

'I don't think I concluded that deal the way I meant to.'

'I have a feeling that young woman fucks better than you make deals Cassian.' Spartacus erupted into laughter to be joined by Cassian who was still stunned by being put firmly in his place by a young servant girl.

The day was coming to an end and Plinius took a stroll in the

101

grounds hoping, at some point, to catch a glimpse of Chia. He ambled along, past the orchard to a small meadow. The night was warm, with just a faint breeze brushing his skin. He had failed in his quest, Chia was nowhere to be seen and he resigned his heavy heart to not seeing her tonight. He turned to leave and, suddenly, there she was standing in front of him. She stood, completely naked. His eyes took in the feast that they beheld. Moving downwards they came to her breasts. They defied gravity, upturned slightly, beautiful orbs topped with pink, erect nipples. His eyes moved further down, taking in the wondrous shape of her hips, the golden colour of her skin and the triangle of dark hair between her legs. Then she was walking towards him and fear took hold of him. He felt the urge to run, it was funny he had faced many dangers on this mission but, here and now, he felt at the most peril and yet totally overwhelmed by the excitement of the moment.

She kept advancing, the look in her eyes was one of pure devilry. She was in command here, status in life meant nothing, the slave was the master. She took him by the hand and led him to a small area where the grass was long and soft. Her clothes lay to the side and it was clear to Plinius this was one ambush he had failed to avoid, and why would he want to? She removed his tunic and then his loin cloth, his member springing out towards her. She smiled and took it in her hand. Plinius gulped down his excitement, he could hardly believe this was happening. She made him get down, lying on his back the grass sticking into him, prickling his now sensitive skin. She caressed and kissed his body and then straddled him. She reached for his manhood and guided it to where she knew he craved, then began lowering herself gently. She took all of him and then paused, knowing that the feeling was driving him wild. She did not want to rush, the first time was too often rushed but she had the skill to ensure lasting enjoyment. When she felt him relax slightly she began to gently move her hips, manipulating him with her muscles with an expertise which far out stripped her years. The lights of ecstasy exploded within Plinius' mind. He had never experienced such a thing, and that night the experience would go on and on. She handled him superbly, bringing him back to hardness again and again then finally, when both were exhausted, they lay on the grass holding each other close in a knowing embrace and slept.

The morning sunrise awoke the sleeping pair, each still entwined in the others grasp. They rose slowly, not wanting to leave the warmth of the other. Chia smiled at the man who lay beside her and he, in turn, gazed back with adoring eyes.

'I must go, I have duties,' Chia said with reluctance in her voice.

'I will walk with you,' an eager Plinius replied. For a short time, while they dressed, silence descended, each not knowing what to say. There had been little time for conversation the night before.

'You do not have to walk with me, I am a slave...' Chia began, but was interrupted by Plinius.

'You're not a slave to me, we could marry.' Foolish though the statement was it was said with no less conviction.

'Plinius, you are young. You will bed many a slave girl, I knew what I was doing when I came to you last night. There is no debt, I came as all women should come to the man of her choice.' Chia said the words but her eyes were filled with sadness at the realism of her life.

'Listen Chia, when the mission ends I will be wealthy - I will buy your freedom,' Plinius said almost a pleading within his voice.

'The thought of such things takes too much cost on a slave's heart Plinius. You must not speak them – any happiness or pleasure a slave receives in this world is fleeting and only serves to remind us of the miserable life we live.' A tear slid down her cheek when she spoke but the grasp she had on his hand strengthened.

'Will you meet me tonight?' He asked, wondering if he had hurt her too much with his words.

'I will spend each night in your arms until you leave.' She spoke quietly, forcing a smile upon her face.

'Then we will talk more of this because, like it or not Chia, I will not allow you to remain a slave as the Gods are my witness.' He said it with bravado, the confidence of youth streaming back into him. 'Trust me,' he pleaded.

'If the time comes Plinius I will gladly go with you, but I will not dwell on such thoughts. I will concentrate on the time I know we have together and hold that time special in my heart when you are gone.'

They spoke no more but held each other close all the way to the villa. When the time came to part she kissed him gently on the lips and was grateful that he did not try to hide away from the inquisitive eyes of the villa, but instead was proud that she was in his arms.

'Until later my love,' she whispered in his ear and was gone.

Plinius watched her go. He marvelled at her beauty, the very movement of her holding him transfixed in time, not daring to look away for things of such beauty rarely lasted and he was afraid she would vanish upon a breeze.

He eventually joined Spartacus who was sharpening his blade. Plinius noticed how he looked after the weapon.

'Why take so much time? There are plenty of swords, just take a new one when that one becomes blunt.'

'If I can teach you one thing let it be this; all swords have a life and in the end we must choose another, but until that time it is right that we nurture it with love. Its weight and length must become as an extension to our very body. The better we know the blade, the better it will serve us.' As he spoke he held out his hand, gesturing for Plinius to give up his sword. As he received it he felt the weight and ran his finger down the edge.

'It's a fine sword but you must learn to make it better. While you feel how to improve the blade you will learn how to use it as part of you. Weapon, blade and man will become one, and once you have achieved that you will be a match for most in the arena.'

Plinius did not speak, he just moved to Spartacus' side and seated himself, observing how Spartacus manoeuvred the blade to gain the ultimate edge. Not too thin which would blunt too easily and not too thick which would lack significant cutting power to disable an opponent. Spartacus smiled to Plinius as he sat down.

'I thought you would have had enough training with your weapon last night.' Plinius blushed at his words and smiled taking Spartacus' words in good humour,

'You can never have too much.'

Both he and Spartacus laughed as Plinius learned his new craft.

Chapter 14

The days passed and, with each of those days, the men became quicker and stronger. The weapons they used became as one with their bodies. Not one man shirked training, often they worked harder than was expected. All of them knew the cost of being found wanting in the arena. The men toiled endlessly in the day and rested well come the night. Plinius joined Chia every night and each night their affection for one another grew. Each night the fear of separation also grew. Although the emotions welled up inside Chia she had promised herself she would not show them to Plinius, she would not be the reason he was not focused on the mission and therefore came to harm.

Cassian spent more and more time in consultation with Albus, trying and failing to get him to march into Caralis and therefore give the convoy a clear run to the port and Lathyrus who would be waiting to carry them to Utica. On the final night, and close to giving up, Cassian brought Spartacus to the meeting, hoping he could help persuade Albus.

'I have told you Cassian, I cannot march my men down those narrow streets. They wouldn't get half way before being cut apart,' Albus said defiantly.

'But this convoy needs to reach the docks, we must board the boat,' Cassian replied, with exasperation.

'If I may, what or who prevents you Albus?' Spartacus asked in his most calming voice, as it was clear the conversation was about to turn into an argument.

'Even with the numbers of Apelios' men you killed, he can still throw up to fifty men into the field. Those men, taking shots from behind buildings and using ambush tactics, would soon whittle my small force down to nothing,' Albus stated, determined not to be swayed from his duty to his men.

'And are there any other men in Caralis who would offer resistance to your men?' Spartacus pushed this line of questioning, trying to manoeuvre Albus to a position where he would listen to suggestions.

'No. Apelios is scum but he's scum with a big pair of balls,' Albus replied. 'No other would raise arms against me.'

'Then the way forward is clear,' he paused to get full attention. 'We simply kill the bastard tonight.' Spartacus smiled. Cassian looked at Spartacus and knew the man was right. It was an old saying but if you cut off the head of the snake the body would wither and die.

The three stayed a while making final preparations. It would mean a couple of men entering the stronghold of Apelios, dispatching him and leaving before the alarm could be signalled to his men. This task was not easy to achieve and the men agreeing to take on such a task would know that. Even if Apelios was killed then the chance to get clear of his men would be close to impossible.

Two horsemen made their way from the villa. Dressed in black they were difficult to make out and Albus, watching from the villa walls, soon lost sight of them. He turned and grumbled.

'Crazy bastards...' And then added, 'Gods protect you.' He went to make ready, for in the morning, Albus would once again ride into battle.

The two horsemen moved slowly, picking their way in the dark, it would not do for a horse to take a fall now.

'But why you?' Spartacus asked with a disbelieving look on his face.

'As much as I make the plans Spartacus, I still need to gain the respect of the men,' Cassian replied.

'You have it. They know you have steered them this far.'

'You are most gracious Spartacus. Then maybe I have to gain self-respect.'

'But you have never even served, I have never even seen you lift a weapon.' Spartacus was exasperated that he now had to watch Cassian as well as carry out this bloody mission.

'Well I stick them with the pointy end, I think.' Cassian tried to make light of the situation but he could tell Spartacus was in no mood for humour. The conversation died.

Spartacus was bloody annoyed, he would rather have come alone. If the bloody idiot went and got himself killed what of the mission then and why the bloody hell is he so fucking cheerful, we're going to almost certain death and he's whistling a fucking tune? He kicked his heels as they reached the flatter, safer dirt road, eager to take his frustration out on someone and if that whistling did not stop it would be Cassian.

Quite some time later they arrived just outside Caralis. They tethered the horses in a quiet spot under the cover of a clump of trees and stood for a while discussing the best way to approach the town. They required ease of access to Apelios' main building.

They picked their way through the dark, dank streets, the putrid smell of human filth filling the nostrils. The occasional beggar grumbled his discontent at being disturbed, but to all other inhabitants they were like spectres, ghostly, moving ever onwards to an unsuspecting victim. On they went, avoiding any sign of life, in a town so submerged in deceit and mistrust it was better not to be noticed until the options to do so were exhausted.

The timid approach made the journey to their desired location take some time and put an edge to the nerves. Spartacus much preferred a straight forward fight but this was no straight forward mission. This required a whole different type of skill, one which he hoped the Roman possessed too. They moved into a dark alley and there, directly across from them, lay a large building with just two slumbering guards at the front entrance. Spartacus had guessed that Apelios would not have too many men guarding him for in a place like Caralis sometimes the show of force was to have little on view, as though stating to the world I am untouchable. They decided to find another way in, for removing the guards may well be noticed and they needed time to complete the task. They skirted the building and found an old tree. They silently used it to scale the wall. Now they must find the prey they sought. Albus had given instructions as to the layout of the building. He knew the details well as he had dined there many times when it belonged to the previous occupier. The previous occupier was a wealthy merchant who met with an untimely end. His property had almost instantly been inhabited by Apelios. Of course no blame for the merchant's death could be placed upon him, but it was an unspoken reality that all knew but dared not even whisper.

Apelios again woke from a disturbed sleep. That burning stare had interrupted his dreams of power again. The fear of it had woken him many times since he had observed the unknown stranger at the entrance to the warehouse just a few days before. He was not usually subject to such frailties but that man unsettled his very soul. He took a huge mouthful of wine and cast a nervous look about the room. All was quiet. He wondered whether he should have doubled the guards but almost laughed at his own suggestion. That man was far away, running with all his might. Both he and the arrogant Roman would not dare to enter Caralis again. They had been lucky and the Gods rarely granted such luck a second time.

He glanced down at the slave girl next to him, the bruise already showing on her face where he had slapped her into submission. He smiled and knew he had the power to take what he wanted when wanted it. He lay back and slipped into slumber.

The slave, sure that this time her master had fallen into a heavy slumber, rose and pulled her torn tunic back into place, covering the red welts on her body made by the pig now asleep before her. She raised a hand feeling the bruise forming on her eye. She shot the man an evil glance and prayed to the Gods that they would kill this man and then walked, while feeling the agony he had bestowed upon her, from the room. She often walked the grounds at night and dreamed of scaling the wall to freedom. She began to sob, but quietly, for if a guard heard they would come and force her again to perform for them. Such was the life of a slave unlucky enough to be sold into the household of Apelios. She cursed her luck that she had been born attractive, for it meant she gained attention she neither sought or needed. As she sobbed she felt the small wooden pendant around her neck, the only gift she had managed to retain from her mother.

As the girl quietly sobbed, the sun had not yet risen and the villa of Albus was bathed in the eerie glow of burning torches. The household was already in full flow, preparing the wagons and supplies for the mission. Those men who would be completing the journey to Utica had been allowed to sleep longer, while Albus and the rest made all the preparations. Now even those men were roused, for the time for rest was over. Bull emerged from his quarters, attempting to stretch and yawn the earliness of the day out of his aching muscles. He glanced around looking for Plinius and as he did so Albus approached him.

'The boy will be down with Chia.'

'You excused her duties?' Responded Bull, surprised at his host's generosity.

'By the Gods, if we were all granted the chance to say goodbye to loved ones before we went to war,' he answered solemnly, 'best go fetch him.'

Bull nodded and strode to where he knew the two lovers would be. It was not long before he found them. He had expected to have to wake them but they sat huddled together, as if trying to steal every last moment they could. Bull smiled as he approached feeling awkward at disturbing the moment.

'Forgive me, it's nearly time.'

'I will be along,' Plinius answered, a sad resignation in his voice. Bull turned quickly, not wanting to encroach on the couple's precious moments, especially, he thought to himself, as it may well be the last time they shall see one another. His heart was heavy for he liked Plinius and thought him deserving of a brighter future.

Plinius looked into Chia's eyes.

'It will not be long then we shall be free to be with one another.'

'Just come back, whether to me or another, just as long as you come back,' she responded, the emotions churning her up inside.

'There will be no other. You will be with no other. You will be my wife and free, this I swear.'

'I would gladly spend two lifetimes as a slave in exchange for you to be safe.' She had not told him of the nightmares that had haunted her slumber, nightmares of a young man bleeding in the sand. He smiled, trying to reassure her.

'I will return and will never leave you again, I promise.' He kissed her and held her tight, trying to take her sadness from her.

Within the household of Apelios the slave girl struggled to stop the tears which dropped freely onto the wooden pendant. She was so desperate in her misery and pain she did not hear the figure behind her, and could do nothing when the hand clamped around her mouth to prevent a scream that would alert the guards. A quiet, tender voice said.

'I have no wish to hurt you, but you must not make a sound. I need information and then you can go on your way.' The owner of the voice had not pressed too hard upon her face, a fact which was not lost on the girl and she nodded in compliance. She turned to face the man and he raised his other hand, placing a finger to his lips and then released her.

'What do you want of me?' She asked, the fear coursing through her body, she had learned not to trust men.

'Your master is Apelios, yes?' As he spoke he took in the state of the girl, seeing evidence of the recent ordeal she had obviously gone through.

'Yes – he is sleeping,' she replied.

'Do not worry about that, this is not a social call. Tell me, where are his chambers?' The man smiled and tried to not frighten the timid creature any more than was necessary.

'I will tell you, if you take me with you.' The girl stiffened as if expecting a hand to slap her into submission.

'That will not be possible, but tomorrow things will be different here.' Cassian removed the cloth from his face.

'I cannot stay here my lord,' the girl said, the pleading tone evident.

'Come the morning a convoy will pass this building, you will join it,' Cassian instructed. 'You will find safety.'

'My master will never allow...' She began.

'Like I say, things will be different tomorrow. Now where are his chambers?'

The girl, for the first time, found herself wanting to believe the man and quickly gave instructions to where her master lay, including a way through the slave quarters which the guards never patrolled, which would lead Cassian straight to Apelios.

There were two entrances into the chambers, the one revealed to Cassian by the slave girl which was used by the servants and the other manned by two guards who were supposed to be watching but who were, in reality, lazily drifting in and out of sleep. This

110

entrance Spartacus discovered at the same time as Cassian moved towards the other. Spartacus realised there was no sneaking past two men so close to the door, even though they were only half awake, so he quietly unsheathed his sword and hoped to close the distance before they became aware of his presence.

The first guard fell with a single blow to the neck, blood spraying the surrounding area. The second guard was quicker and managed to scramble out of the way of a second thrust and drew his weapon. He called the alarm and attacked the intruder. Apelios woken, once again, jumped from his bed and raced to the door, swinging the heavy wooden door to the side, only to be greeted by a sight of carnage. There was blood splattered on the walls and one of his guards was crumpled on the floor, his throat gaping. There was then a terrible squeal as his other guard had just been impaled through the gut. Apelios observed the sword and followed the arm that held it, tracked with his eyes on to the powerful shoulders and then to the head, just as it turned to look straight at him. He was looking straight into those eyes he had hoped he would never see again.

Spasms of fear took hold of him and he backed into the room he had just emerged from. He scrambled for his sword, all the time watching the man moving towards him. He tried to call for help but his throat and mouth were like dust and he managed only a feeble, faint sound which would alert no guard. He held his weapon up, transfixed by the man to his front so much so that he never saw the figure move behind him. The hand came quickly, clamped over his mouth and his head jarred violently back. Before he could react a voice whispered to him.

'This is for Trabus, you murderous bastard.'

The blade entered the middle of his back. It tore aside all tissue, splintering part of the spine and carrying on through the internal organs until its tip burst through the man's chest. Apelios never dropped his gaze from that of Spartacus and held his stare until the moment of death took him. Blood quickly covered the marbled floor, Cassian smiled at Spartacus.

'Told you, the pointy end does it.'

'You're a bloody idiot,' Spartacus laughed, 'we best leave.'

In truth, the exit from the building was easier than both expected. The guards, on finding their master slain, were more interested in looting his possessions than finding the culprit. It was clear the house of Apelios was at an end and each of his men had made many enemies in his service. They would need plenty of coin to avoid being slaughtered like the beasts many had behaved as.

They slipped through the streets with ease and with more haste than they had arrived. They had arranged to meet Albus and his men and time was racing on, they could not afford to waste any more. It was time to continue the mission. They hoped the path was now clear from the likes of Apelios, his death would serve as a warning to any others who would try and delay the convoy from proceeding on its intended path.

Chapter 15

The two men climbed onto their horses and retired to a safe distance where they had agreed to meet Albus. They set up camp with a small fire to prepare food and to keep them warm until Albus arrived and escorted them through Caralis with the convoy. They would not sleep, for they needed to sit and watch Caralis in case there were those who would seek revenge for the death of Apelios.

No avengers came. Apelios was as popular in death as he was in life, with not one soul to mourn his passing into the next life. Both Cassian and Spartacus began to relax and waited for the convoy to arrive. They added wood to the fire and took some provisions which Albus had provided. Each reflected on the task they had just carried out. Cassian was in a joyful mood

'Well that could not have gone much better,' he said, a broad smile spreading across his face. Clearly the excitement still coursed through his veins.

'We were lucky, it is unusual to carry out such a mission without some sort of loss,' Spartacus replied.

'All the more reason to be thankful to the Gods for safe passage through,' Cassian said, still gleeful.

'Ah the Gods. They usually demand some sacrifice in such matters.' Spartacus was in a brooding mood, one which Cassian struggled to understand and it more than a little annoyed him so he left the man to his thoughts. Cassian was just happy they had completed the task which would allow the convoy to continue towards its proper goal.

It was not long before the sound of wagons and troops could be heard and the convoy soon entered their vista. Albus and his men were in full armour as were the men of Cassian. All were anxious, wanting to see Spartacus and Cassian alive and well. Hearty handshakes were given by all and a sense of relief spread throughout the convoy. All now believed they would safely cross the streets of Caralis to the docks. In truth, few had looked forward to a street battle where soldiers often fell to an unseen foe.

'How in Hades did you manage it?' Albus inquired.

Cassian told of their exploits, how they had become separated in the house of Apelios but entered his room virtually at the same time from different doors. How the slave girl had shown him the rear entrance to Apelios' private chamber, and the how the guards had shown no interest in catching the killers of their master. Indeed the guards had taken the opportunity to steal all that was not too heavy to move, and who could blame them? For those that had been wronged by Apelios were still likely to look for someone to blame. Albus listened, amazed at the tale and, just a little part of him, felt annoyed that he would not be entering battle. He had retired from army life what seemed a life time ago, but part of him still craved the clash of steel, the excitement of that fight against death and facing all the dangers it had to offer.

Spartacus observed Plinius, surprised to see him in good spirits and approached the young man.,

'How are you Plinius?' He asked, in rather too much of a fatherly way. Inside he chastised himself for the act.

'I feel eager to see this mission through,' Plinius replied.

'I thought you may be brooding on that young girl of yours.' Spartacus wondered whether he should remind Plinius of the girl.

'Oh, I was sad to part from her, but now it seems I have something good and true to fight for. I will free Chia!' There was no question within the young man's words, it was a statement of intent, one from which he would never falter or be diverted. Spartacus slapped the young man on the back heartily.,

'Then we shall complete this task together. We will kill those who prevent it and together we shall drink heartily at its end. Yes?' The response invigorated Spartacus. It reminded him of simpler times when, as a young man, the world was black or white, right or wrong and all young men thought only of how the world should be. It was joyous to observe the simplicity of it all.

'I will be honoured to drink at your side Spartacus,' Plinius replied.

Within a short time the convoy began its slow trundle to the port. Still the men were alert and looking for signs of danger. Just because Cassian and Spartacus came through the port easily this did not mean they would enjoy the same experience. However, with the success of Cassian and Spartacus though the men were cautious, they were also confident.

Spartacus lay down in the back of a wagon and slept, but Cassian was eager to see this part of the mission concluded and he marched with the other men. Besides, he was enjoying the new way the men looked at him, with looks of respect for his deeds and for himself. They reached the outskirts of the town and all was quiet. Cassian guessed this was partly down to the time of day. So early few people had an honest reason to be on the move, and secondly with all that had happened recently he supposed the normal populace would be keen to stay indoors. They passed the burnt out wreckage of the warehouse where the mission had so nearly come to an abrupt end and so many of their comrades fell. Aegis broke away from the convoy and paid homage to the site with a little prayer. The convoy though kept moving not wanting to slow and become an easy target. They wanted to reach the dock before too many locals were about.

They soon came upon the headquarters of Apelios. The quiet seemed to settle more on that looming building, more than on the rest. The guards were gone and the doors stood open to the world. The power and the memory of the man would be forgotten within a week, as was the way with such men. With luck Albus would now be the only man with real power and he could restore some normality to the port and allow it to return to the prosperous state it once knew.

The dock was not that far away and they reached it in good time, unmolested in their journey. Despite Albus' deep yearning for battle he allowed a sigh of relief that their journey had been a simple and safe one. They settled at the dock and glanced out to sea. Lathryus and his boat could be clearly seen, cutting through the waves, but it would be some time before the vessel reached them, so they created a little area to rest, which could also be defended against any locals who still felt brave enough to try and take the convoy. Cassian called Spartacus to him.

'I need to do something, keep an eye on the men for me. You take charge.'

'What... where are you going?' Spartacus exclaimed, 'you can't go off on your own,' he added.

'Don't worry, I won't be long,' Cassian added, and was already moving away.

'Bloody idiot,' Spartacus murmured to himself. 'One mission and he thinks he's bloody invincible.'

Cassian had made a promise to the slave girl and he intended to go and fetch her. It was still early and, after the beating Apelios had given her, he was not surprised that she had slept through the arrival of the wagons. He reached the doorway of the household and drew his sword. It was still possible enemies lay within and he did not want to be taken by surprise, and a gleaming sword always made would be attackers think twice.

He moved from room to room, the building had been picked clean, as if beasts had descended on its carcass, ripping the flesh from its bones. He did not shout for the girl for fear of alerting the enemy within. Here and there bodies lay. Obviously there had been fallings out over which items would be taken by which members of the household. The smell of blood was rank in the air. At one point Cassian slipped in the pools of deep crimson liquid which virtually covered the whole floor. The gentle buzz of flies was becoming more pronounced, as the stench of the dead wafted through the streets of Caralis. The eager insects rarely required much more of an invitation.

He entered the slaves quarter. It was deathly quiet, as though not a living soul had been here for an eternity. The lack of sunlight only added to the oppressive feeling. The rooms were small and lead into a hallway which was enclosed. The area suppressed the mind of any visitor, making them seek only refuge from the place. Steadily he moved down the hallway occasionally slipping in the viscous liquid, or brushing against a heavy objects on the floor. He chose not to examine these things, for he already fought back nausea and dared not let his eyes see what his mind imagined.

At the end of the hall the room seemed to open out and, even before he reached it, he could see the shards of light penetrating the room. He picked up his pace a little, hoping for the freshness of a breeze. He came to what looked like the kitchen area. His eyes came to rest on a large table in the centre of the room and on top of it was a figure, blood obscuring its features. Every inch of him wanted to move quickly past the figure, but he was drawn to it as flies are drawn to a corpse.

He knew who it was long before he swept the blood matted hair away from the beaten face. A bag lay on the floor, all her possessions sprawling from it. Cassian could only guess, but it seemed to him she had been collecting her belongings before she joined the convoy. Her clothes had been torn from her and her nakedness revealed the suffering she had endured before death had finally taken her. A red welt around her neck clearly showed where a necklace with a small wooden charm had been ripped from her throat. Cassian remembered seeing her grasp it when she sobbed the night before. He counted at least three puncture wounds upon her pure, feeble body, with numerous swollen areas where obviously she had been beaten. He took off his own cloak and laid it over her, straightening her limbs as he did so. He stroked the girls head and his tears fell and mixed with her blood. He gently kissed her upon the forehead.,

'Forgive me.'

He stayed with her, the rest of the house had no lure for him. Inside him his emotions fought one another for precedence. One moment anger, then sorrow, but the victor was shame. Shame that he had allowed such a crime to an innocent.

The noise broke the grief he felt for this brave girl in front of him. He raised himself, forcing himself to be aware of the dangers around him. He moved silently to the far door. The noise had come from the room beyond. He gradually eased open the door, to observe a figure rifling through the belongings of the slaves. On making sure the figure was alone, Cassian slipped inside hoping to stay unnoticed for as long as possible. An old male slave lay slumped against the wall. His throat had been cut and the look of surprise was still etched on his face. Cassian moved quietly towards what he supposed to be the killer of the old man, but the figure had noticed a movement from the corner of his eye.

The figure leapt up, holding a dagger in one hand. He then crouched and picked up a sword with the other.

'Clear off, this my room. Or I'll gut you.' The man's clothes were covered in blood and he sported scratches down his face.

'No worries my friend, just passing by.' Cassian's sickly sweet tone had returned. 'We all need to earn a little coin.'

'Hmm.' The man grunted and dropped the arm holding the dagger. The movement made Cassian glance down at his arm and there, wrapped around the wrist, was a necklace with a small wooden pendent on it. The smile never left his face, an art he had mastered for so long which served him well, even when an anger burned within. Cassian smiled.,

'I will let you get on.' He turned and walked towards the door, but as he reached it he pushed the door closed and slid the heavy bolt into place, sealing both him and the looter inside. He casually turned, the sickly smile still on his face but his eyes burned with the fury of the Gods themselves. The looter looked upon those eyes, he did not lift his dagger or attempt to run but merely stared.

Cassian strode back into the camp, the dark mood engulfing him. He moved silently through the rest of the men and away from all who would try to converse with him. He looked out to sea and began watching the approach of Lathryus. Spartacus observed him, his cloak gone and his tunic covered with blood. Gone was the smiling Cassian. Spartacus approached him, placing his own cloak upon his friend's shoulders.,

'Are you injured?' hHe asked. Cassian glanced down at himself.,

'Oh no....it's not mine.' He spoke as if in a another world.

'What happened?' Spartacus sensed great sadness within Cassian.

'It's as you said Spartacus – the Gods will have their sacrifice.' As he spoke a single tear rolled down his cheek. Cassian needed to be only with his demons and his shame.

The boat pulled alongside the dock and Spartacus prevented Lathryus from talking to Cassian. In fact he kept all of the men from the Roman. For Cassian had just become aware, if he hadn't been before, that this was not a game being played. That bits of paper and plans rarely did the pain and agony suffered by all involved the justice they deserved.

The cargo was loaded and farewells said. Cassian did briefly speak to Albus and asked him to take care of the girl. He believed she deserved better than to rot away on a kitchen table. Albus promised he would do all that was required and it was not long before Lathyrus gave his orders and Spartacus and the wagons turned away from Caralis sailing into new dangers ahead.

Albus watched as the vessel slipped its mooring and moved out into open sea. He turned and looked at the state of Caralis. The smell of burnt embers still hung in the air. He shook his head and thought of Cassian.,

'What a mess you have made my young friend, but I thank you for it.' He turned to his men., 'Right let's put this place back together like we should have done months ago.' He sent messengers to gather the main power brokers within Caralis to him. Meanwhile he and the rest of the men made their way to the once powerful household of Apelios. Albus could see a small crowd gathered around the main entrance, looks of horror upon their faces. He could not see what they were looking at but, judging the reaction of the crowd, this wasn't going to pretty. He braced himself, pushed out his chest and, leading his men, advanced.

'Out of the way! Make way there!' Albus shouted. The crowd parted and even the war hardened veteran of many a campaign was made to stop in total shock. A man was pinned to the main door. His genitalia had been removed, as had many other extremities. There was hardly a place on his body which had not suffered. This man had not been killed or even executed, this man had been torn apart and it had been done slowly, to exact as much pain as possible. Beside his battered body, hung a notice. It read :

'Murderer, Rapist, Looter, Defiler of the Weak. Look upon this Caralis and see the result of your actions.'

'Shall I remove him Ssir?' aAsked one of Albus' men.

Albus took a big gulp of air, fighting back the bile in his throat and studied the people around him.,

'No he stays until all have seen. We shall have law in Caralis.'

He marched his men into the villa. Bits of paper fluttered here and there as the main doors were opened, as ash flutters in the breeze. Albus knew it was up to him to make sure that Caralis was re-born from those ashes and, though the inhabitants did not know it, they owed the young Cassian a great debt and they should praise the day he entered the port.

Chapter 16

The vessel cut through the waves with delightful ease, and those of Cassian's men who could settled down and tried to sleep. Cassian himself drifted away from the men, his mood matching the darkness of the clouds on the horizon. He moved to the cargo area, where he could be alone. Cassian glanced down at his hand and there, within it, saw the small wooden pendent grasped tightly. In his mind he argued with himself. It would have been impossible for him to have taken the girl to safety when she asked, but the guilt was eating away at him. He remembered her big pleading blue eyes, a face so filled with beauty and vulnerability and he had walked away, put his own safety first. He tried to lie to himself, to claim it was for the good of the mission but, the truth was, he knew she would slow him up. He had not thought about the danger she would be in, come the death of Apelios. He closed his eyes only wanting to sleep but the images invaded his restless mind. They alternated between her pleading eyes looking up at him and then to her broken, smashed body lying on the hard wooden surface. The beauty that she had once been totally gone from her. He curled into a ball against some cargo, trying to block out the world.

The feelings Cassian experienced were new to him. He struggled to comprehend why he felt as he did. The type of world Cassian operated in meant people in his service died all the time. However, he had always been able to argue the loss was for the greater good. This was different, the death was pointless and served no end. The victim had already suffered too much for one so young and feeble but then to die like that, in so much pain without any possibility of survival. No person in the world cared whether she died or not. He had been the one person before her death who could have made the difference but he had failed utterly and totally. He had simply turned away and left her to the whim of the fates.

Lathyrus joined Spartacus at the rail. He could see Spartacus watching the foreboding clouds come closer and closer and smiled.

'Worried about a bit of bad weather boy?' Lathryus spoke in his usual highly confident manner. Spartacus was surprised at being addressed as boy, he had not realised Lathryus was a good deal older than himself, but he admitted to himself those clouds were an ominous sight.

'Shouldn't we try to avoid them?' He said, trying to keep the calm in his voice.

'Usually yes, but other factors need to be taken into account.' Lathryus pointed to another place on the horizon as he answered. Spartacus followed his hand, carrying on his vision to the horizon. At first he could see nothing but then a sail, then another and another.

'Bollocks!' He said, for he had no wish to do battle at sea, walking was difficult enough.

'Not to worry Spartacus. This little beauty rides the waves like a whore on a senator's cock.' Lathryus boomed his usual laugh and slapped Spartacus so hard he nearly tipped head long into the waves.

'You dozy fuck.' Spartacus screamed his annoyance, but Lathryus just laughed all the more. 'I think I best go inform Cassian, we need him here,' Spartacus said, but to be honest had no confidence approaching Cassian in his present mood.

'That is true enough, but there's more than one storm brewing tonight. Our young master needs to get his head in calmer waters.' Spartacus didn't reply, merely nodded his agreement and, with that, turned and searched for Cassian. Now was not the time to dwell on the past, for the future had enough dangers of its own.

The dark, damp interior of the vessel made Spartacus feel even more sickly than before, especially as the waves hitting the vessel were becoming more and more substantial. He eventually found Cassian, huddled in a ball in the darkest corner of all. The bundle never moved when Spartacus neared, despite the huge man struggling to keep his footing and more than once swearing his displeasure.

'Cassian, you're needed above, we have problems,' Spartacus shouted but no response came. 'Get the fuck up, you're needed now!' Spartacus said, his temper erupting. 'By the Gods, I hate the sea!' He shouted.

Cassian turned and looked at the big man,

'She asked for my help...I failed her,' Cassian said, so weakly Spartacus' temper disappeared as quickly as it had come.

'Who, the slave girl?' Spartacus asked.

'Yes I found her...he broke her poor little body, raped her and then killed her. I mean, why kill the girl?' Cassian searched Spartacus for an answer.

'Who knows why these men do such things, it does no good to think on it,' Spartacus replied. He had no answers, he had seen many shameful things and was usually powerless to stop them.

'I found him,' Cassian said, a different glow in his eyes.

'Who?' Spartacus was confused by the sudden change in direction of the conversation.

'The man who killed her,' Cassian said pointedly.

'I take it you killed the bastard, that's good and now put it behind you, we...' Spartacus was interrupted.

'Oh I didn't just kill him, I took him apart bit by bit. The more he screamed the more intense I made his agony. I didn't stop until the room was covered in blood,' Cassian paused, 'but it made no difference you see!'

'What do you mean?' Spartacus was lost by Cassian's remarks.

'It was me who killed her. I should have taken her away when I had the chance, by killing him the way I did I was trying to wipe my guilt clear – but it never changed a thing.' Cassian held his head in his hands.

'Do you think anything will ever take away the guilt each and every soldier feels? That I, young Plinius, Bull, Aegis, and now you, feel. Last night, when we returned from the port, you felt the exhilaration and glory of battle and today you feel the guilt. They are the two sides of a coin, you cannot have one without the other,' Spartacus stated. It was a fact he had learned many years before.

'But how do you cope?' Cassian begged for an answer.

'Mostly, you just do what you must for your comrades. When you have a chance you get blind drunk, so drunk you don't feel at all. Now on your feet we are in the shit!' Spartacus barked out the last word with such ferocity Cassian was compelled to obey. The authority in Spartacus' voice made him move despite his reluctance. He slowly followed but his mind was still swimming with the apparitional face of the young slave girl.

They joined Lathyrus. He was watching the progress of both the sails and the storm, a calm, confident look upon his face. He smiled at Cassian and Spartacus.

'They sense blood, see how they hurry.'

'They are a good deal closer than before,' Spartacus remarked.

'That they are young man, that they are. But they won't ever get close.' It was spoken as fact, the man had a confidence not shared by Spartacus. Years had taught him how to view the sea, learning to love and hate her in equal measure.

'How can you be so sure? They have already halved the distance between us,' Spartacus said, his usual annoyance showing at over confidence.

'When you fought in the arena I hear you were rather good,' Lathyrus stated. The change in the conversation took Spartacus off guard but he managed an answer.

'I won more than I lost.'

'The way you managed this was through watching an opponent, working out his failings, Yes?'

'And these vessels approaching are your opponent and they have failings?' Spartacus replied, trying to see Lathyrus' point of view.

'The vessels my opponents? Oh no but, by the Gods, they have plenty of failings. The sea is the opponent, everything else just factors to be taken into account. The sea, that's where the real danger lies.' The smile was gone and a more studied look enveloped his face. He continued. 'You see, the waves breaking on the sides of those vessels?'

'Yes,' Spartacus replied.

'Well, the size of the waves means all of those vessels are taking in water. Not much, but it's building with each wave. They will become a little slower and, more importantly, they won't move in the water as well.' Lathryus was now giving a lesson and his two students were becoming more and more interested. 'Now this in itself would not be a problem, but the winds they will be changing before long. Those speeding boats, rushing to carve us up, will be caught in the winds not able to turn. A good captain would be able to spot the problem but, as they are still racing towards us, I think a good captain is what they are lacking.'

'But won't we suffer the same fate?' Cassian now asked, his interest pricked.

'This little beauty of mine skims the waves, she rarely takes on much water. Besides, I have the advantage.' He smiled.

'And that is?' Spartacus asked, this time pushing for an answer.

'I know which way the wind will blow and will catch her gently in my sails. Those poor buggers will be lucky if they're not sailing the River of Styx by nightfall.' He spoke for the first time with a slight look of regret upon his face. Lathyrus was a sailor and knew what a carnivorous lover the sea was, he had no wish to watch fellow sailors devoured by her.

Time passed and, with each moment, the sails in the distance came closer and became more menacing. Spartacus kept glancing at the sails and then at Lathyrus.

'You're sure?' He shouted. The storm was raging in his ears, numbing the sounds around him.

'This is nature Spartacus, it would be truly boring if she did the same thing all the time.' He whooped his delight as the powerful winds whipped at his face.

'He's fucking insane!' Spartacus called out, more for his own benefit rather than for anyone else.

Just then Spartacus saw Lathyrus giving commands, but could hear nothing due to the high winds stealing away the sounds. Lathyrus' men though seemed to react with awesome efficiency and, before long, the boat was turning, slowly at first, fighting the waves which now punished her. The crew were cheering. He heard bits of conversation about the wind and strained to hear more. If the wind had changed direction it was news to Spartacus. It seemed to be hitting him from all sides, exactly the same as before. Then Spartacus noticed the increase in speed, though slight at first but growing. After some time he could tell the waves seemed to be losing their power, not rocking the boat with anywhere near the ferocity as before. He glanced out at the sails and they seemed fine for a while but then they seemed to virtually stop dead, as though running into an invisible wall. He could see the enemy, scurrying around the decks of the opposing vessels, and although he could not hear a sound, he sensed their panic. Suddenly on the second boat he saw a mast smash apart, the great winds smashing it to splinters. He could tell the crew were screaming to the Gods for protection but it was in vain. Another huge wave took the vessel in the side and many of the crew were thrown overboard to certain destruction, for no man could survive in such waves. It was hit again and again. With no hope of catching the wind, it was dead in the water and each wave covered the deck and filled the hull. Spartacus watched the dreadful sight, unable to look away, captivated by the sheer destructive power of nature. Then in a blink of an eye the vessel vanished, the sea had claimed her, only the wind and waves occupied the space she had once been.

The sun shone. It was hard to believe that in such a short space of time the sky was blue and the sea totally flat. Spartacus had watched the battle between man and nature for some time, nature had delivered a crushing defeat to man. Two of the vessels would be seen no more, the third limped away from the field of battle, wounded and incapable of fighting any more. Occasionally a body was spotted in the water, but little could be done and Lathyrus performed some sort of ceremony, which thanked the Gods for delivering his vessel whilst also honouring fellow sailors who had been lost. It was the first time Spartacus had seen him so serious and he likened it to when a brother of the ludus had fallen in battle. Members of the same ludus would honour the loss of a fellow gladiator, almost as a family member.

Eventually Lathyrus returned to his normal self and he and Cassian took time out to discuss the mission. Cassian seemed to avoid Spartacus, the latter believing Cassian to be feeling some shame for letting emotions be seen in the raw. It was nothing to Spartacus but to a man with breeding, like Cassian, it was frowned upon. It was not done within the higher ranks of Roman society to seem so vulnerable. So Spartacus gave him space and allowed the plans to be made in his absence. Besides, he took the time to speak to the men and could sense their confidence in entering the final stage of the mission. He had grown to admire each of them, to survive this far demanded that admiration. It was a strange to respect Romans, but they had earned it with blood and pain and no little skill. He glanced around at each of them and was reminded of the night before Crassus' legions had fallen upon the slave army with such devastating effect. He prayed to the Gods that these men would not meet the same end.

As the calm water and the warming caress of the sun settled upon the men, it gave Spartacus the chance to think of his family. The chaos of the mission had all too easily driven them from him. Only his dreams afforded him such luxury. His beloved's face swam into his mind's eye making him crave her smile. He wondered if he would ever see his daughter again, she was so young when he had left. Even if he did see her, would she recognise him or be afraid by his presence and turn from him? His mind relaxed too much, allowing the images of his son to enter. The grief overwhelmed him. It weighed so heavily upon his heart it would surely crush him. Just when it seemed the emotions were becoming too much, a gentle hand touched his shoulder.

'Be still my friend, I bring you wine with just a few herbs of my own.' Aegis smiled and added, 'they settle both the gut and the mind.' Spartacus was amazed at the man's insight, or was he allowing his grief to become too obvious to the men? He glanced around to see if any of the others were observing him and noted, gratefully, they were not.

'Sometimes the quiet moments are the worst to deal with,' Spartacus responded, drinking the wine greedily.

'It is so, but they are needed and we just need to learn how best to overcome them, like a new opponent.'

'Give me the arena any day.' Aegis smiled at Spartacus' words.

'It is always easier to deal with an enemy to our front, much more difficult are those from within. But master, those enemies and the victory tastes just as sweet, perhaps more so.' The huge man again patted Spartacus on the shoulder, rose and walked away. Spartacus watched him go and wondered whether the man was healer, warrior or magician. He did not know, but if it was one or all three he was glad the man was here, for his skills would be needed.

Chapter 17

Lathyrus negotiated into a small secluded cove. They would travel the small distance up to Utica at first light. The men were glad to feel the welcoming sand beneath their feet as they strolled along the beach. Aegis and Plinius had wandered away from the main party. It looked to Spartacus as if Plinius was picking up any extra tips from Aegis on how to fight in the arena. Cassian had ordered a pig to be slaughtered and for a small quantity of wine to be distributed amongst the men. Tonight they should relax before the deadly business of the tournament. He finally chose to speak to Spartacus.

'Think they are good enough to face what's in front of them in the arena?' He said, clearly hoping for a positive response from Spartacus.

'They fight well, and they instinctively fight as a team. I have not seen the qualities of the opponents we will come up against, but I'd say they have a chance.' He did not know what Cassian required of him, these men were good, strong fighters but they were not gladiators. They had not experienced the arena. It was completely different to the fighting these men had trained for and experienced before. He only hoped the instructions he had given to them would keep them alive.

Cassian had seemed to Spartacus to be in a lighter mood, although once or twice he had seen the man drift away as if pulled back to a world of shadow and misery. Thankfully the tasks ahead needed his careful consideration, and therefore, he had little time for reflection on the ghosts of the past.

The planning went into the night, with Lathyrus not happy when he was forbidden by Cassian from attending the games. He was told he must return to the cove and wait until he received further instruction, after he had deposited the men and the wagons at the port of Utica. The men slept uneasily that night. Despite the best food and wine, all knew the task ahead of them. They received their orders for the following day, Cassian clearly trying to set them at ease by keeping them informed. A valiant try, but few men slept easily when the shadows of death hovered but a heartbeat away.

The morning came all too soon for those who had laboured in drifting away to slumber. Sleep filled eyes and aching muscles greeted the start of day, but they followed the orders laid down to them the previous night. A new cargo was brought ashore on Cassian's orders. When the sheets were removed from the crates they discovered the very best quality of weapons and gleaming new armour and the men gasped in delight. Even Spartacus was awed by the quality of the swords, crafted to the very highest of standards. Spartacus kept his own swords but took a small shield and a new helmet, though he had rarely fought in one at Capua, finding both shield and helmet restrictive. However, with so many warriors in the arena at one time, a blow may easily be overlooked and it was important to try and defend against such things.

Unlike usual arena games each gladiator could carry whatever weapon and as many as he wanted to into the fight. However, Spartacus was quick to point out to a number of the men that, after you have been in the arena fighting for your life, the extra weight could get you killed. This said, Spartacus had decided to carry an extra sword by carefully fixing in to a sling over his back. When the men looked at him he quickly added.

'The extra sword I carry is because I have no doubt that one of you useless buggers will lose yours,' but his face betrayed him.

The men jeered at his lies and he laughed, the morning's tension slipping away with each insult and laughter made. They dressed in all the finery and soon were joined by Cassian, who also wore new armour, and two gladius at his hips. Bull whistled as he approached.

'Why thank you Bull but, I have told you I don't think of you in that way,' he chided.

The men continued in good form throughout the morning. Even the call to make ready to board did not dent their high spirits. Boarding the ship was more hazardous than usual in the full armour and it was Spartacus again who nearly toppled into the surf, the men hooted loudly at his curses.

The voyage was thankfully short as being out on deck under the glare of the sun made the men regret their earlier excitement at the new armour, sweat pouring from every available pore. The port was a mass of boats and scrambling men. Each boat was unloading men and armour and all boats came with a huge chest, obviously payment for entry into the games. Lathyrus ordered the unloading, his men again excelling in their duties. Clasping both Cassian and Spartacus in turn by the forearm, he wished them strength and good fortune. They thanked him for all he had delivered, he winked at Cassian.

'That little thing you wanted me to arrange is waiting at the end of the dock. You need to speak to Theltus, he will sort you out.' Again Cassian thanked him. The convoy, now alone again, made its way through the throng of the busy docks.

'What was Lathyrus talking about?' Spartacus enquired.

'A surprise, that is all. I told you we need to make an impact to get everyone's attention,' Cassian replied smiling, but said no more.

The convoy continued. Most moved from their path, the gleaming armour and the three wagons laden with chests imposing a will of their own. Towards the end of the docks, Cassian strode out to meet a thin, willowy man who was clearly disgruntled by the hustle and bustle of the streets. He bowed to Cassian and a conversation ensued, but the words were lost on Spartacus mostly due to the sheer noise emanating from the multitude of wagons, animals and people. There was a nodding of agreement and Theltus scurried away, obviously intent on doing the bidding of Cassian. A few moments later and the warehouse buildings began to thin. The masses of people however did not and there, stretching out in front of the convoy, was a paved road, unusual in this part of the world. At its end there was a huge arena, the like of which Spartacus had never seen before. As they approached the ominous building, Theltus was busily clearing a gap both in front and behind the convoy. For a moment Spartacus feared a trap, his hand instinctively moving towards his sword. Cassian placed his hand upon Spartacus' arm.

'Do not worry my friend, this is my doing. I promised you an entrance.'

Filing both in front and behind the convoy were men armed

with great horns, known as buccina, which began to herald the arrival of Cassian's men to the arena. All around stopped in their tracks, the noise was deafening. Even Spartacus found himself puffing out his chest in pride. What a sight they must have been - the gleaming armour, the accompanying band and the wagons, with chest upon chest which many guessed to be filled with coin. Their eyes hungrily took in the feast, few had seen such a procession and the delight at it brought tremendous cheering which showed no signs of halting.

The convoy entered the arena, its huge walls and gates stealing the sun from above their heads. It seemed to take an age to traverse the space between the gate and the arena floor. Both the warriors and the crowd were in awe of the sheer size of the place. They emerged into the light, the horns never faltering once and the masses inside turned to look at them. It took a time to adjust the eyes from near darkness to the bright sunlit surroundings, but Cassian steered the convoy to the centre of the arena. A makeshift platform had been erected and, at its pinnacle, upon a ridiculous looking throne a figure sat, who they knew had to be Dido.

Cassian strode out in front of the procession. The crowds parted, as if a Godlike hand swatted them aside, as the convoy moved ever closer to its target. The seated man rose as Cassian approached, as he did he lifted his hand to silence the horns. Cassian turned and nodded. The horns silenced immediately, like a flame extinguished by a sudden draft.

The figure was obviously eyeing Cassian closely and why wouldn't he? The entrance was designed to get his attention and so far it had succeeded. The rest of the convoy came closer and, for the first time, Spartacus could see the self proclaimed ruler of the arena. The man was slender, almost feminine to look at, his oiled black hair immaculate with not a strand out of place. Slaves jumped at his every order. He reminded Spartacus of the figures he had seen in the mosaics at the villa of Crannicus, almost too pretty to be real especially for a man. He did not know why but, at that very instant, he decided he loathed the man.

Cassian moved closer but did not get close enough so that Dido was looking directly down upon him, so as to give him the advantage in front of the onlookers. Cassian spoke loudly and great confidence.

'Greetings my lord Dido. My men and I have travelled far to take part in the games you have graciously given to the world.' Cassian doubted such unabashed flattery would count for much but it was worth a try.

'Thank you. To whom do I have the pleasure?' Dido may have looked like a girl but his voice could have been used as a weapon in its own right. It grated like a saw against the bone.

'A mere lover of the gladiatorial game. I am Cassian Antonius, merchant to Rome.' Cassian watched to see if Dido recognised the name. If he did it didn't show upon his face. Either Dido was ignorant of his name or had learned well to hide surprise.

'Have you brought the monies as well as these fine troops, for the love of the game is not enough and all must pay, including myself?' Dido was arrogant, he picked that moment to wave his hand towards his own chest, the lid being open so the crowd saw the immense wealth being brought forward.

'I do my lord, I bring that and much, much more.' Cassian then waved his hand and a wagon was brought forward. In turn each lid was opened and the chest placed at the foot of the platform. With every lid that opened a deafening cheer erupted from the stands. The crowd were not ignorant, they knew something strange was happening and the rising tension was palpable.

'Tell me Cassian Antonius, why so much?' He asked the question but, as a betting man, he already knew the stakes were about to be raised, he just didn't know what the bet was yet.

'I have travelled long, far and wide,' Cassian was now putting on a show, his gestures becoming more and more pronounced, 'and the world talks about the games you hold here. The only other topics are your great gambles, which challenge the very fates.' Cassian bowed his head in mock admiration. Dido shifted, he sensed a trap but with so many eyes watching his every move he would have to play the game.

'The gamble you have in mind, please enlighten me?' He tried to remain calm but those close enough could observe a small bead of sweat as it traced its way down his cheek.

'A simple wager, as all the best are. My men to win. If we lose you keep this vast fortune, enough to buy half of Rome,' Cassian finished letting the tension build.

'And if you should, by chance, win?' Dido's eyes narrowed.

'Then I get everything. The coin, the games, all your assets, even the tunic you wear will belong to me.' The crowd sucked in their breath, seeming to take the very air from the arena at Cassian's words. The trap had closed. This was beyond imagination, the crowd hung on every word, sensing the enormity of the situation.

There was no way out for Dido. The games, the very way of life in Utica had been built on such deals and he always won, but usually he was the one raising the stakes and he would have to once again.

'So I risk everything and you only risk coin? It seems a little biased, I would like to amend the bet if I may.' Dido was in his element, he lived to play for high stakes. He would test the character of this man and see him shuffle back to Rome, his arse in his hands for daring to play this game with Dido of Utica. Spartacus tried to catch the eye of Cassian. He had seen the game change, now the trap awaited Cassian but the crowd sensed blood and Cassian dared not step away now. The deal must be made.

'Of course my lord.' Cassian beamed, but in truth the elation was slipping away.

'As the risk is so great and I have made a great deal of enemies over the years in service to Utica,' he nodded to the crowd as they cheered him. 'To lose my power would be almost as a death sentence and so, if I risk death so must you Cassian Antonius.' It was Dido's turn to pause and let the intensity build. 'Therefore of the six men you select to do battle in the arena, you must be one.' He couldn't help leaning forward slightly to hear the response of this young Roman. He was shocked to see a smile broaden on the face of Cassian.

'It seems fair, then the deal is made.' His voice boomed around the arena.

'It is.' Dido said no more, merely waved them away, but inside the manner in which Cassian accepted this deal disturbed him.

Lathyrus had set sail immediately, still a little annoyed at not being permitted to stay in Utica. His mood did not improve, especially when he heard the great buccina sound and the crowd roaring with delight. His journey took him back to the cove and, as they neared, he was hailed by a lookout. Lathyrus stared in amazement, for the horizon was full of sails all heading to what he guessed to be a larger cove, situated not far along the coast from his own. He had never seen so many Roman ships of war in his life and knew they were not simply out for a day in the sun.

'What do we do Lathryus?' His lookout asked, the concern visible on his face.

Lathyrus smiled. He realised this was why he had not been permitted to stay in Utica. Cassian had wanted both him and his vessel as far away as possible from the port. For a net had been thrown over the majority of the pirate vessels of the region. The Roman Navy would soon close that net and Lathyrus doubted many would escape to plunder the trade lanes again.

'Why, we go to the cove. I need wine!' Lathyrus boomed with laughter. The thought of operating in these waters with no competitors excited him, he could almost see the coin in front of him. He then offered a silent prayer to the Gods. He hoped that Cassian had made a big enough splash, that all eyes had turned inwards and not out to sea. For otherwise, if seen by the wrong pair of eyes, news would reach Dido and he would surely work out the betrayal. Cassian's fate would then be sealed.

Chapter 18

Dido sat in his lavish quarters, everything about the man shouted arrogance. Slaves pampered and pandered to his every whim. Before him there were a selection of oiled, beautiful people selected by his own hand. All were naked, totally exposed to the lecherous tendencies of the man. He stroked the face of a nearby slave, in this a case a young man who had quickly learned to hide his revulsion at his master.

A fat, bloated man entered the room, his discomfort at the heat outside evident. Sweat poured from him, like water from a leaking aqueduct. He was flustered and could not understand the relaxed state of Dido.

'What troubles you, Yaroah?' Dido asked. He loathed the man but he had proved useful despite the foul stench of sweat which seemed to accompany him, no matter the heat of the day.

'What are we to do? I don't understand why we just don't arrange for this Cassian to meet with an untimely end,' he said, almost pleading with Dido to give the order.

'You are unduly concerned. The chances of this man being victorious are virtually none.' Dido spoke with not a trace of concern, confident the young Roman would never survive the arena.

'But that's what I mean - virtually none, so there is a chance!' It was not a question but a statement from Yaroah.

'You never understand the game do you?' Dido said and then continued, 'I cannot have him killed, that is why he made such a public show. On the contrary I must look after the man and those who serve him all the time they are not in the arena.'

'But why?' Yaroah questioned, completely lost in Dido's reasoning.

'The reason we have all become rich beyond our dreams is because of how the populace out there perceive the games. Gladiators from all over the world take part, men of somewhat questionable backgrounds are safe here. For here there is no law but the law of the games,' Dido paused.

'But...'

'Though we profit from those laws because of the usual mayhem which takes place, when such violent men are within close proximity we, like everyone else, must adhere to those laws. This man Cassian made the entire city aware that everything rides on that single bet. If he was to die outside the arena then the games, the life we have carved out in Utica would come to an end most abruptly.' Dido emphasized the final word to give impact to Yaroah.

He watched the man and sighed at the man's failure to grasp even the most basic fundamentals of the game. To Dido that was the point of everything, how to play the game and how to win. But, unusually, he took pity on the man and explained further.

'The tournament leaves few men standing. At the end of such a terrible fight the last team will face our champions, tell me how many times have they lost?'

'Never,' Yaroah answered.

'Precisely. If this Cassian does reach our champions what state will his men be in and how long will they last in the arena with our champions who have destroyed all who have faced them?' A smile finally appeared on the face of Yoroah and understanding the enormity of Cassian's task seemed to settle his nerves. 'Now be a good fellow and run along and ensure the teams are comfortable, especially our young Roman friend.' The words were spoken in a quiet tone but there was no mistaking that Yaroah was dismissed. He scurried from the room like a startled rabbit, he knew better than to over stay his welcome.

Every team of gladiators were allotted a certain area where they could sleep, train and eat. The area granted to Cassian's team was surprisingly spacious and it was well away from the inquisitive crowd. Cassian's men settled down. They tinkered with weapons and armour, anything to keep busy, the days ahead playing heavily on their minds. Spartacus watched the other teams as best he could, for most were under specially built enclosures. He was amazed by the fact many were from far and wide. In his time at Capua he had

137

seen many types of armour and weapons. They were all on show here, but many were also new to him. Weapons of infinite varieties carried by men, the likes of which he had never seen before. The armour glittered in the sun. Much was clearly a show of wealth by the owners, determined to improve their own standing in this community. Spartacus considered it most likely these were men who worked in the darkness, feeding on the corruption of societies across the known world. He spat on the ground trying to cleanse himself of the distaste he felt for these men, but the realisation struck him that he worked for such a man, and indeed Cassian was a master at the art.

He saw the young Roman picking his way through the men and wondered if Cassian had finally misjudged the situation or was he a master with a sword as well? He doubted Cassian considered training with a sword high on his list of priorities. Spartacus waited until Cassian was close.

'Have you ever been in battle or even fought a duel?' Spartacus asked the young man, hoping to be surprised by a positive answer.

'Hmm... no, not that I can recall,' Cassian answered candidly.

'Then what a fucking stupid idea to accept Dido's terms.' Spartacus had not meant to be so forthright but he could not believe Cassian's stupidity.

'He would not have accepted the challenge if I had not agreed to his terms,' Cassian replied, surprised by the emotion Spartacus was showing.

'I cannot train you to face the arena in half a bloody day,' Spartacus blurted out. 'It's suicide.'

'No need. We have more pressing matters, we need to pick the six men for the arena and enter their names.' Cassian dismissed the thought of training, an attitude which shocked Spartacus to the core.

'Fine! Get your bloody head chopped off.' Spartacus knew the conversation was over, he stormed away from Cassian although he knew he must return. He had a sneaky feeling this was all about how Cassian felt such shame over the death of the slave girl. He wondered if that shame was so deep the young Roman would sign up to a suicide mission to try and wash away the hatred he felt for himself.

Spartacus' anger soon abated. Now was not the time to be apart from the men. He returned to them, attempting to judge their mood. A strong tap came at his shoulder, he turned to see who wanted his attention. He looked into a chest, the size of which belonged to myths and not to a real man.

'Spartacus, I am glad that you have awoken from our last meeting.' The huge man boomed out the words and, as he did so, Cassian joined Spartacus fearing trouble might erupt.

'Ah Colossus, nice to see you again. Is that what you still call yourself?' Spartacus smiled the smile that all opponents offered one another. It meant at another time blood will be spilt.

'I go by the name my victories earned me Spartacus. You should know as you were one of them.' Colossus sneered at Spartacus who suddenly looked weak and feeble next to the mountainous Colossus.

'Things that don't kill us, only serve to teach us valuable lessons. I thought you won your freedom?' Spartacus asked.

'I found the easy kills in the arena for good pay too good to refuse. Mind, some kills I would gladly do for nothing.' He leaned in close to Spartacus as he spoke. Spartacus, with no trace of fear in his voice replied.

'Then I will be glad to test your skills and your boasts when we meet in the arena. I always enjoy a workout before the proper fighting starts.' The insult landed as it was intended to do but before the beast of a man could react a voice sounded from behind.

'Opposition fighters are not allowed in each other's enclosures! Please remove yourself immediately or lose your place in the games.' Yaroah spoke with all the authority of an administrator, but it did the trick. Colossus, with one last icy stare at Spartacus, turned and trudged away. Yaroah then turned his attention to Cassian, barely concealing his loathing. 'Here are the rules of the game. Any rule breaking and your team will forfeit its place at the games and any monies given. Is that clear?' He spat the words out.

'It is,' replied Cassian, not really bothering with the little man.

'You must deliver a list of your named fighters before your first bout. You will be instructed when that bout will take place.' With those words he turned and left not waiting for a reply.

Plinius called to Spartacus.

'This man Colossus, he defeated you in the arena?' He asked, almost scared to hear the answer. Spartacus laughed.

'Knocked me out cold. I missed the sun rising five times.'

'But what if you meet him again?' This time it was Cassian asking the questions, obviously concerned Spartacus may not be the best man for the job.

'Who knows? All I can say is I was younger than Plinius here when I fought him last and had only a handful of victories to my name, but since then I have learned a great deal. I suppose he may have as well.' Spartacus was calm and calculating. He believed the men needed the myth of Spartacus to strengthen their resolve but he could not lie to them, Colossus was a very dangerous opponent with both strength and skill.

The men watched Cassian and Spartacus talking, each wondering who would be chosen. As daunting as the arena was, each feared they would not be allowed to fight. They had come too far to simply fetch and carry. The meeting seemed to go on for an age, much nodding and shaking of heads were observed by the men. A couple of times the talking stopped and the men braced themselves for the decision but then the talking would commence again. Eventually though the talking did stop and Cassian and Spartacus rose and gathered the men about them. It was Cassian who spoke first.

'Before I read out the names, I wish to say that all of you have performed heroics to get us here. Each one of you has earned the right to the monies you have been promised. If any of us survive this place I would be honoured to call each and every one of you brother and friend.' He paused letting his words sink in. 'Firstly, I will say to those who are not to take part in the arena, we still have need of you. Your share of the winnings, should we of course win, will in no part be diminished. We will need you, men will no doubt suffer injuries. I know it would be a comfort to me knowing a friend tends to me rather than a stranger.' Cassian finished and nodded to Spartacus.

'The six that will fight in the arena are as follows : myself and

Cassian, Aegis, Bull, Thulius and ...Plinius.' The last name stuck in Spartacus' throat. He had wanted to spare Plinius the arena but, the fact of the matter was, he had developed into a fine warrior and to refuse him entry when he was clearly one of the better fighters would have destroyed the young warrior. He had fought so long to prove he was a man. Spartacus would not take that from him and besides in the arena you needed your best men.

Cassian then went over the rules.

'There have been changes this year to the rules. All six men will enter the arena together. They will be joined by three other teams, apparently more teams are taking part hence the reason for the bigger bouts. If we get through the first few rounds then only two teams will enter the arena to do battle. Within the arena, as each bout takes place, there will be two areas marked off. If a man enters these areas then he is disqualified from the tournament and likewise you cannot strike a man who has entered within those areas. So if you are injured and unable to fight, use them. I have no wish that we spill more blood than necessary.' He paused. 'Many of the teams are forged in blackness they will not give quarter, so put your opponent down and make sure he stays down.' Cassian finished and glanced to Spartacus.

"The arena is a truly terrifying place. It closes in on you. Work together, pick your targets and do not get separated. You don't want to find yourself against multiple enemies, no matter how good you are.' His eyes came to rest on Plinius as he finished speaking, the concern he felt for the boy hard to disguise.

The night moved along slowly. The men were anxious at what the future held. Most had gone to rest by themselves. Aegis took a stroll, the young Plinius at his side but this time he held his tongue and just walked. Bull carved on a piece of wood and Cassian and Spartacus drank wine while staring into the flames. Cassian glanced about at the men.

'I hope they will come through this,' he said. Spartacus was there but the words were not directed to anyone, his lips simply agreed with his deepest feeling.

'If the Gods are on our side then some will, but some will die – it is the way of things,' Spartacus spoke his eyes never leaving the dancing flames.

Cassian watched him for a while and wondered where in his mind Spartacus escaped to. Did he think of his family or of a home he once knew, or even the son taken from this world? As the thought came to Cassian guilt grabbed at him and the sadness that came from it made him think of his own family and the doubts he held that he would ever hold them close again. He rolled onto his side and closed his eyes, he so needed to sleep. As his eyelids came down a young, pale female with pleading, wide blue eyes danced into view he spoke so quietly that the words were just for the figure.

'Forgive me.'

On the sands of the cove, Lathyrus sat and drank. He had given up counting the Roman sails for there were far too many. He worried himself over the fate of Cassian. He had grown to like the young aristocrat over time and would be saddened by the loss of him. If the port had become aware of those sails then Cassian was probably already dead. He shook his head and gulped down more wine.

He remembered back to the first time he met Cassian. The aristocrat was at his father's shoulder just a snotty nosed whelp of a boy. However, even then, he had a lightening intelligence and an eye for an opportunity. Well he hoped that the boy had not finally made an ill judgement for it would clearly be the death of him. Dido was not the sort to forgive.

He was roused from his thoughts by movement. One of his men had left the rest and headed to the darkness of the rocks. Lathyrus had given instruction that all the men were to remain on the beach and he disliked being ignored. He rose quietly and moved away from the light of the fire. He moved to the outskirts of the camp trying observe the man better. The sailor had found a dirt track in the rocks and, with a suspicious glance over his shoulder, had proceeded to climb it. Lathyrus followed him using the shadows as cover. He trailed him up and over the summit.

Lathyrus stood and watched the man's progress. He was gathering wood for a fire. Lathyrus grew angry inside, this man planned to signal Utica. At this height the fire would easily be seen by those in the port. He remembered the man now, he had joined the crew in Utica saying Dido had taken his wealth and he needed to earn coin. It was a common story and, besides, Lathyrus had run into a storm a few days before and lost some good men. So the man joined the crew. He had been no trouble, got on with his duties when asked and only drank when told he could.

Lathryus growled and stepped into view.

'So you would betray me. I have always said that any man that takes coin over his vessel will die at my hands.' The sailor retreated a little.

'Dido will pay so much coin, if we warn him.'

'And what of our friends down there?' Lathyrus nodded towards Utica as he spoke.

'They are no friends of mine, and with that type of wealth who needs friends?' The man spoke with confidence now, believing greed would get the better of Lathyrus.

'So all you have to do is light the fire, oh and kill me,' Lathyrus braced himself for the attack that would surely follow.

'You're a fool to let an opportunity like this go by, and a fool not to bring a weapon.' As he spoke, the man drew a wickedly curved dagger from his waistband.

A splash in the water made the men on the beach sit up but their attention was quickly taken by the figure approaching the camp fire.

'Where have you been Lathyrus?' A sailor asked, for it was unusual for their leader to wander off without wine.

'By the Gods, can a man not go for a crap in peace?' As he spoke he threw a bloodied dagger to the floor.

'Bloody hell, take some getting out did it?' the sailor smiled.

'That it did.' Lathyrus grasped the wine and began to drink.

Chapter 19

The morning arrived all too quickly. The men busied themselves, rarely looking up from the tasks they had chosen. Only the arrival of Yaroah broke their intent on letting the world pass them by. The man did not stop for conversation, his day too busy for such luxuries, he merely passed the instructions to Cassian as to when they should present themselves at the arena.

Cassian supplied the men with a fine breakfast and tried to encourage them as best he could. After a while though he stopped, realising they just wanted to prepare in their own way.

'Is it always like this?' He asked of Spartacus.

'Pretty much. Some men reflect on their lives, some dream of the glory they will receive and others burst out laughing for no reason. Don't try to understand it Cassian.' He placed a gentle hand on Cassian's shoulders.

'And you, what do you feel?' Cassian said, obviously seeking assurances.

'Mostly scared shitless. Always have, probably always will,' Spartacus said with a rueful look on his face. Cassian smiled.

'Good, at least I'm not alone.'

'Oh no, most are scared to the point of panic. Those who aren't are either insane or too dumb to realise what shit they're in,' Spartacus smiled.

'And are there many insane?' Cassian pushed for an answer.

'I have seen many things in the gladiator schools. I have seen men who have faced death and spilt so much blood that they leave the sane world behind. All they crave is the destruction of those in front of them. They are oblivious to anything else, even the baying of the crowd means nothing to them.' Spartacus thought of such men as he spoke.

'What do you do if you meet one in the arena?' Cassian said, now beginning to fret.

'Well, if he is lacking skill you kill the fucker as quickly as

144

possible. If he's good you try and stay out of his way and hope someone else dispatches him or at least tires him out,' Spartacus replied.

'And if you can't stay out of his way?' Cassian was still trying to find an answer, he was not accustomed to vague solutions.

'Then that type of rage in a man tires them out quickly. You move with speed and, when you strike, you strike to kill. No honour will be found in these men, they would strike at you from the other world if they could. What I tell you will go straight from your head as soon as we enter the arena. All men find themselves on the bloodied sand and, if you are to survive, you will learn to kill and be just as savage as the next man.' Spartacus looked at the man in front of him and wondered if a pampered upbringing was suitable for a man about to enter the arena. 'Stay close to the men, concentrate on leading them. If you feel the moment becoming too much look to lead, responsibility for others often steadies the arm.'

They tramped their way to the arena, their armour glistening in the sunlight. The cheers now echoed from inside the mammoth building. The roar was becoming deafening, obviously a kill had just been made. They descended down a large flight of steps, plunging into the darkness beneath the throng of battle above. The coolness of the dark, narrow passageways was a welcome reprieve from the heat of the day. However with each step they came closer to the din of the crowd and the waiting area where they would be announced to the crowd. There was a seating area but all remained standing, the nervous energy coursing through every vein.

In time the cheers began to die down. The smell of blood wafted through the heavy grills and a number of them fought down the urge to vomit. Then suddenly a voice could be heard announcing the next bout. The heavy lock was drawn from the wooden doors at the end of the waiting area. Suddenly Spartacus was speaking.

'Now is your time. Today each and every member of that crowd will know your name. Today we will kill every fucker that dares come close.' He ended his words with a thunderous battle cry which echoed from the walls. Each and every man responded, adding their own roar, the time had come. Now they must kill.

For a minute the sunlight blinded the eyes, each man taking his

145

time to become accustomed to it. They glanced around to get their bearings. They spotted the marked areas, which they hoped they wouldn't need, or if they did that they could reach them in time before being slaughtered like swine. Suddenly the bout had begun and, just for moment, the world stood still. The fighters held their ground and silence reigned in the crowd. Then one of the groups of fighters simply charged into another one at the other end of the arena. The crowd hissed its anger, they wanted all the fighters together to deliver more carnage. Spartacus raised his arm and steered the men towards the remaining group.

'If you can, kill them quick. The victors from over there will soon be coming this way,' he advised, but the remaining group were already moving at pace towards them and little thought could be given to much else.

As much as they were trying to work as a team they naturally ended up fighting individual skirmishes. A squeal to Spartacus' left let him know someone had been injured but, while fending off an attack by his opponent, he dared not take a look. His opponent was skilful and moved with an elegant grace which kept him away from the reach of Spartacus. The crowd went into raptures time and time again. He had hoped he could kill his opponent quickly and from the corner of his eye he could see the other battle was over and those who were victorious were moving in, hoping to cause slaughter against the unprotected flank of those battling here. Suddenly Cassian yelled in victory. He had taken the throat out from his opponent who grasped at the wound, trying stem the deluge of blood.

Cassian moved quickly past Spartacus and, with horror, Spartacus knew what he was going to do. The fool was going to slow the charge of the rushing oncoming enemy and so protect his men, but he would do it alone for everyone else was engaged in a fight to the death. He tried to end his opponent quickly, but the man had skill and evaded a killing blow that should have torn him apart.

Dido watched from his lavish vantage point. He saw the young Roman dispatch his enemy with ease and sighed a little. However, his hope was raised as he watched the young Roman rush to protect his men's flank. He laughed and called to Yaroah.

'You see! That young man will be dead soon and I will be substantially richer.' He chortled to himself. Why do these people play the game against me? His eyes narrowed as Cassian took the head off the first incoming gladiator with a single swing. The action stopped the charge dead, for the sight threw a warning to the dead man's comrades that danger neared.

Plinius took his opponent with a slash to the back of the knees. As he faltered Plinius finished him, a sword thrust in through the side of the neck. Quickly glancing around he rushed to aid Cassian. On his way he slashed a hopeful blow at Thulius' opponent. The cut was not deep but the man instinctively dropped his guard, only for Thulius to seize his opportunity, taking the man's arm off at the elbow. The scream grated the teeth and was only silenced with Thulius' second and fatal blow.

What had been four against one soon became three against three, and the enemy began to retreat once Cassian took another of their number with a thrust to the groin. Thulius again delivered a blow to end the suffering of the man. Aegis wrestled with his opponent, both disarmed in the fight, a contest only one man was ever going to win. Before too long Aegis had broken the spirited opponents arm, and quickly got behind him, a quick snap of the neck, and the foe slipped peaceably to the floor. Taking up his sword Aegis too joined his comrades. The two remaining enemy fled to the safety area, accompanied by jeers from the crowd.

All that was left was Spartacus and his agile opponent, so difficult to hit because of his speed. Spartacus could see his comrades standing not knowing whether to aid him or not. For so long Spartacus had led the way, now they had finished their opponents first. Spartacus looked to Cassian and smiled. He accompanied it with a movement so quick if his men had not seen it they would not have believed it possible. In one motion his hand went for the spare sword slung to his back, the opponent never even noticed. All he saw was a blur, the sword took him just below the left eye smashing through his face. There was silence from the crowd, disbelief etched on all faces. Then the cheers came and the body fell. The crowd were going wild. Spartacus looked across at his men and they too were cheering him. He held his arms in salute to the crowd and then to his own men. They all grasped each other by the arms and applauded the others endeavours. Spartacus caught the eye of Cassian and saluted him personally, for the Roman had proved himself a true warrior of the arena.

The march back to the rest area seemed to go by in the blink of an eye, the mood far lighter than on the journey to the arena. The men joked despite the aches of battle starting to settle in. Cassian had worried that the men left behind would be filled with resentment but, if they were, they never showed it for an instant. They had prepared hot meals and laid out clean tunics and dressings had been prepared for any injuries. They applauded the men back into camp and talked non-stop about how they had seen the battle from the stands.

Nothing more than deep scratches were the injuries for the day, Aegis though still insisted they received a heavy dressing of his special herbs, forcing Cassian to sit at one point.

'You have shown yourself today, my lord, to be a great warrior but if you will not be seated I shall twist your head round so it faces the other way.' The men erupted in laughter, including Cassian.

'Well as you put it like that my friend please, be my guest,' Cassian replied. Spartacus went to move away from camp only to be heralded by the big man.

'Spartacus sit!' He vigorously pointed to a bench as he spoke.

'Fuck! Aegis you will make someone a fine bride one day,' Spartacus joked.

The night bore down upon them and it found the men in a relaxed state, many retiring early at peace with the world craving the sleep they had not managed the night before.

'A good day's work,' Cassian spoke, stepping into the light of the fire.

'You told me you couldn't fight,' Spartacus said, in a mock accusatory way.

'No, I said I had never served or been in a battle. The two are not the same,' Cassian replied.

'You are as slippery as an eel Cassian. Why not tell me?' He asked the young Roman.

'There was a time when you wanted nothing but my death Spartacus. It was a good idea that you believed me to be a spoiled rich kid who only knew how to give orders. If you were to try and kill me I would need all the advantage I could muster,' he replied. The two chatted for a time in high spirits, joyed by the success in the arena.

Yaroah stood next to a gilded chair and waited for Dido to finish, the squeals of pain emanating from behind the curtain. He chose not to look. Some practices which Dido called sport could make the most travelled of people, who had witnessed many uncommon things, blush in an instant. The sobbing started and as it did Dido exited the curtains.

'Takes a while to train them to it,' he said, straightening his tunic.

'I feel we need to talk,' Yaroah said, almost begging for an audience.

'Oh what is it now?' Dido was quickly losing patience with the man.

'Did you see them fight? There could be a problem.' Yaroah would not let it drop. Dido smiled and placed his arm around Yaroah's shoulder.

'Listen my friend. It's the first bout, there are many more ahead of them.' He patted the man on the back, inside repulsed by the man and everything stood for. He was fat, lazy and had no will for the fight, a waste of human flesh.

'But...' Yaroah never finished.

The first blow knocked him to the ground. As he turned his head upwards he saw Dido wielding the second blow, the large bust clasped in his hands. It smashed into Yaroah's skull. Blow after blow rained down upon the shattered fragments of the now pulverized skull. Yaroah was dead long before the blows ceased. Eventually, with blood and brain matter decorating the floor and furniture, Dido stopped. He looked down at the remains of Yaroah.

'Perhaps now you will shut up.'

He called for a servant. The servant arrived in good time and gagged at the sight, but Dido was nonplussed.

"Be a good girl and fetch me a clean robe. Oh and best clean that up.' He waved his hand casually, as though the deep red ooze was merely a goblet of wine, accidently tipped to the floor. He sauntered away leaving the servant to behold the carnage. She went and fetched a silken robe for Dido and then the slave and a number of servants cleaned away the blood and scrubbed the brain matter from the gaps between the marbled floor. Dido lay back and relaxed, he smiled, it had been a good day.

Across the city, away from the rich splendour of Dido's would be palace, there was a much more modest accommodation. The owner's wife busied herself in the kitchen. They had servants, but tonight was to be special. Her husband had been troubled the night before and she wanted to ease his woes. She cooked his favourite meal and wore the blue dress he always liked. The children were packed off to bed early, though they complained, they liked to say good night to their father. The night wore on and still he was not home. It was not like him for he was not like the man he worked for. Her husband had always been both a dedicated father and husband. The dinner ruined, she waited watching the door for her husband's return, willing the heavy door to move. As the night passed and the early light of the following day moved into its place, she lowered her head onto her arms and sobbed. Later that day she would rise and visit her children to tell them that their father would not be returning, for she knew her husband, Yoroah, was dead.

Chapter 20

Cassian's men negotiated the second, third and fourth bouts but the euphoria they had felt in the earlier round was gone. The injuries were sapping the strength. The emotional strain and the willpower required for facing death on consecutive days was beginning to take its toll. They trundled back to the rest camp, muscles burning with the exertion they had been put through. Even Bull, the ever cheerful, looked sullen. The enemies they faced in each match were becoming more and more skilled, confident from the victories they had tasted in the arena. It was now becoming mere chance that all had passed through the bouts without serious injury or death.

Spartacus was thankful that, from now on, it would just be the one team of gladiators they faced in the arena. It was becoming increasingly difficult to fend off multiple attackers, especially as word had got around of Spartacus' skill and therefore he often found himself facing a number of foe intent on taking out the best first. He felt his right shoulder, the cut was reasonably deep but caused only an irritation, that was all. He had become accustomed to pain in the arena's of the empire. He had to admit though fighting day after day was a new experience, one which he did not enjoy. Even the pig Batiatus realised that men needed to rest after such feats of physical exertion and to risk losing his prize assets to tiredness rather than skill would not have interested him, unless of course the coinage was sufficient.

They entered the rest area. Most didn't bother attempting washing or eating, they just slumped to their cots and wished for sleep. Spartacus signalled Cassian just as the Roman was to take to slumber himself.

'You must get them up. They must eat and dress their wounds.' He said it not as a request but as an order.

Cassian didn't reply or complain to Spartacus that he had suddenly decided he was in charge, but instead turned and, with his most enthusiastic voice, cajoled the men into movement. They received treatment from those not fighting in the tournament. Massages were performed with perfumed spices, anything to try and reawaken the bodies to the enormous tasks which faced them. Only when the warriors had been completely cleaned and feasted would Cassian allow them to sleep. Though he knew Spartacus was correct, he hated being the one delaying the men the opportunity to sleep. To their credit they simply carried out the tasks with no malice towards Cassian for, despite their tiredness, they knew what he ordered them to do was the right course of action.

Dido sat, as usual relaxing and tasting the fine foods which seemed to follow him wherever he ventured. He had not bothered to go to the games today, it was a message sent to the crowds who still thought back to the enormous gamble Dido had made with the now respected gladiator Cassian. The message was simple; no nerves, no distress, Dido was in complete control. Still the Roman was beginning to irritate, he should be dead by now.

'Melachus!'He called.

'My lord?'Came the answer, as a tall, willowy character slipped through the door. The figure never ventured too close. The news of Yoroah and the manner of his death spread quickly through the household and it had been with a fearful heart Melachus had accepted the post offered by Dido. To refuse appointment would have meant death but, as many from the after-life could testify, accepting was no guarantee of safety either.

'And how did our young Roman friend do today?' Dido asked, eyeing Melachus closely.

'Another fine victory my lord,' replied Melachus, taking a step back as he did so.

'Good… Good,' Dido said with false joviality. 'Tell me, are you a betting man?' He enquired.

'It has been known my lord.' Too bloody right thought Melachus as he answered but I'm no good at it, that's why I have to work for a fuck like you.

'Then tell me, who are the favourites to reach my champions?' Dido smiled his lecherous smile.

'Oh the Parthians by far. They have danced through the rounds easily. Then Suetos' group, that's the one with Colossus and then, I

152

suppose, Cassian Antonius' men.' He tried to keep the admiration he felt for Cassian from his voice.

'Excellent! Tell you what, let's pair the Parthians up against Cassian's men.' The smile was now replaced by a look that sent the message; disobey me and the carrion will be feasting on your flesh before the sun falls.

'I...I will see to it.' Melachus bowed from the room, his veins pulsating with anger. You cheating bastard the draw is supposed to be chance. It was evident Cassian had Dido worried. If he was fixing the draw then the seeds of doubt were obviously beginning grow. Melachus smiled as he strode through the chambers of the villa.

The morning came and so did the orders for who and when the men would next fight. Their muscles still ached and each simple movement produced the type of noise old soldiers made as they rose from a chair. Thulius toiled away cleaning his armour and Plinius deposited himself next to him, groaning at the aches as he bent his tired muscles. He watched Thulius meticulously scrub each speck of dust from his equipment. He had thought Thulius a good soldier and knowledgeable in most of what he did, but he had never truly realised that there could not be more than a couple of years in age between them, and yet the man next to him seemed so worldly.

'You will wash the breast plate away soon if you clean it anymore,' Plinius said, in a tired attempt at humour. Thulius gazed unflinchingly at Plinius.

'Plinius my friend.' A kind of sadness seemed to have settled over him. 'It is good armour and I noticed yours has been quite badly damaged. When I am finished with it today I would like you to have it.' He finished speaking and immediately went back to cleaning.

'What do you mean? You will need it tomorrow,' Plinius looked at the man, confused at such behaviour.

'No...I won't. I will die today in the arena.' The words were spoken quietly but with absolute certainty. Plinius was so taken aback that he stood and left. He feared the insane mood that had befallen Thulius could infect him too. He sought out Spartacus. He needed to help Thulius.

Spartacus was busy putting a deadly edge to his sword, a duty he would allow no other to do. He observed Plinius heading for him.

'Ah Plinius …some wine?' He asked brightly.

'Please,' Plinius replied, not knowing how to tell Spartacus what Thulius had said. He greedily took down a large mouthful of wine. He was about to speak but was beaten to the words by Spartacus.

'You should not think too much on what Thulius told you,' Spartacus said, a knowing look upon his face.

'You know what he says?' Said Plinius. He required the answers.

'Many soldiers and gladiators have woken to say such things. Some claim a vision and others just have a feeling deep within them,' Spartacus replied.

'But tell him he's wrong!' Plinius demanded.

'Is he Plinius? The man believes it is so. No amount of talking with me will change that and I cannot order him not to feel that way.' Spartacus looked across to Thulius as he spoke, a familiar feeling of foreboding touching his soul.

'Then drop him from the tournament,' Plinius argued.

'And risk five to save one? Plinius, the man has a belief and it's one he has accepted. He will fight for his friends in the arena just as hard as before. If the Gods do decide to take him then they will do it and no intervention from you or me will interfere with that.' Plinius looked at Thulius and yes he looked sad, but the man had obviously accepted whatever fate was to befall him, and he would do it with a sword in his hand. Plinius rose, poured an extra goblet of wine and re-joined Thulius, handing him the drink.

They stood facing the enemy, the sand reflecting the brilliant sunshine up into their faces. They watched the enemy who wore no armour, just blue uniforms made of a sturdy cloth. Each of them carried a long, curved sword and a small round shield. Everything about them said they should not have reached this far in the tournament. But Spartacus observed the way they moved, it was like a serpent. They barely caused a ripple in the sand below them. Each of them seemed to undulate, almost moving with the breeze.

154

He had heard of the style, spoken as legend within the gladiator schools of the empire. He remembered the crowd speak of these warriors, it was said they fought as wisps of smoke. Make a thrust with a sword and they simply bent around the blade and became whole again. Bull also had heard those rumours. He spoke, but to no one person in particular.

'Do you think it's true what they say?'

It was Spartacus who answered.

'Look at them, everything about them suggests speed and tricks, and to get this far they will be good. But trust me, make contact with your blade and it will make the smoke bleed just like any man.' He paused then roared his defiance at the enemy.

It was the ultimate test of power against speed. The slower, armoured gladiators of Cassian's men tried to use their power to crush the enemy, to pin them down and prevent the enemy from using their greater speed. Whereas their opponents would strike, move and strike again, trying to take advantage of a shield moved too slow, or an exposed piece of flesh.

Two individual skirmishes got too close to one another and four fighters crashed into one another, sending all to the floor in a heap. The crowd roared, sensing the blood that was to follow. Bull lay motionless on the floor, knocked cold by the fall but before his opponent could take advantage Thulius, who had risen first, ran him through the throat with a well placed lunge. Almost simultaneously Thulius received a blow to his thigh. He staggered and his opponent sensed victory. Spartacus removed the head of his enemy with a backward slash of his weapon, a move which was met by the crowd erupting in raptures. He managed to get between Thulius and his aggressor to prevent a fatal blow being delivered. He was rewarded with a slight cut to his cheek.

Spartacus roared his anger and, trapping the opponent's sword under foot and bringing his shield up, took the man under the chin. The man was launched into the air, his back arching. He would not have chance to regain his feet for, before he hit the ground, Spartacus thrust again and the blade burst through him. He landed with the point pinning him to the sand.

A terrible roar came from behind Spartacus as he tried to

retrieve his weapon, but the blade held firm anchoring on the ribs of the fallen man. The enemy from behind lunged towards Spartacus, whooping at the thought of an easy kill, but the weapon stopped short of its intended victim. He didn't realise what had happened at first but Spartacus had seen the unarmed Thulius place himself between the enemy and himself. The blade drove cruelly into him, but his actions gave Spartacus all the time he needed. He quickly took a step and dove at the man, no sword in hand. The unsuspecting enemy crumpled beneath Spartacus and, within a heartbeat, he was dead, his neck broken.

Spartacus wanted to go and tend to Thulius but the bout was not over. The enemy still fought on, but the numbers were on the side of Cassian's men now. However, there was no retreat and these shape shifters died hard, inflicting wounds upon all of Cassian's men. Spartacus turned as the battle ended. He looked at the forlorn body of Thulius still warm, blood covering the sand beneath him but, even from that distance, he knew Thulius was dead and would be paying Charon coin to cross the river of Styx that very night. Victory had been achieved but the cost was heavy, they trudged back to the camp. A mixture of relief at being alive and sadness at losing a fellow warrior filling their hearts.

The men sat around the fire and watched the flames flicker skywards. Bull raised his goblet to the heavens.

'To Thulius, may the Gods accept him to their bosom.'

The others around echoed his sentiments. Spartacus thought of the man that, in truth, along the dangerous path they had all trodden had been somewhat of a mystery. He had neither shone for his brilliance or stuck out because of his stupidity. The man had never requested a conversation or praise of any kind and yet he placed himself between a blade and Spartacus, even though the result of his actions was clear. Thulius would lose his life and would do it saving a man who had never taken the chance to spend time with him. He looked around at the men and wondered if he would sit by the fire, regretting the chance not to know them better if they were to fall in battle. He then checked himself, he would not fill what might be his last days with recrimination. Each of these men signed up for a mission and it brought dangers, all of which they knew. Men died, that was the way of things. He wondered if he told himself that enough times, whether he would actually believe it, or whether as always, he would place that which brought him pain to the far reaches of his mind. Then, only on the very darkest nights, when he was all alone would they be able to escape and torment him.

He glanced to the large white villa almost as dominating a building as the arena. Up there a pompous, egotistical bastard was making it rich from these deaths. He prayed that one day the masses would be baying for that man's blood. He made a promise that, if still alive, he would gladly cheer as loud and as long as any on that day.

As it was Dido was not happy. He threw a cask of wine at Melachus.

'I thought you said the Parthians were the best.'

'No my lord, I am no judge of such matters, I merely said they were favourites.' Melachus replied, concerned his promotion would be short lived, and he took a small step closer to the door.

'And what was their condition at the end of the bout?' Dido asked, hoping his plan had not been a complete waste.

'One dead, all carrying minor injuries,' Melachus answered quickly and efficiently.

'Ah a minor success then. It seems this group aren't blessed by the Gods after all.' He smiled. 'Very well, leave me and send me some sport.' As he spoke he licked his lips hungrily and Melachus turned quickly to hide his pure loathing and revulsion.

Whilst alone Dido looked down at his hands. A tremor moved them. There was no doubting the master of the games was beginning to feel fear. He consumed his wine, trying to force the feeling of dread that had lodged in his guts. This was uncommon, it had been many years since he had felt such fear and he did not like it. He decided actions were required to ensure Cassian would not be alive to collect his wager.

Chapter 21

Cassian stared at the arena. The throng and buzz of the crowd making their way to the colossal building was audibly larger than ever before. They sensed blood and carnage, a battle to see who would meet the champions of Utica. He swatted a fly from his face, the early morning already producing too much heat. Within the great arena men would struggle against both the enemy and the oppressively close heat, which would tire the already exhausted warriors to the point where mistakes would be made. In the arena mistakes were fatal.

He had risen early, wanting the time to be by himself, yearning for the simple life. His life before was one of dispatching orders, where men's lives were cheap, he rarely even met them. He would make the plans, send the messages and then actions would be taken. Here though, as he looked at the rest of the men beginning to stir, it was different. Here he stood side by side with the men, learnt of their homes, how the journey of their lives had brought them all to this place, all converging at the same point in history. He raised his hands and stared at them. There was so much blood on them he thought all the water in the Tiber could not cleanse them. He doubted he would ever feel clean again. They had come so far and yet so little had been achieved. The next few days would see if their labours were successful or whether, like so many plans, it all ended in dust, swept away by the breeze like so many good intentions.

He was not the only person to rise early that morning. Dido had sent for a man, a man who had the means to end this gamble he had made with Cassian quickly and without fuss. He waited, rapping his fingers against the table. He was not used to being kept waiting but he knew that showing anger to this man would more than likely see his head split in two. So he waited, guarding against his own anger, holding it inside.

Spartacus hardly tasted his breakfast, everything tasted so bland these days. He passed wine to Bull who gratefully accepted.

'Well this is it then. Win today and we get to grips with those so called Utica champions,' Bull remarked.

'Easy to be champions when all you fight is remnants of men who have been through the tournament.' Spartacus spat out the words as if they added to the distaste of the food. He had little respect for such men.

'We'll see. I haven't even caught a glimpse of them, difficult to judge a man out of sight,' Bull said thoughtfully.

'We will see them soon enough,' Spartacus said confidently.

'You aiming to put the record straight against Colossus then?' Bull asked, a smirk on his face.

'I won't need to go looking for him, he will come for me. He knows I should have defeated him the last time we fought but my inexperience cost me the bout. That will not happen again,' Spartacus replied.

'Is he as good as the crowd think he is?' Bull looked down to hide his concern.

'You saw him! He is powerful, made all the worse for his height. His blows rain down from above, the reach of the man is ridiculous. But for all his power he has weaknesses and if you're quick and don't linger for too long then the bout is there for the taking,' Spartacus replied, eager to get to grips with the man.

'So your plan is to stay out his bloody way,' Bull joked.

'Hmm yes! Sounds about right,' Spartacus laughed. Plinius perched himself down next to them. Bull threw a casual arm around him.

'Why so glum Plinius? Not long now before that beautiful young maiden of yours wraps those golden thighs about you,' he said cheerfully.

'I'll settle for a drop of that wine,' he motioned to the wine before continuing, 'Cassian was up with the sun this morning.'

'A leader's heart always weighs heavily before an important battle,' Spartacus said, before he could stop himself.

'He should look to himself today, there's enough to worry about just staying alive,' Bull added.

'If only it was that easy,' Spartacus replied. 'A proper leader grows attached to his men, which in turn makes him doubt the

159

plans he has devised for the upcoming engagement and to second guess whether he was right to bring his men down this road,' Spartacus spoke thoughtfully as he remembered the battles he orchestrated with his army of slaves.

'A man could go mad with all that going on his head. Simplify it, see the enemy, go kill the bastards,' Bull replied.

'If only Hannibal had you advising him, Rome would have fallen in a day,' Spartacus teased.

'Bollocks,' Bull retorted.

A knock at the door made Dido glance up. Melachus entered.

'My lord your guest is here,' Melachus said, trying to gauge the mood of Dido. He wondered how his master would handle the man who stood waiting just beyond the door. A broad, sickly smile spread onto Dido's face.

'Ah thank you Melachus, be so kind as to show him in. There will be no need for you to stay.' Melachus showed the man in and quickly left, hoping Dido would say the wrong thing and have his head ripped off. The man entered.

'I am quite busy. I have some business in the arena today,' the man boomed.

'Colossus, do forgive me but I had some rather important business for you myself and I believe it would be most beneficial for you...wine?' Dido was in deal mode. He wanted a task completed and if he must pamper this oaf then he would, despite his loathing for a man with muscle for a brain.

'Very well. What is it you want?' Colossus replied.

'As I understand it you have certain issues with this Spartacus which you mean to resolve in the arena,' Dido said. It was not a question but a statement of fact, there was little which escaped Dido's knowledge within Utica. Colossus did not answer, merely nodded his head.

'I would appreciate it if you concentrated your skills on Cassian Antonius, at least in the beginning. Kill him and then you can do what you like with Spartacus,' Dido's eyes narrowed in anticipation of the answer from Colossus.

'And why should I do this?' Colossus replied. Dido felt the sensation of joy inside, when the other party asked why, it meant

160

how much coin would they get. He had coin by the wagon load, the negotiations were already won, it was just a matter of the price.

'Did you see the wagons of Cassian? I will present you with one of those chests. All that gold for one man.' He thought it too much but much more than coin depended upon the right reply, so he made it an offer the man could not refuse.

'Ah I'll take your money. I was going to kill him anyway, may as well get paid well for it,' Colossus whooped with joy.

Dido watched the man leave. He thought to himself what an unbearable piece of scum, I must remind myself to tell my champions to chop him up into little bits. A cruel smile spread across his face, after all a whole chest of coin for a man like that would be merely wasted.

Cassian led the group up to the arena. The crowd were going crazy, all pushing and shoving to catch a glimpse of the warriors who threatened to become legend. The tournament had never had two groups with such talented fighters reach this stage with so many members intact and, maybe, the champions of Utica would finally have a battle to test them. They walked out onto the sand, the dried blood patches now in evidence all over the arena floor. It was strange, despite the din of the crowd Cassian still believed he could hear the flies buzzing in his ear as they searched for a suitable corpse upon which to land. He thought they would not have long to wait.

Colossus and his men filed into the arena from the far side. He seemed to have grown even more since the last time they saw him. He raised his arms, milking the crowd. He carried a gladius and a large hammer like weapon which had undergone alterations, sharp spikes attached to the shaft of it. It was a weapon designed to cause damage and agony, not only death. The two groups moved towards one another like two powerful lions fighting for control of the pride. They circled one another looking for weakness. Then the two beasts collided and the crowd exploded with pure excitement.

Spartacus could not understand it, he thought Colossus would seek him out, but the huge man had avoided him and, instead, Spartacus found himself fighting two men intent on gaining reputation by slaying the mighty Spartacus. Cassian avoided the mighty blow aimed at his head by Colossus. He flicked out his own blade, causing a cut to appear on the huge man's thigh and quickly danced away to avoid the hammer blow which was sure to follow. Time and time again fighters from both sides would fall into a trap set by their enemy but, as the crowd sensed a death blow, they showed their skill, managing to avoid the fatal blow and making the crowd fall to silence with disappointment.

Aegis faced a man who was at least a head and shoulder shorter than himself but the skill the man showed with trident and net was breathtaking. Aegis only just managed to avoid entanglement in the net on a number of occasions. Then the crowd would have its first victim, for Aegis was struggling. The smaller man was just too quick for him. Further and further back he retreated until he could go no further, his back thudded against the stone perimeter of the arena. A faint twist of the shoulder and a lunge, and the trident speared Aegis' left hand to the wall. Bones, muscle and sinew were smashed to pulp by the powerful weapon. The smaller opponent saluted the crowd as they cheered him, then pulled a dagger from his belt and thrust it towards Aegis heart. In one quick movement Aegis caught the hand of his opponent and used its momentum. The blade missed Aegis by a fraction. It continued up, taking his opponent under the chin, rising up through brain and skull and tipping the man's helmet off, as it burst from the top of his head. Aegis was victorious but bleeding profusely. His tournament was over, he stumbled to the safety area holding his shattered hand down by his side. He slumped to the floor of the safety area and managed to tie a piece of cloth around his mangled hand, the pain and loss of blood making his surrounding world blur.

Cassian parried a massive blow, the weight of which forced him back. He was feeling tired now and hoped that his gargantuan opponent was too. However he was not confident of the fact as Colossus' blows remained constant in both speed and weight. He side stepped another thunderous blow and saw an opening. He took it and opened a gash along the forearm of Colossus. The crowd cheered and Cassian delayed slightly too long due to his euphoria at scoring an injury upon his opponent. The huge hammer like weapon swept down from above, taking Cassian in mid thigh before he could scamper from the giant's massive reach. The agony was unbearable, blood poured from the wound as muscle and layers of fat were exposed to the sunlight. He managed to parry the next two blows and began to stumble towards the safety area. He chanced a look to see how far away it was and Colossus noticed the look and sensed victory. Blow after blow rained down on him, his vision becoming blurred, the loss of blood sapping all energy from him. Suddenly he was grasped from behind and pulled towards safety, his would be protector standing between him and Colossus. Bull was no match for Colossus, so he did not try to fight him but merely guarded the retreating Cassian. The crowd cheered, the strange sight of one gladiator virtually chasing two others across the arena, one race which Colossus seemed destined to win. Now within steps of sanctuary Colossus had to make his move. He trapped Bull's sword and raised his huge foot. The kick took Bull in the chest, the force of it knocking wind from his body and sending him and Cassian flying. Both landed beyond the lines of the safety area but this seemed not to concern Colossus, he raised his weapon high. Cassian, his mind dazed and flitting from reality due to his wound, was pinned to the ground by the unconscious Bull. He glanced up and saw the weapon rise. He never saw it fall or felt the blade impact, a cloud drifted over his mind and a young servant girl stood before him smiling.

If he had remained conscious Cassian would have seen the net hook around the weapon arm of Colossus and Spartacus, who had picked the weapon from the floor, use all his strength to pull and turn the giant round to face him. Up in the stands, in his private viewing area, Dido angrily jumped to his feet.

'No! You stupid bastard finish Cassian.' He slapped a servant girl to the floor, his anger on view for all to see. Melachus was tempted to throw his master from the platform but settled for helping the girl to her feet.

Colossus stared at Spartacus, his anger writhing like snakes in his gut. He charged, swinging the deadly hammer as he did so. Spartacus rolled out of the way, the weapon whistling by just above his head. The crowd cheered for another life had been taken. Plinius had felt, once again, great joy as the crowd cheered his name as his vanquished enemy lay dead at his feet. He moved to help Spartacus, but a motion from the man told him to hold his ground. The crowd cheered the gesture, realising this was a battle between titans, with death being the only outcome. Both would fight to the bitter end with no quarter asked or given. The hatred each felt for one another was evident with every blow. The blows came thick and fast, both wielding them with precision and power, the upper hand switching from one to the other with regular occurrence.

Spartacus had already killed two opponents but, if the Gods ruled the skies, then he was the God of the arena. He moved with the grace and power of a lion and Colossus was getting tired. Each blow Colossus threw was designed to destroy his opponent but Spartacus seemed to read them all. Colossus overstretched, trying too hard to score a hit, knowing his strength was failing him. Spartacus took advantage. His blow was not like the meagre blow Cassian had delivered, but a slash to the back of both legs that saw the huge man brought to his knees. His weapons dropped from his hands and he looked up to the skies. For a moment beautiful clouds held his view but then a figure came from them. It was Spartacus, he had leapt high into the sky to bring down a blow. His sword cleaved through the helmet of Colossus, it continued down and all was torn apart, the sword not coming to a stop until it finally found rest on the sternum of Colossus. A giant may have died but the crowd cheered the giant of the arena.

Spartacus acknowledged the crowd but his thoughts were for his men. He quickly moved to them. Both Cassian and Aegis were bleeding heavily, the pain suffered by both was evident for all to see. Bull was still unconscious. Although Spartacus could see no external injuries, he still worried that the man had received a blow which left the type of internal injury which healers could not see, let alone heal. He glanced to the stands, to see Dido milking the applause of the crowd and he looked happy. Why shouldn't he be, the arena had just witnessed one of the greatest bouts in its history. His enemy lay on the sand bleeding, most likely he would die of his wounds.

Dido wanted him to die but hoped the time before death would be slow and painful. That would teach the Roman to dare to challenge Dido of Utica. He straightened his back and raised his chin in self importance, the crowd cheered his name.

Chapter 22

The victory in the arena, no matter how great, seemed hollow and distant. Spartacus and Plinius stalked nervously outside the enclosure, waiting for news of their comrades inside receiving treatment for their injuries. Bull lay still unconscious, soundly asleep unaware of the hardships two of his friends now endured. Cassian had lost a lot of blood and the healers tried vigorously to clean and bind the wound. By far the worst was Aegis, his hand totally shattered and, at that very moment, he was being held down, a saw poised to take the hand off for it had long since passed the point of saving. The screaming started and Plinius made to enter the enclosure.

'Steady friend, there is nothing we can do in there. Let the butchers have their way, for this time they speak the truth. Aegis must lose the hand or lose his life.' As he spoke he held Plinius and prevented him from going further. At first he struggled but then his body went limp knowing what Spartacus said to be true. The rasp of the saw came to an end and, as it did so, the screaming slowed and then stopped, to be replaced by a gentle whimper. It was accompanied by the groaning of Cassian as the bandages were pulled tight over his wound.

Spartacus steered Plinius towards the fire and made him sit. He poured a large goblet of wine and insisted Plinius drank. He paused and let the wine calm the boy.

'We need to talk,' Spartacus began quietly, 'for we have a problem.'

'Really! I hadn't noticed?' Plinius remarked, his tone more severe than he meant it to be, he was angry at the situation his friends were in. His emotions were raw, he wished he had disposed of his opponent quicker in the area and then maybe he would have prevented the pain his friends now endured.

'We will deal with the injuries. We have another problem,' Spartacus said, ignoring the tone, for he felt the same anger. Plinius did not reply but gave Spartacus a quizzical look that showed he was at least listening.

'Tomorrow the tournament rests but the next day we shall be in the arena fighting the champions of Utica.' Spartacus put emphasis on the word 'champions'.

'What of it? That's what we came here for,' Plinius was still direct but his anger more under control.

'I want you to withdraw from the tournament, our friends will need a good sword to protect them if I fail.' Spartacus' words hit Plinius like a hammer blow.

'You think I cannot fight well enough for the arena?' Plinius blurted.

'We both know that is not the case. You have proved yourself many times.' Spartacus defended his position, though part of him realised Plinius had a point. Oh there was no doubt the boy could fight, but Spartacus had seen these men hurt enough and would like to put an end to that hurt, especially for Plinius. He did not know why but he felt he must do what he could to defend the young man, even if it meant entering the arena alone. Suddenly Plinius stared at Spartacus.

'I would not have been here if it wasn't for you Spartacus. I would gladly do what you command in every other respect, but do not ask me to do this.' The boy stared unflinchingly into the face of Spartacus and, at that point Spartacus knew there would be no dissuading the young man so intent on proving himself.

Melachus stood watching his master explode, the furniture taking a beating.

'How can that bastard still be alive, he bled like a stuck pig?' He rounded on Melachus fists clenched, the latter flinching at the unbridled anger.

'Please my lord, his group of men have been destroyed. Only two remain standing.' Melachus spoke quickly he feared he was close joining Yoroah in his fate. The thought stopped Dido in his tracks he ran the figures through his mind. Two men, no matter how good, could not best his champions. A broad smile broke out on his face and his temper was gone as quickly as it had flared.

'You're right of course. Now is not the time to be angry, it is for celebration. The crowd are happy so we must be happy. Remember Melachus, we must keep the crowd happy at all times.'

'Yes my lord.'

Melachus made to leave but he was called back by Dido,

'Who is the best healer in Utica?'

'Stoiclese the Greek, my lord no question,' Melachus answered, suspicion in his mind. He wondered what Dido planned now.

'Then employ him and send him to Cassian.' Dido laughed, 'No tricks Melachus. This time the crowd need to know I appreciate great warriors who put on a show for them,' Dido finished, a serene angelic smile upon his face. Inside he was soaring with joy, the gamble was won and he decided he would like Cassian alive, to see his disgrace happen. Though he may arrange for a little accident to take place once the crowd was dispersed and they forgot the bravery of the young Roman.

It was dark by the time Cassian and Aegis slept. The rest of the men stayed close by, ready to help their friends if need be. The meal had been of the highest quality but little was touched. Two men walked from the darkness and those seated jumped to their feet ready to unsheathe their swords. It was Melachus who spoke first.

'Easy, we bear no misfortune, we come to help.' He spoke whilst holding his hands out to show no weapons.

'And why would one of Dido's men want to help us?' Plinius spat out the words.

'I am not one of Dido's men. I work for him because I must, but I will never be his.' Melachus' words came with such conviction it shocked Plinius.

'What do you want?' Spartacus said, bored with the exchange.

'Dido wishes to impress the crowd by sending you the best healer in Utica. I have brought him to you.' Plinius was about to send them packing when Spartacus intervened.

'They are through there but, be warned, any hint of wrong doing and this place will be your grave.' It was said with such severity both men believed it instantly and nodded in compliance. A while later Stoiclese emerged from the enclosure, his tunic covered in blood. All of the men looked to him, waiting for a verdict. He reached and drank from a goblet of wine.

'They should be fine as long as the wounds don't go bad which means constantly changing the dressing. I see no reason for their condition to deteriorate.' It was said in a matter of fact way like all healers tended to do. People were less human beings, more pieces of meat or a fascinating project. But nevertheless his words brought comfort, which was nothing to what happened next. A voice sounded from behind Stoiclese.

'Here! Who left me in here with these two bastards? Neither one of them can hold a decent tune,' Bull said, a beaming smile radiating from him. All the men rose at once, glad to see him up about. They slapped him heartily on the back and relayed what had happened once he was knocked cold in the arena, a fact he turned scarlet at. His colour was not helped when Spartacus joked.

'Tell me Bull, why do you keep going to sleep every time we enter the arena?'

'It's because we have to wait for you to kill your opponents, I get a little bored,' Bull replied, not showing the fact he felt ashamed at not being able to join them in the arena for the next and most dangerous bout.

The morning brought more good news, Cassian stirred from his slumber and, with the special herbs Stoiclese had mixed for him, was in a very joyful mood indeed, insisting the men carry him out of the enclosure so he could speak with the men. Aegis stirred occasionally but losing part of his body meant he needed to heal both physically and mentally. He stayed inside but his condition improved through the day. Cassian broached the subject of the upcoming bout against the champions.

'Listen men. We have had a good run, but I feel sending Spartacus and Plinius into that arena outnumbered would be unwise. I cannot promise you the wealth you would have gained should we have succeeded, but I can make you all wealthy men. What say we leave this place, let Dido have the cess pit?' He ended, waiting for the angry response. All the men, save Spartacus and Plinius agreed immediately, many stating you don't miss what you never had. However, Spartacus stood.

'If you think I've gone through all this shit to turn back now you are mistaken. I'm fighting and will kill every one of the bastards.' The bravado in his words always came when his back was against the wall. In a more settled state of mind he would have happily got on a horse and ridden away. The men now looked at Plinius. He smiled and took his time over the answer.

'I have already told Spartacus what I am doing. Besides, don't think I'm letting him get all the glory,' he nodded towards Spartacus.

'You're mad, the pair of you. You don't need to do this,' Cassian blurted in amazement.

'Listen, don't worry about us. I've been speaking to Melachus. Tomorrow a platform will be erected to present the champions with their winnings and we need you at the top of it so Dido doesn't try and get out of his deal. How the fuck will you get to the top of it?' Spartacus asked. Stoiclese began to speak.

'Strictly speaking he shouldn't be moving around, but have one of your men knock up some crutches and, maybe with a couple of men to help him, once at the platform steps he should be fine. Just don't go putting weight on the damn thing,' he ended.

As Melachus returned to the household of Dido, he was about to go and report to his master. Before he could he observed Postus, the head of guards leaving his master's quarters and alarms sounded in his head. Luckily Melachus was familiar with Postus and the two had shared more than one cask of wine over the years. He picked up a spare pitcher of wine and went to Postus' room. The man was seated, not looking best pleased. He glanced up as Melachus entered.

'What's the matter Postus?' Melachus enquired.

'You know what the bastard wants me to do?' Postus replied.

'No, what?' Melachus replied with false concern. He needed to know Dido's plans.

'He's told me if Cassian's men are victorious then I am to slaughter them on top of the platform, in full view of the crowd. They will want my balls,' he said, shaking his head at the enormity of the task he had been set.

'Then don't do it,' Melachus said, leaning in close. 'If you slaughter Cassian and his men all hell will break loose. The crowd will bay for blood and who do you think Dido will throw to them?' He let the question hang in the air.

'Then what will I do?' Postus said, the panic beginning to set in.

'Do nothing,' Melachus replied.

'What?' Postus replied, aghast at the suggestion.

'Look if you do nothing Dido will be forced to command you to act and all will hear his treachery. Just make sure the men at the top of the platform are men you can trust. Do nothing, I'm sure Cassian and his menwill take care of the rest.'

Melachus paused seeing if his words had found a home within the mind of Postus and saw that they had. He realised it would be difficult for Postus, he was former military and following orders was as natural as breathing to him. He followed orders even if they were bloody stupid ones, he was programmed to do so. He only hoped Postus' pure hatred for Dido overwhelmed his urge to obey. He left the man with his thoughts and the wine. It was a delicate moment and the decision or man could not be pushed, some things are better left to fester.

Fortunately Dido ordered Melachus later that night to deliver the invitational scroll to Cassian personally, so there would be no need to sneak out of the household to warn Cassian of his master's plans. He relayed the conversation he had with Postus regarding the orders he had received.

'The treacherous little bastard. He plays to win,' Cassian declared.

'He has never lost and doesn't intend doing so tomorrow,' Melachus stated.

'Tell me, why do you help us?' Cassian asked, his eyes watching the man's response.

'Because of my habit of betting on the losing man, my family went broke. It was because of me that my sister had to enter Dido's household as no more than a slave. She was young and innocent and he took that from her. She was found in an alley, so badly beaten my own mother couldn't recognise her body and refuses to believe her to be gone. I pray to the Gods that I haven't backed the losing man again.'

Cassian looked at the man, his shame apparent in every bone of his body.

'You haven't. Tell me, you're alone with him why not just cut his throat?'

'Oh trust me I have fought the urge to do so but if I'm caught who will provide for my mother as she sits looking at the door waiting for my sister not believing she is dead? I have failed her once, I will not again.' He looked away, trying to hide the tears in his eyes.

'Then tomorrow we shall take the glory but you will have justice.' Cassian raised a goblet to the man and hoped he could live up to the statement, or rather Spartacus and Plinius could.

The night wore on. Cassian and the men made the plans which would only succeed if Spartacus and Plinius could be victorious in the arena against the champions. Bull had been quiet for some time and when asked what was wrong, he apologised he would not be at their side in the arena. The comment made Spartacus regret his earlier statement about Bull falling asleep.

'Bull, if it was not for your skill many of us would not be here,' he said earnestly.

'I definitely wouldn't, Colossus would have smashed me to bits,' Cassian added.

'All the same, I wish I could be at your side. You may need me,' Bull responded looking forlorn.

'I don't. I need you with me on that platform. Dido will try any method or trick to hold onto power. I need a good man.' Cassian grasped Bull by the shoulder as he spoke. Bull held up his hand to stop him.

'Alright, alright. Anymore of that and I will throw you off the bloody platform myself.'

The men laughed and summoned all their courage, for the next bout would be the most dangerous and what they had all given so much to be a part of.

Chapter 23

It was a long walk to the arena. Cassian refused to be carried and it seemed to take an age but, thanks to the herbs of Stoiclese, he was in good form, milking the crowd who cheered all of their names. The crowd were so intense even Spartacus felt giddy. He had never experienced such levels of pure excitement, even at his pinnacle at Capua. The men of the crowd roared in appreciation of what they had seen these men achieve, the women screamed at the immense manliness of those in front of them. Some of the less inhibited even bared their breasts and made certain movements with their bodies to show how they would like to celebrate with the men.

'You mind if I stop of here for a bit?' Bull joked.

'Not even your mighty sword could handle that lot, you best come with us,' Spartacus replied.

'It's a shame Aegis won't be with us to see our triumph,' Plinius stated.

'But he is Plinius. All those we travelled with are by our side and add weight to our blows.' As Spartacus spoke he thought of all the men who were no longer with them. Deep down he vowed that, no matter the cost, victory would be achieved in the name of each and every one of them lost on this mission.

They reached the location where the group must separate, Cassian and Bull would enter the arena through a different door to make their way to the central platform. Before they went they wished a great victory and safety from harm to Spartacus and Plinius.

'I feel you face just as much danger as we do.'

Bull, be on your guard. Dido is the sort of man who will not give up his power lightly, watch the devious little bastard.' Spartacus was concerned, for if trouble did start on the platform then Cassian could not defend himself , only Bull would be able to keep him from harm.

'Don't worry, if he starts anything I'll gut the little prick.' He spat on the floor as he spoke as if to show his distaste for men like Dido. Inside Bull was excited at the chance of running a blade through the man, for although he had never met Dido he loathed the man completely.

Spartacus and Plinius made their way down the dark narrow steps to the waiting area where they could hear the crowd chanting their names. Suddenly a hush came over the crowd as Melachus began to speak.

'People and guests of Utica, what a tournament this has been!' The crowd cheered his words. 'Great battles and heroic feats by men worthy of legend.' Again the crowd acknowledged him. 'And finally we come to the last bout, one of epic proportions...the challengers,' as he spoke the heavy wooden doors to the arena floor began to open, 'destroyer of so many fine warriors...Plinius.'

'I think that would be you,' Spartacus smirked.

'Don't rush, the crowd loves me, give them time to show it,' Plinius replied. He strode out, arms aloft bathing in the adoration.

'And now, a man who slew the great Colossus without breaking sweat... Spartacus.' The crowd erupted and Spartacus did not disappoint. He roared his battle cry and flexed his muscles for all to see his prowess. It was not something he usually did, but today the odds were stacked heavily against the two warriors and perhaps it was best to concentrate on the pomp and ceremony rather than the dangers ahead.

'Now they face their greatest foe, three men forged in battle. They fight as one, even their own mothers don't know their names but we know them! For they are the champions of Utica.' Again the crowd whooped and roared and from the far end three figures strode into the arena, not even bothering to acknowledge the crowd. A message had been sent, they would do this job quickly and efficiently and the champions of Utica would have another victory.

Dido smiled a beaming welcoming smile as Cassian finally reached the top of the platform, his face white with the effort with sweat pouring from his forehead. Behind him followed Bull, his hand never too far from the hilt of his sword.

'Cassian! So glad you made it, I feared you would expire in the effort,' Dido said in a over friendly way, which did nothing to hide the fact that part of him wished the Roman had done so.

'Oh thank you for your warm welcome but, fear not, I have proved most resilient to dangers over the years and feel I have plenty of time left yet,' Cassian replied.

'Good, good... please sit near to me, let's enjoy the spectacle although I fear your men are out matched and the bout will not last long,' Dido replied, obviously enjoying the moment.

'I thought you knew fighters Dido but you have misjudged Spartacus. I would bet against all if Spartacus walked into that arena alone. The man is a God in the arena, I was telling Bull earlier how I saw him best six men in the arena at Capua, what a day that was.'

It was an idle and untrue boast, for Cassian had seen no such thing, but he was pleased to see just a flicker of anxiety in the eyes of his enemy. It was very brief, Dido had obviously trained himself well, but it was there and Cassian enjoyed the moment. He quickly added.

'And that Plinius, what a warrior he has become.'

'Excellent! Then a great spectacle we shall experience, come wine is in order I believe.' Dido gave the signal for wine, as he spoke Cassian never replied but smiled and nodded in agreement. Bull, on the other hand, had his eyes elsewhere. There were four guards on the platform top, all dressed in armour with a gladius at their side. Added to that a further two stood at the half way point on the steps of the platform. The man to his right, obviously the leader of the guards, nodded to him and performed a weak smile. Bull returned the smile thinking now there's a man in dilemma.

The combatants closed in on one another and, before Plinius could react, Spartacus charged. It was not his usual tactic but he needed to split the oncoming champions. The move worked and now Plinius just faced one champion. He knew this was Spartacus' plan and, although he felt a stab to his pride, secretly he thanked the much more experienced gladiator. Spartacus rained in so many blows that both of the champions were forced to retreat. The crowd roared its appreciation to see two champions forced onto the back foot. Up on the platform a concerned Dido shifted uneasily in his seat. Spartacus slowed his attack trying to conserve his energy, but his attack had borne fruit. One of the champions now moved slowly thanks to a slash to his thigh. It would not stop him fighting but his movement would be reduced. Then his opponents moved onto the offensive and Spartacus became aware of why they had been so successful. Neither were particularly great fighters but they worked superbly as a team. Over and over again one went high as the other went low, and only great skill kept Spartacus from harm. Plinius fared better, with only one enemy in front of him. He traded blows well with the champion. Both were well matched, similar in speed. Plinius probably had the edge, but his opponent had the experience and a number of times it saved him from potentially fatal moments.

The crowd cheered and sucked in the air about them when a blow went close to causing damage. Spartacus received a cut to the arm and the crowd went berserk. Dido rose from his seat sensing blood, but his euphoria was short lived as the champion who made the cut delayed too long and Spartacus, ignoring his own blood flowing, took the man's head clean off. A cascade of blood shot into the air, resembling a grotesque fountain. That was it, the crowd went totally insane. They called out his name almost forgetting the other battle raging in the arena.

The crowd noise rose to an incredible level and stayed there. Now it was impossible to tell when something new had happened from the cheers of the crowd. Spartacus could not tell how the other fight was progressing but, as he had neither been joined by friend or foe, he could only guess it still raged. Spartacus now pressed his remaining foe, the man much less confident without the teamwork of his comrade. Blow after blow tested the man's skill and initially he withstood the barrage, but eventually his defences were breached, as he slumped to the ground blood pouring from three separate slashes on his body. Spartacus finished him with thrust to the throat. He turned and elation took over, for there was Plinius standing above his opponent his sword pinning the man's torso to the floor. Spartacus raced to congratulate the young, brave man.

Spartacus cheered and turned Plinius to face him. The young warrior smiled, a small drop of blood in the corner of his mouth and the whiteness already creeping up his face. He slumped into Spartacus' arms who lowered him gently to the floor, holding his head from the dirt of the arena. Spartacus searched Plinius for an injury and found a dagger had been plunged into the warrior's side, just as his breast plate finished. Plinius looked at Spartacus.

'Did we win?' He asked.

'Yes. Now calm yourself, the healers are on their way,' replied Spartacus. But as he spoke he knew it was already too late.

'I …I made a promise to Chia, freedom,' he struggled, blood now staining the sand where he lay.

'She will have all you promised and more, you have my word,' Spartacus replied looking at the boy. He realised why he felt such an urge to protect him, it was the eyes - it was like looking straight into his son's and the grief welled inside like a great wave. He struggled to hold back those waves.

'I wanted to make you proud...' Plinius was fading, his voice growing weaker, the rasping in his chest growing as his lungs fought for air.

'A general could not be more proud of a soldier,' and then Spartacus sobbed, 'a father of a son.'

He held the boy long after he had slipped from this world. All the pain Spartacus had suffered for so long seemed to meet at this point. His heart could not hold back the sheer agony of it all. He roared, but not to intimidate an enemy this was pure anger at a world that had taken too much from him. He slumped over the body of Plinius and he sobbed, until there no tears left within him and still he held the boy. If Pluto the God of the afterlife had tried to take the body now he would not have been able to break Spartacus' grip upon it.

Cassian and Bull now stood at the platform's edge. The usually light hearted Bull stood with tears rolling down his cheeks, he never made a sound but he could not prevent the tears being freed. Cassian however turned the grief to anger, he spun around and as loud as he could shouted.

'It's time to pay your debts Dido.'

'What?' Dido could not believe it, one man and a boy had defeated his champions. This could not be happening.

'The laws of this place say all debts must be honoured, no matter by whom.' Cassian pushed the argument. His anger threatening to get the better of him.

'I'm not giving you a single coin. Guards kill them!' Dido was desperate and, despite the crowd howling its discontent at what they were witnessing, he was not going to lose it all to this arrogant Roman, or anyone come to that.

Postus had been watching the battle in the arena and had seen the valiant Spartacus defeat two champions as though he was a God. He then observed his humanity as he wept for his slain friend. His resolve stiffened and when the order came for Cassian to be slain and the other guards moved to carry out the orders, he could not stand by.

'Back to your positions! By the laws of the games all debts must be paid,' as he spoke he looked at Dido. His master stood aghast at the betrayal, and Postus smiled.

'How dare you! I rule here, me and no other.' He went to move towards Cassian, but Bull drew his weapon so quickly Dido only just managed to prevent himself being impaled upon it. He slumped back into his chair unbelieving in what the Gods had done to him. 'Very well.'

'Then you shall remove yourself from this place immediately. Do not go back to the household for it and everything in it belongs to me, do I make myself clear?' Cassian's stare still burned with anger from which Dido shrank, merely nodding. He complied and, rising from his chair, he began to leave.

'Wait!' Cassian shouted, making Dido turn once again to meet his stare 'I believe that tunic belongs to me.'

The crowd had whooped and cheered when Cassian rose in front of them and pronounced two days of celebration all at his expense. There was to be food, wine, music, dancers and whores to fill every guest of Utica with joy and all paid for by their new patron. By far the loudest cheer though came for Dido as he ran naked first from the arena and then through the streets of Utica. His slender frame became bruised as the crowds took the chance to throw anything to hand at him. He eventually sheltered in a small barn, his battered and bruised body struggling when the cold of the night set in. The parties raged all over Utica and Melachus strode around the streets until he found the quivering Dido.

'Master come, how could they have done this to you?' Melachus helped Dido to his feet and placed his own robe around him, and led him to a small warehouse. 'In here it is safe and warm I will fetch you some food and beverage.'

'Thank you Melachus,' Dido replied weakly.

The trader who owned the warehouse had thought he heard a noise but, on looking from his window, he dismissed it. There was so much noise tonight it could have come from anywhere and he tried his best to sleep with the din in the streets. The following morning he rose and, intent on getting supplies, he entered his warehouse to be met by a truly horrific sight. A naked man was tied to the table. The figure was spread eagled and his manhood was gone. There were no other significant marks upon his body so it was evident he had been left there to bleed out in agony, his screams hidden by the euphoria that had taken place in the city.

Lathyrus had observed the craft pass his cove and head towards the Roman fleet sheltering just down the coast. That had been quite some time ago and now, finally, he could see Roman sail beginning to occupy the horizon. Obviously the small craft had brought a message which had motivated the fleet into action. Lathyrus disliked being a static observer, not knowing the fate of his comrades. He was of half a mind to run the risk of the Roman fleet and go to Utica to find his friends. He wondered whether Cassian had been successful, for even with the fleet on the move it proved nothing, for the fleet would not pass up the opportunity to sink pirate vessels whether Cassian was dead or alive. Even now if the fleet was spotted by those in Utica many of the pirate vessels could slip away, for the Roman beast was a lumbering animal at best. The sails took their time but eventually the last of the great Roman vessels disappeared from view. As they did, the small craft which had passed the cove so long ago came into view and began to make its way to Lathyrus' cove. The wait was unbearable and Lathyrus fidgeted nervously. Finally a man approached him on the beach.

'Greeting Lathyrus, I have news from Cassian.' Lathyrus, his patience finally giving way, demanded.

'Well tell me, for the Gods sake.'

'Cassian sends word that the plan is in place, and you should...'

The man did not finish for Lathyrus cheered his delight, lifting the man off the floor and hugging him.

'Bring wine,' he shouted, his booming laughter startling the birds from the trees.

Chapter 24

While the once powerful Dido vented his death screams with no man able to hear, a lone figure sat by the fire seeing the ghosts of the past wander by his mind's eye. The powerful man, built for battle and glory, was so lost within himself a child could easily have approached and thrust a dagger into his heart and the great warrior would not have tried to defend himself, but instead would have happily drifted away on the mists of misfortune and loss. He was unaware of the figure that approached him. It would be the third friend to try and shake him from his melancholy; both Cassian and Bull had left, shaking their heads, at a loss what to do. The third figure had only recently heard of the great battle within the arena. His pride and grief at both victory and loss were still raging their own battle within him, but he raised himself above his own mental and physical hardship to be at his friend's side.

'Spartacus it is time to leave this place. You can do no more here.' Aegis was as large as a mountain but spoke as gently as the morning mist which caresses and places a gentle kiss upon the flower. Spartacus stirred, slightly shocked to see Aegis up on his feet.

'Aegis, I am glad to see you recovering.' The words were meant but the speaker was lost again in the flames as soon as they were uttered.

'It was not a request. Spartacus come from this place,' Aegis said, his voice becoming stern.

'The mission is over Aegis. Leave me in peace, I am a free man. I do as I like,' Spartacus spat back at Aegis.

'And that involves self pity and dishonouring Plinius?' The words were harsh and the owner for a minute thought to retract them, but Spartacus was already on his feet his hand on his sword.

'You dare say I dishonour Plinius,' Spartacus raged, but Aegis stood his ground. He met the stare of the great gladiator and would not yield.

'You see this?' Aegis held up the leather capped stump where his hand once been, 'When you turn your back on your friends you dishonour the sacrifices that I, Plinius, Thulis and all made to get us to this point, but most of all you dishonour yourself.'

Aegis' words hit home. The anger left Spartacus as quickly as it had risen, he slumped back down.

'You do not understand,' his words were feeble, the fight had gone from him. 'His eyes you see...'

'Spartacus, you saw the eyes of the young Plinius. They are the eyes all of us men see in the innocent and vulnerable. Did you not think I saw my child in the boy? – But we are not Gods Spartacus, we are mere men and we cannot protect the innocent from all the woes of the world, no matter how much it shames us.' Aegis' words were gentler now, he understood the man and he too felt the shame that he was not there to help Plinius.

'I'm tired Aegis.'

It was more than a statement of a man requiring sleep, it was a declaration that he had withstood enough misery.

'I know my friend,' Aegis replied, and he took the warrior by the arm. The warrior became as a sheep, gently moved from the place by Aegis the gentle shepherd. They walked in silence to the former household of Dido and Spartacus finally found sleep. He did not dream or stir until the morning sun washed into his room. Aegis did not retire to his quarters but, instead, left to find the body of Plinius not wanting the young man to be cast away with the other fallen of the arena. The young warrior and friend deserved to be honoured.

As the sun rose the following morning, Cassian and Spartacus stood on the balcony gazing across the city. It was quiet now, it was amazing how much people could drink when the cost did not hit their own purse. Bodies could be seen in the streets, however these were not the bodies of the dead but bodies of the drunk. A single man could walk amongst them and steal everything they owned and all he would get for his trouble would be the groans of drunkenness. Cassian sometimes struggled to believe the depravity of people, their thirst for blood, coin, wine and sex made fools of most of them.

182

'So our mission is over,' Spartacus stated.

'Our part is but not the mission as a whole. You see the horizon there?' Cassian pointed out to sea where a few small sails began to appear.

'Yes,' Spartacus replied, he was in no mood for idle chatter.

'Well, soon it will be filled with a Roman fleet,' Cassian said pointedly.

'But why? Dido has lost his power.' Spartacus wondered why bother.

'Dido is an example of the type of man who can rise to power in a place like this, because of the pirates and men that use this place as a base,' Cassian instructed.

'So, you will destroy the place?' Spartacus replied.

'No, not at all. There are, within those streets as many as a couple of thousand pirates sleeping, within that dock hundreds of vessels which usually disrupt Roman trading at every given moment.'

'That's why you told Lathyrus to stay away from the docks,' Spartacus said, amazed at the forward thinking of the man.

'It is. Soon the docks will burn and Roman marines will enter the city. In one swoop most of the danger to legal trade in this area will be swept away.' As Cassian spoke he struggled to hide his pride at succeeding in the plan but a thought caught him and, within his mind, just a little voice whispered, 'but at what cost?'

They were joined by the other men. All watched on the balcony as the first of the Roman triremes ploughed into the vessels which stood at anchor in the dock. The smashing timbers could be heard across the city and the noise roused a number of its sleeping population. They raced through the city to behold the stuff of nightmares, especially for those who made their living on those boats. Some even managed to join their vessels, only to be consigned to the depths along with them. Greek fire sent some to the watery grave, others were just run down by the huge ram on the front of triremes, which turned the once proud vessels to fire wood. Interestingly Spartacus noticed many of the boats could have been taken without sinking but it was clear this was a mission of destruction. Everything pirate would go to the bottom of the sea.

For much of the day more and more boats burned or were smashed to pieces. Every now and then an occasional vessel would escape its mooring and slip past the great barrier that was the Roman fleet. Bodies could be clearly seen drifting in the harbour waters. Only the night before those same bodies were having the time of their lives on wine provided by Cassian. Little did they know that wine was the road to the afterlife and the final voyage they would take.

The day was beginning to lose its light as the first of the Roman triremes began to deposit the marines onto the dock. A few unwise pirates had decided to make a stand. Although the marines were in no way comparable to the regular legions of Rome they were still efficient in killing and the pirates were swept aside with little or no trouble. A defendable position was established by the initial marines, which enabled more and more to pour from the boats into the port area of Utica. They moved relentlessly through the city streets, all that tried to stop them fell beneath sword and boot. The spectacle resembled a plague of locust making its way through a prized harvest, leaving only destruction in its path.

A larger trireme pulled into the docks and it too spilled out marines but also a figure came ashore, his bright white tunic standing out against the drab exterior now made even more so by the smoke drifting over the city as more pirate boats burned. In such a short time a bustling, if not entirely honest city, had become a ghost town. Those pirates still ashore headed away from the sea to seek sanctuary in the hills, while the inhabitants of Utica shut themselves away in their homes and hoped the heavy boots of Rome would not come calling.

The day came and went, with order being restored gradually throughout the city. Come the morning Cassian received a guest, who praised Cassian beyond all measure.

'What you have done here is truly amazing. I doubt a Roman legion could have done the job better.' His name was Critilo, a true Roman diplomat, steeped in its tradition and politics but deeply in debt to the man Cassian served. 'He hoped to be here himself of course but he felt it necessary to stay in Rome to prevent Crassus becoming too curious. It was truly a master stroke to get this amount of triremes and men out to sea without that old dog noticing.'

'I am sure we will have plenty of time to catch up but, for now, I suggest you come and meet the men who made it possible,' Cassian said, eager to share the glory around.

'Delighted to.' The two strode over towards the men who, in return, stood to greet the man.

Critilo looked around at the men.

'So few left, I understand you began with over thirty men.'

'We have lost many good men along the way, mostly in Caralis, but all along the road we made sacrifice.' Cassian spoke with a heavy heart but he resolutely introduced those that remained. Critilo studied Spartacus for quite some time before vigorously shaking him by the hand. He seemed in true awe of the gladiator.

'Of course I had heard of the legend, but never believed I would actually meet you.' Critilo was like a young boy given a pony. Spartacus was taken aback by the greeting, he expected nothing but resentment from a Roman.

'Ermm...thank you, it's nice to meet you.' Cassian erupted into laughter.

'You will have to excuse Critilo, he is a keen student of history and you are somewhat of a celebrity to him. I'm sure once he gets to know you, the shine will go off it.'

'Bollocks,' Spartacus replied, but in good humour.

'So,' Critilo asked, 'what now for you all? Will you go and spend all that wealth? I'm sure Cassian here could still use your services.' Cassian held up his hand to steady his friend.

'They, if they want to that is, will return to my villa where they will rest and then, and only then, will they make such decisions. I feel in need of a little relaxation myself, besides I am keen to spend time with my family.'

'Of course. Of course. Well I must leave you, important business in the port but please, if you require assistance do not hesitate, I am your servant,' Critilo was up and gone in a moment.

'Is he for real? He's like a bloody whirlwind,' Bull remarked.

'Don't let the exterior fool you, he's got a very sharp mind. I will wager he will have Utica running perfectly within no time at all.'

185

Cassian thought to himself; lucky bastard to have a nice administration job now the tough work has been done. Somewhere to work and be close to family. He suddenly felt tired, wanting his family close and a chance to sleep in his own bed with his love next to him.

The sun rose and fell across the port of Utica many times before Cassian was fit enough to undertake the long journey back home, first calling at Caralis. Spartacus had made promises to Plinius and Cassian would not be the reason they were broken. The men who chose to leave with Cassian were Bull, Aegis and, of course, Spartacus. The others had seen the possibilities in Utica now trade wasn't governed by one man and, with more than a little help from the now governor of the region, they stood to make a lot of money. Joining the now very small group was Melachus. His mother had passed away the same night Dido came to his most unfortunate end and Cassian believed they owed the man something. Postus also tagged along. He yearned for excitement after guarding the lavish home of his former master. Cassian had only been too keen to offer the man a place in the group.

'Of course! If it's excitement you require I'm sure I can accommodate you,' he laughed.

The small grouped journeyed through the streets of Utica. It had begun to gather its momentum again, soon it would be a bustling city port, with traders from all over the known world visiting, no longer afraid of the pirates who terrorised them on previous visits. They were glad to leave. Utica had gathered too many ghosts and they would leave for happier lands and hopefully a peace which young and old warriors crave for most of their lives, with few ever really attaining the desired goal.

The familiar black sail drew closer with the huge figure of Lathyrus standing close to the rail, his hand aloft in salute to the warriors. They acknowledged him but could not raise the cheer which would have been usual when the craft which would take warriors home arrived. Lathyrus recognised the look of the men and toned down his usual exuberance, at least for the time being.

It took time to load men and armour, though thankfully the wagons would stay behind. Each man carried plenty of coin upon them, but the majority would stay in the safe hands of Critilo. Cassian had given assurances of its safety. A small chest was delivered to Lathyrus to be shared amongst his men, his eyes lighting up as he spied the wealth inside. The vessel slipped its mooring and, with the passing of time, the once great port of Utica began to fade into the horizon.

Chapter 25

The voyage seemed to take an age. There existed a vacant hole in the heart of each of the men despite the mission's success and wealth few had dared imagine. The completion of the mission had left an empty feeling, the determination it had required from all to complete was suddenly gone and, for the moment at least, none could fathom what to replace that determination with. Coupled with the loss of so many brave comrades it was a sullen voyage indeed. Lathyrus, as was his way, persisted in trying to raise the mood with crude jokes and even cruder sea songs but even he surrendered in the end. The battle he waged could not be won. He also felt a trespasser upon their grief for, although he had played a major role in the mission, he had not been there in the most dangerous times and the coin he received somehow felt dirty and undeserved. Through the voyage he took to watching his passengers while away the hours, simply gazing over the rail back towards Utica long since removed from the horizon. The strong gales and rain never prevented them, for they stood like great statues, forever in deep reflection and never deflected from their thoughts. It was not until the port of Caralis was sighted that they arose from their mental slumber.

Spartacus sighed to himself. The news he would have to deliver to Chia weighed heavily on his spirits. He had no wish to bring torment to the girl. Since the night he had so nearly gutted Aegis for his harsh words he had steered well clear of any conversation concerning Plinius, but it would seem this would be a conversation that he must undertake. Even as he thought of Plinius his insides squirmed uneasily and every hair upon his body stood to attention, as if searching for a calming breeze which would massage their master's spirit, which still screamed its anger at the unjust world.

It was not long before the small group of men were trooping through the streets of Caralis once again, though the change that had been brought about in such a small space of time was truly remarkable. The dregs of society were still there but, like most busy sea ports, they had retreated from view to occupy the dark alleys and to all but the untrained eye they were hidden. It was necessary, if Caralis was to attract the wealthy merchants from around the trading world, its image must portray that of a prosperous and flourishing place of business. A place unsullied by the crime and dirt that affected so many of the places which had known success before being conquered. Its new master was now ensuring it was policed in the right manner.

They paused at the once headquarters of the despot Apelios. The building itself still stood proud and ominous but now it was Albus' men who secured the main entrance. When Cassian questioned one of those men he was informed Albus was at his villa, for the administration of the island had tested the former military man's nerves. Cassian could understand why, for even he felt it tiresome dealing with quarrelling merchants and he had years of experience, whereas Albus was a military man, used to settling disputes with a gladius. But this was a new world Albus had entered, one where charm, intelligence and sleight of hand were the weapons of choice, where a purse of coin or well aimed flattery succeeded where a thousand armed soldiers could not.

As Albus was not within the port they decided to move directly to his villa which stood half a day's ride to the north. They gathered a few provisions and purchased some quality mounts which would speed their journey along, for they had no wish to amble along as they did the first time they had made the journey, with heavy wagon and oxen hindering any attempt to make good time.

Only Spartacus feared the speed for, with each step, it brought closer a task of misery and so each step made his mood darken. He had tried thinking of other moments of the mission but they slipped through his mind as sand slips through the fingers, to be replaced by one constant image - that of Plinius lying upon the ground in front of him, a fatal wound in his side and a small trickle of blood in the corner of his mouth. Spartacus' memories would see him clench his huge, strong hands to the mortal wound to try to prevent the blood flowing but, no matter his strength, the dark liquid seeped through his fingers. The boys' eyes misted and his head lolled, and as the thoughts ended, the anger burst within Spartacus again. Now he would tell the girl, though he would rather face the finest Roman legions with just a dagger than have to bring the girl such misery.

News of their arrival had spread quickly through the villa, though Albus himself sent word he was just completing some important paperwork and would be along presently. The rest of the household came rushing out to greet them, all eager for news of their quest. Spartacus scanned the crowd his eyes almost immediately coming to rest on those of Chia. Her eyes read his immediately and complete understanding happened without a word being uttered. The tears welled in her eyes and her body stiffened but she casually turned from the crowd and walked slowly down the path she and Plinius had so often trodden.

Once down past the orchard, to the place that had been theirs, she threw herself to the grass where they had made love and she sobbed. Spartacus did not follow straight away, he thought it best for her to gather her thoughts and remember Plinius as she wanted. He allowed himself to try and trace the words in his mind of what he wanted to say to her and then, after a short time, he too walked the path to the orchard. It was a debt he felt he owed to Plinius and one from which he would not falter.

'He loved you very much,' Spartacus began nervously.

'Then why did he leave?' Chia snapped back, her anger at the world evident.

'Because sometimes a man cannot choose what he wants to do, but must choose what he has to do.' It sounded foolish as he said it but knew it to be the truth. He remembered having the same conversation with his own beloved.

'Oh duty, I suppose men make such a thing over duty, but who pays for their duty? – those left behind, that's who!' Her anger showed no sign of abating.

'He felt it was his duty, he felt it the right thing to do.' Spartacus tripped over his words.

'He wasn't a soldier any more, he owed nothing to Rome, what has it ever done for him?' She replied.

'Plinius did not care for Rome. Plinius did this for the men who

190

marched at his side and, I regret, he did it for me but most of all he did this for you and the love he held in his heart for you.' Spartacus now answered on a surer footing he felt he understood the man Plinius had become.

'For me? I am a slave,' she replied and for the first time sadness overtook the anger.

'Not to him. You were his first love, his only love,' Spartacus whispered these words with gentility.

Chia looked at him and again began to weep uncontrollably. Spartacus moved to her and placed his huge strong arms about her. He had half expected her to force him away, blaming him for the death of Plinius, but she held him too and, as the sun started to fall, they embraced each other in grief, sharing the sadness they both felt.

Cassian visited Albus in his private study, the latter rising to meet Cassian by the door. As he did so he glanced into the courtyard and observed Cassian's men within it.

'So few?' he stated.

'The Gods' favour was expensive,' Cassian replied.

'Spartacus?' There was a look of surprise on Albus' face for he could not believe Spartacus had fallen.

'No, he has gone to speak to Chia.' As he spoke the torment was so obvious upon his face Albus guessed the reason why.

'Ah young Plinius, grave news indeed.' Albus spoke sullenly but Cassian tried to lighten the mood.

'But you should have seen him in the arena. He was like a lion, with a skill far advanced of his years,' he enthused. Albus stood up straight and said with determination.

'Then he deserves to be honoured as do all that fell.' He obviously had something in mind to show respect to those that had fallen but first Cassian needed to secure Plinius' wishes.

'It is of Plinius I wished to speak and of your slave girl Chia...' Cassian began.

'Yes, I know of the young man's promise to Chia,' Albus replied. For a moment Cassian believed Albus would refuse to grant Chia her freedom.

'I would gladly pay for the girl, it was the boy's dying wish,' he

191

added hurriedly to try and sway Albus' decision.

'There will be no need for payment. Of course she will have her freedom but, tell me, why this matter weighs so heavily upon you?' Albus had not seen a commander care for the wishes of his men so clearly as this young Roman. Cassian paused thoughtfully before he answered.

'I have dealt with the grime that this world has become filled with for so long.' He was going to leave his statement there but felt compelled to be completely unguarded in his response. 'I have seen the deceit that most men live by and so, over time, you protect yourself against befriending any for they will surely deceive that friendship. Out there in the courtyard you see what remains of my command. Those men and those who fell have fought and died at my side. I have seen much more than deceit in these men, I have learned to trust and respect each and every one of them. I owe them a debt that the trust and respect demands. They are not merely men I ordered to do my bidding, but men I am honoured to call a friend and brother. A friendship forged in blood,' Cassian spoke with vigour and purpose and a truth. Qualities that Albus had rarely seen in men, let alone in one so young.

'Then let us honour them.' Albus strode from the room.

Albus had seen to all the preparations. A huge pyre had been built in the centre of the courtyard. At its summit was a heavy wooden tablet and upon the tablet were carved the names of all who had fallen on the quest. All warriors deserved to be honoured with pyre and blessing and, as most of the warriors lay where they had fallen, it had not been possible to afford them what they had earned in blood and pain. The entire household gathered to pay homage to the fallen. Even Chia attended, her grief would not prevent her from sending Plinius upon a safe journey to the afterlife and for the chance to say goodbye.

Cassian headed the ceremony, speaking each and every man's name in full, a fact Spartacus found surprising, for he felt the shame that he could not remember them all. He watched the tongues of flames flick upwards, hungrily feeding upon the tablet, taking each name in turn. They first blackened and then devoured each of them. Finally it came to Plinius' name, the one Spartacus wished to

192

honour above all others. When his name finally succumbed to the onslaught of fire Spartacus felt an easing of the spirit. Goblets rose and rose again in honour of the brave who had paid the ultimate price, wine flowing like the raw emotion of the night.

The mourners honoured the fallen with blessings and tales of their bravery to those who were not there to witness it. When enough blessings had been said and much wine had been drunk, the mourners finally slept. The fire became embers and gradually turned to ash, a slight breeze began to blow lifting the ash and carried the souls of the brave upon their last journey.

Chia left the villa of Albus with Cassian and his men. She could not bear the pain of the place anymore and, besides, she was now a free woman and one with considerable wealth. As Cassian had promised, Plinius' earnings had passed to her. Plinius had kept his promise to her and she would not betray his honour by wasting her life away in misery. She would thank him every day for removing the manacles of slavery. The grief was still raw but she would face it, and overcome it. The love she still felt for Plinius demanded it be so.

Cassian had wondered how many of his men would leave once they returned home. He considered the coming danger of Crassus, a man not known for his forgiving ways and a tendency to exact reprisals against any who went against him. Cassian would bury the records of any of his men, they would become like ghosts. New identities and new locations for them to live would hopefully deliver them from any intended harm that Crassus would inflict upon them. As for himself, it would be impossible to hide but he would ensure his family went on an extended vacation to his father's lands in Greece. It would be more difficult for any action to be taken against them there. With the protection of his own patron maybe Crassus would think better of it and let things be, rather than risk virtually open warfare.

Cassian almost laughed at the suggestion they had damaged Crassus too much for him simply to accept. Before long Rome would know of what happened in Utica and those who knew the darkest politics within Rome would look to Crassus to see if he possessed the backbone to fight back. It was perhaps fitting that at the same time these thoughts were visiting the mind of Cassian, an important looking Roman was picking his way through the streets of Rome, eager for news of Utica, the rumours were almost too unbelievable to comprehend.

Rome bustled with its usual self importance. Traders tried to coax every last coin from every passer-by, and then occasionally a member of the Roman elite would saunter through the busy streets and the traders would go crazy at the chance to make real money. Such visitors would epitomize their class, attendants galore waiting on their every need and whim.

This man was different. He walked with only a couple of bodyguards, as if he was beyond the mediocrity of such melodrama. All around him knew his name and the power of the man, and he enjoyed the honour they paid him. Some tried to ingratiate themselves with him, whilst others hid from his view, fearing he might remember a debt owed. On a normal day he might have a gentle word to such feeble plebs but, for now, he had to get the information he required. He had already sent for such information to be gathered and would make his way to his grand villa to await the news. He however could not resist a smile to himself, he pitied these poor detestable fools. Where would they be if it wasn't for men like himself? They would wallow in shit, not capable of the intelligence to move Rome to the heights at which it belonged. He would drag them to it, for he was one of the few with the foresight required. He made his way to his villa, just one of many that he owned throughout the mpire. This was his favourite, he never liked to be too far from the senate. He revelled in the politics of the senate and had become master of it. Those that did not openly support him feared him, which was a situation he gladly accepted. He craved the power and the more he received the more he wanted. He went straight to his private bathing area within the villa for he hated the grime of the city and awaited one of his most trusted agents. The man wasn't cheap but Crassus knew the value of both coin and man. Shortly there came a knock at door and a man entered. He bowed in reverence and waited to be addressed.

'You have news for me?' Crassus asked.

'Yes my lord, though I fear it is not what you would have wanted,' the agent replied.

'Well, tell me then what the winds have blown?' Crassus smiled, he never lost his temper, always a pillar of calm. He had trained himself well not to show concern, no matter the news and had realised, over the many years in political life, that a hardship often brought rewards if one was intelligent enough to see it.

'The Roman Navy has destroyed over one hundred pirate ships at the port of Utica.' As he spoke the agent looked at Crassus. His employer never even blinked though he knew that the loss must have been a concern. He then proceeded with his report, 'Dido has been removed, believed dead, and a Roman governor, Critilo, installed,' the agent finished as Crassus sighed. Crassus had always liked Dido, he was so easily corruptible and Crassus so enjoyed corrupting. He saw it as almost a civic duty bending men to the will of Rome, that is as long as it was the same as his. Also he thought the loss of the ships and arena would remove a substantial source of revenue, one not easily replaced.

'Who was responsible?' Crassus asked, leaning forward to hear the name clearly.

'First reports suggest it was Cassian Antonius,' the agent replied, nervous at Crassus' sudden movement.

'Well make sure. It would be a great shame to remove such a promising fellow without certainty, especially as he has begun to show real promise.' Crassus' praise of Cassian was genuine. He had hoped to enlist the young man but it seemed one of his competitors had got there first.

'And if the reports are correct?' The agent asked, already knowing the fate of Cassian if the reports did prove to be right.

'You will spend some time on gathering all necessary information. The man himself, his family and his men and hopefully who they work for,' Crassus paused, 'then business as usual, first of all his family and men and, only when he has lost everything, will he meet his fate. Understood?' Crassus put the death sentence on Cassian as casually as ordering a new tunic.

'Yes my lord,' the agent replied. Already he felt a trace of sympathy for Cassian.

'It must be public. All must know the price of going against Crassus, and that price is total destruction.' Crassus smiled at his own bravado. It was not his usual manner but once in a while he liked to be dramatic. 'Best inform Titus Flabinus. I believe he is best suited for the role and if these men were successful in the arena they will have worth, so I must send my best man,' Crassus ended.

'At once my lord.'

The agent turned away, recognising Crassus had ended the meeting. He nervously thought of meeting Titus, a thoroughly loathsome fellow who was held in awe by the underclass of Rome and in fear by those he had set his sights upon. He and his men loved killing a little too much, with the wealth that Crassus bestowed on them being just an added benefit. The agent thanked the Gods, it would take time to gather the information required and his meeting with Titus would be not for some time.

As Cassian and his small group journeyed home, another man worked his way through the filth of Utica, down the dark alleys. He was free from attack for the good work he had done for both rich and poor alike. Stoiclese entered a small warehouse. It was lit but poorly and the smell of blood and death filled the nostrils threatening to overwhelm the senses. He had entered these rooms many times. It was important work, he saved who he could and those he could not he used their bodies to enhance his knowledge of the human form and workings. He picked his way through the injured, many from the recent games. The injuries were severe, most would not last to smell the fresh air beyond these rooms but he hoped one or two could return to the land of the living. His eyes came to rest on one such case and remembered back to the night that the warrior had been brought to these rooms.

'You waste your time, he is too far gone. Only the Gods could save him,' Stoiclese said, assured in his own mind that the warrior was near his end. Only vapours of life still inhabited the body.

'The Gods are too busy and my knowledge is not enough, he needs you.' The huge dark warrior, with a leather cap where his hand used to be, had a stern face but his eyes were pleading with the healer.

'I tell you it will be for nothing. I can ill afford to throw away my

196

supplies on a lost cause,' the healer replied.

'You know that I have come into riches Stoiclese. Save this man and you shall have all to carry out your works,' the man replied, still a pleading edge to his voice.

'Very well, but you know his chances?' The healer quizzed.

'I do, but they are better with you than any other I know.' The huge man turned to leave as he spoke but Stoiclese called to him.

'You wish me to inform Cassian that the boy is still alive?' He asked. Aegis turned.

'No. They have grieved for him once. I would save them the pain a second time, I will contact you soon.' With that he was gone into the night.

Stoiclese brought himself back from his memories to gaze down on the young warrior. He still had not woken from his slumber but, with each day that passed, his breathing became stronger and colour returned to his skin. It seemed that this Plinius was not an easy kill.

THE END

Historical Note

History tells us Spartacus was killed during the final major battle near the Siler River. In truth, the battle was not a grand affair, where one mighty force lined up against another. It's likely the slave army was breaking apart, its cohesion lost in the face of Crassus' legions. The main part of the slave army did indeed engage with the legions and were easily defeated. The body of Spartacus was never recovered. This was not surprising, the amount of dead would have been tremendous and so picking out one man would be extremely difficult for the Romans. It was also possible Spartacus slipped away as many slaves ran from the battle. Pompey encountered a large group and destroyed them. My own personnel opinion is that the Romans knew so little about the man that identification, even if his body was recognisable, would have been impossible. There are little actual facts known about the man. Historians believe he was Thracian and that he was of noble blood and may have served as a Roman auxiliary before being sold into slavery. The evidence is sparse and therefore the legend of Spartacus lends itself so well to interpretation.

Marcus Lucinius Crassus, on the other hand, is well documented in most articles of Roman history of that era. He was a man with enormous wealth and political skill, who held many high offices within the Roman senate. His wealth helped the young Julius Caesar rise to prominence. Though he gained much influence within the senate, for many years his popularity suffered because he was not known as a great leader on the battlefield. This fact seemed to annoy the powerful politician, especially as Pompey, his great rival, and the young Julius Caesar had a gift for victories. This may have been the reason he embarked on an ill thought out campaign into Syria and the battle of Carrhae in 53 BC. He lost the battle, his army and ultimately his life. As for his secret underworld activities, it is difficult to see how a man who had so much success within the senate did not employ such tactics. The time dictated that to stay in power you used every weapon at your disposal. The one thing which is certain is Crassus had the coin to purchase any service he required.

Gnaeus Pompeius Magnus (or as he was more commonly known Pompey), was a skilled military leader and great rival to Crassus. The plebs of Rome loved him because of his victories and, if it had not been for the emergence of Julius Caesar, he may have achieved total power within Rome. Pompey is believed to have tried to claim the victory over the slave army having actually only destroyed remnants of it. Crassus would be horrified by the senate granting Pompey a triumph and a great honour for his victories in Spain and over the slave army, whereas Crassus was left with a minor honour and still no recognition as a military leader. It was approximately 68 BC when Pompey was charged with removing the pirates from the Mediterranean, a task which he completed within four months, although this was probably due more to the payment of gold than the sinking of pirate vessels.

The majority of the other characters are fictional. However I have tried to remain true to the era. The Roman Empire could be a dangerous place and the impact of squabbles between the power hungry politicians and generals could be profound. Life was cheap, with coin and power being sought by those brave enough to reach for them. Even the powerful risked all.

Coming Soon

Spartacus

The God's Demand Sacrifice

The world was at peace. With the coming snows anger and deceit were driven away. The lands slept, for the unusually heavy fall had taken all by surprise. The birds were silent and flightless, not venturing into the cold. Animals sheltered where they could, gathered close to one another to guard against the bitter chill which accompanied the serene winter flakes. Inside the white covered buildings people huddled next to the fires and consumed wine to warm from within. Only slave footprints could be seen in the snow, for wood for the fires and provisions for their masters still had to be gathered.

In one such household the slaves were happier or, it would be better to say, more comfortable. It would be an over statement to suggest a slave could ever truly be happy, only freedom could bring about that state. Their master had returned from his task a changed man. The squalid quarters they had once frequented had been demolished and an entirely new building had been erected. The building guarded well against the cold and yet remained light and welcoming. New clothes, including cloaks, had been provided. They had no idea why their master had become so generous, but thanked the reasons behind it.

Cassian slept an uneasy slumber. The nightmares of a powerful man, demanding revenge haunted him regularly now. Only the special herbs Aegis prepared for him took the edge from the blades that pierced his rest times. He had hoped that his patron would protect him but, upon meeting with the man, it was made clear he must look to his own defence. He woke, beads of sweat racing down his face. Cassian glanced to the door which lead to an adjoining room, where his wife, now expecting their third child, slept. He thanked the Gods she did not witness his nights of turmoil, he would not allow his troubles to burden her, especially while she was carrying their child. Cassian had spoken to Aegis of his dreams, believing the man to have a gift for soothing the spirit. The gentle giant had done what he could, praying to the Gods and mixing a special brew, but still the nightmares persisted.

Aegis went to the other men and told them of Cassian's visions and, to a man, they chose to stay longer. If the visions foretold future events they would stay at their friend's side. They blamed the weather when Cassian enquired why. For while the winter had provided a white blanket which lay across the land, it also provided an excuse for the men to remain at the villa. If Cassian guessed they were not being entirely truthful about their reasons for remaining, he never let his suspicions be known. If truth be told, he was happy they would remain, the future worried him.

Spartacus kissed his sleeping daughter, revelling in the time he had been able to spend with his family. His wife lay on the bed next to him, her long red hair flowing onto to her naked shoulders. He ran his fingers down the smooth skin of her back, marvelling at her beauty. Her involuntary movement when his hands caressed her showed her delight at his touch. She turned her head, her smile broad and welcoming. She gently kissed his powerful hand.

'You must speak with Cassian, Epionne becomes concerned for him.'

'Women are always looking to know a man's mind,' Spartacus jested. 'Besides she's his wife.'

'And you're his friend and some things, men like to keep from their wives.' Her tone was serious and Spartacus knew this would be a battle he could not win. He held up his hands in false surrender.

'You win, I will speak with him later.'

'He will be taking his stroll around the grounds now,' she persisted. Spartacus let out a sigh. He leapt from the bed, after first catching his wife with a well aimed slap on the buttocks. She let out a playful squeal and, with grin on her face, made him aware she would wait for him to return.

Spartacus picked his way through the snow, he knew where Cassian would be. As tricky and hard to pin down in his business dealings, Cassian was always predictable in his home life. Cassian was leaning against a tree surveying his property. Spartacus trudged the small incline to where his friend stood, deep in contemplation.

'Tell me, what is it that troubles you?' Spartacus asked, a look upon his face which announced he would not be easily persuaded away from his question.

'It's the silence.'

'I have told you before Cassian, I'm a fighter, don't speak in riddles.'

'I have men out there, trying to find out what Crassus is up to, but nothing seems to be coming back, not even whispers.'

'But surely that's a good thing?' Spartacus replied, confused by Cassian's concerns.

'There are always whispers Spartacus, unless...' Cassian stopped mid sentence, as though to utter the words would make his terrible thoughts become real. 'There's a man in the employ of Crassus who is so feared no agents would risk angering him, for his methods are cruel and the man has never failed.'

'Then we just kill the man. He is just a man!' Spartacus replied, his bravado always came to the front when danger reared.

Cassian just shrugged, 'You don't just kill Titus Flabinus. He kills you, your family, your friends even your bloody dog.'

Spartacus stared at Cassian, he had never seen his friend like this, so defeated and seemingly without a plan. He always had a plan.

'Listen, if this man has been set upon us then we need to know, and we need to find a way of besting him.' The words brought no response from Cassian, and his silence brought burning anger to Spartacus. 'Cassian! If you want to sit around and be slaughtered like swine that's up to you, but your family and mine deserve a chance, an opportunity to be free of this man's attention,' Spartacus paused to add weight to his words, and to try and calm the anger which had risen within him. 'I suggest we call the men together and speak with them, they must know of the dangers we all face.'

'Of course, forgive me.' Cassian's mind suddenly snapped back into reality, he realised all the camp must prepare if the worst of his nightmares were to come true.

He asked Spartacus to walk with him and, as they ambled around the snow covered fields, he went through all that he knew of Flabinus. He talked of the rumours and of whole families which had been removed from the face of the world by the man. He recounted the tale of Demotrates, a rising star in the world of trading, who succeeding in agreeing trading terms with the Gaul tribes where so many had failed.

'He was brilliant. Such intelligence, his love for making a deal only eclipsed by his love for his family.'

'What happened?' Spartacus replied, almost fearing the answer.

'The man returned to his home after a prosperous endeavour to find his family butchered.'

'Is that so unusual in these times?' Spartacus had heard stories like this before.

'You don't understand. Not just his wife and child, but his entire family. The slaves who tended his household, even the animals that grazed upon his land, all torn apart. When he returned to his warehouses to gather men for retribution, all his men had also been dispatched to the next world.'

'By the Gods!' Spartacus was aghast at the words Cassian had spoken.

'In just a few hours Demotrates lost his family, his home and his life's work.'

'And the man himself?'

'He would not give Crassus the lasting victory. Before Flabinus' men could get to him he lay in the ruins of his home, next to his beloved, and opened a vein. He would meet his family on his terms and not at the order of Crassus.'

'A small victory, but a victory nonetheless,' Spartacus replied thoughtfully.

As the two walked the perimeter they became aware they were not alone. A figure held close to the cover afforded to him by the tree line at the edge of the land. Spartacus cursed himself for not wearing his sword, a luxury he had finally felt comfortable in affording himself these last few days.

'We should retire to safety behind the walls of the villa,' but, as Spartacus spoke, Cassian was already striding purposely towards the uninvited guest, having spotted him as well.

'Stay your aggression Cassian, for I mean no malice.' The figure spoke when Cassian was but a few feet away from him.

'Druro!' Cassian exclaimed, 'what would one of Crassus' eyes be doing on my lands?'

'I bring you a warning. The wolf has been unleashed. Come the melting of the snows he will come.'

'Why would you give this information freely?' Cassian replied, observing the man and searching for trickery.

'Let me say the information I gather has caused too many innocents to die. I care not for the methods of Flabinus. It was on my information that Demotrates and many like him have suffered. I have been asked to gather such information on you Cassian, and you have little time before I must hand over all that I have learnt.'

'And who does this information concern?'

'You must safeguard the household of Crannicus too, but you have very little time. He comes for you and will not stop.' The figure turned and trudged back through the snow to a waiting horse, he nodded once and was gone.

The fire roared and all were seated around the substantial table. At the head sat Cassian and he patiently waited for the talk to stop. As usual Epionne was the last to notice she was holding up proceedings. She glanced at her husband, expecting a look to reprimand but he just smiled, lingering a while upon her gaze. Cassian began slowly, talking of the events of the previous mission and how that mission had brought his family to the notice of Crassus.

'I had hoped that the protection of our patron would dissuade Crassus from retribution but I fear I was mistaken.' Cassian clasped his hands to his head, fearing to tell those he loved of the terrible position he had placed them in. Epionne rose and moved quickly to his side to comfort him.

'What is it my love?'

Spartacus now began to speak. 'Crassus has given orders that Cassian be made an example. His family, his friends and his home will all be forfeit. Nothing will remain.'

'Not while I still stand!' said Bull, raising himself from the table, 'you have my sword Cassian.'

The statement was echoed by each and everyone at the table. Cassian looked at his friends, who so readily faced death and was humbled by the display. Spartacus then quietened the mood, dragging his friends back from the joyous deviance.

'It is settled then, we will stand side by side. Cassian, we will need information on this wolf Crassus has set upon us. Also will we stay here or attempt to leave these lands?'

Epionne gasped.

'Cassian! What about Flora?'

'They travel here as I speak. Even before I had confirmation who had been sent against us, I made it clear to Crannicus that he should join us. Despite his complaints, he finally relented and will be here by the morn.'

The city of Utica was transformed. Legal traders came from all over the known world. As the city grew from strength to strength so did a young warrior. Plinius had finished his morning exercise, he no longer felt tired to the point of collapse after even a mild exertion. Each day he became stronger and also more frustrated at being caged up. Plinius would forever be in debt to Stoiclese but the young man needed to be upon his way. He had need to see his friends and, more importantly, Chia. He imagined their faces when they set eyes upon him and he smiled. Chia's face visited him constantly and he hoped she had not found another, for that would be more difficult to heal than any wound made by a sword thrust. The sudden thought of it made him seek out Stoiclese, for the time had come to say goodbye to Utica. He entered a small room. Charts and documents covered every available space and there, studying one such document, was Stoiclese. The man never seemed to sleep. Before Plinius could speak, the hunched figure stood and smiled.

'So the time has come young Plinius.'

'I can never thank you enough, only I would seek one more favour,' the young man looked sheepish as he spoke.

'Your friend Aegis has supplied funds for your travel, and much more to aid you on your journey,' replied Stoiclese, guessing at Plinius' concerns. The relief showed clearly on the young man's face and this made Stoiclese smile. 'You don't think I would nurse you back to health only to see you starve upon the way?'

The sun shone brightly. Utica was not experiencing the cold which enveloped the Roman lands to the north. In fact it was so warm, Plinius had decided against wearing his armour, a simple tunic would suffice. However, its weight still tired him too quickly and so he paid to have his belongings carried to the docks, where he would board a vessel to Caralis. He couldn't help smiling to himself. Soon he would meet those he yearned to see and marry Chia, if she would still have him. Suddenly nerves gripped him, if only he had recovered sooner, but he would now speed to his friends and be reunited with his love.

Cassian glanced into the courtyard, the weak sunshine finally beginning to melt the snow. He prayed that the cold would last just a while longer. He needed time to formulate his plans. He tried to remain positive, but this man Flabinus was no ordinary foe. He would not listen to reason, he thought only of blood. Cassian knew if he could not prepare well enough then all would be lost. A shout suddenly split the air and Cassian rushed to the gates. There, in the distance, a convoy moved slowly towards his home. Spartacus joined him and together they rode out to meet the convoy. There was joy in their hearts that the household of Crannicus had negotiated their way safely. Tictus headed the convoy and with him came Flora. They both greeted Cassian and Spartacus, but Flora stepped forward immediately to reach Cassian.

'My dear Cassian. Only the Gods know how pleased I am to see you,' the relief was showing clearly upon her face.

'Where is Crannicus?' Cassian asked, fearing the answer.

'He would not leave! He said he would not allow these men to destroy my gardens.'

'Is he mad?' Cassian cried, exasperated. This time Tictus spoke.

'I pleaded with the man, but he would have none of it.'

'Oh Cassian! What am I to do without my husband?'

'I will fetch him.' Cassian made to ride away.

But Spartacus stopped him, refusing to let him go despite Cassian struggling with him.

'See sense man! You are needed here to make plans. I will go and be back in three days, no longer.' Cassian saw the determination in his friend's eyes and knew there would be no argument.

'Very well, but be quick. The snows begin to melt.'

Spartacus grabbed some supplies from the convoy and galloped to the horizon cursing the stupidity of Crannicus, but deep down he admired the man's love for his wife. He would risk all for a smile from his beloved. Despite the fellow's vulgarity he had shown himself to be generous in both love and spirit. Now he must convince the man to forget his honour and run, for only in running did any of them have a hope of survival.

Authors Note

Need to say a huge thank you to my family who helped so much, in allowing me the time to complete my first novel. Also to Frosty who spent so much time helping proof read and offering advice.

To the readers who have enjoyed my book, I'd like to thank you for taking the time to do so, and hope you will enjoy the sequel 'Spartacus: The Gods Demand Sacrifice' where the adventures of Spartacus and friends continue…